Wild River

Laura Pavlov is the *USA Today* bestselling author of sweet and sexy contemporary romances that will make you both laugh and cry. She is happily married to her college sweetheart, mom to two amazing kids who are now adulting, and dog-whisperer to one temperamental yorkie and one wild bernedoodle. Laura resides in Las Vegas where she is living her own happily ever after.

Also by Laura Pavlov and Published by HQ

The Magnolia Falls Series

Loving Romeo
Wild River
Forbidden King
Beating Heart
Finding Hayes

Wild River

LAURA PAVLOV

ONE PLACE. MANY STORIES

HQ
An imprint of HarperCollins*Publishers* Ltd
1 London Bridge Street
London SE1 9GF

www.harpercollins.co.uk

HarperCollins*Publishers*
Macken House, 39/40 Mayor Street Upper,
Dublin 1, D01 C9W8, Ireland

This edition 2024

1
First published in Great Britain by Laura Pavlov 2024

Copyright © Laura Pavlov 2024

Laura Pavlov asserts the moral right to be identified as the author of this work.
A catalogue record for this book is available from the British Library.

ISBN: 9780008719579

This book contains FSC™ certified paper and other controlled
sources to ensure responsible forest management.

For more information visit: www.harpercollins.co.uk/green

Typeset in Sabon Lt Pro by HarperCollins*Publishers* India

Printed and bound in the UK using 100%
Renewable Electricity at CPI Group (UK) Ltd

*'Her courage was her crown and
she wore it like a queen'*
Atticus

1

River

I parked in front of the hospital and stepped out of my car. I wasn't sure what the hell the old man was thinking, getting himself stuck in here for God knows how long. Booze and pills and his high-strung personality would have done the average thirty-year-old in, let alone a fifty-year-old not-so-fit dude. I'm sure his daughter was horrified by the whole thing, seeing as this all stemmed from her father's ridiculous sex drive.

I hated hospitals, but he was my friend, and this was where I needed to be. Well, if I was being honest, Lionel Rose was more than a friend. He owned Whiskey Falls bar, and we'd grown close over the years. I considered him family at this point.

He'd suffered a stroke recently, and we'd all been devastated by the news.

I took the elevator up and didn't miss the way the two nurses who stepped onto the elevator were checking me out as I stepped off.

The doors closed, and I made my way down the corridor and into his room.

My friend held his hand up as I approached his bed, and his lips turned up the slightest bit as I gave him one of those half-bro kind of hugs, before taking the seat beside him.

The monitors beeped excessively, and irritation rose as I tried to ignore the sound.

The faint smell of cafeteria food mixed with the strong antiseptic scent made my stomach turn.

Hospitals were probably my least favorite place to be, which was saying a lot because I'd spent time in plenty of other hellholes in my life.

Apparently, I'd lived at a hospital for six months as a kid, not that I remembered much during that time. But for whatever reason, I associated hospitals with darkness.

Hell, maybe everyone did.

Or maybe it was my subconscious remembering those months, and the fact that I'd had parents the day I arrived at that hospital, but didn't the day I'd left.

Doreen was there too, giving me an update on his condition while Lionel was trying to choke down his lunch. She was a bartender at Whiskey Falls and Lionel's oldest friend.

"Stop being stubborn and eat this applesauce," Doreen said. "Ruby is going to be pissed when she gets back if you haven't finished it."

Ruby was Lionel's only child.

His pride and joy.

Though she'd always been a little rough around the edges, I hadn't seen her in years. I knew that Lionel was supposed to be attending her latest graduation, as she was somewhat of a professional student at this point. Lionel bragged about her often, and I knew she was getting her doctorate in psychology. But obviously, she'd come straight home yesterday when she'd heard about her father.

"Tell River the story that we told Ruby last night so we can all keep things straight." Lionel's words slurred, and I tried not to let my face show my concern. The right side of his face was paralyzed, and it made it difficult for him to speak. But all in all, the doctor said that Lionel had gotten to the hospital just in time, and he was expected to make a full recovery, but it would take some time.

"What story are we talking about?" I sat forward with my brow raised.

Doreen sighed. "He doesn't want Ruby to know that he was taking all those . . . *stimulants*." She cleared her throat and smirked. "The fact that her father is trying to keep up with the sexual needs of a much younger woman is something he'd rather keep to himself."

Yes. Lionel had doubled his dose of erectile dysfunction medication for several days because the man could be a real dumbass when he wanted to be.

"What did you tell her?"

Lionel looked at Doreen, waiting for her to fill me in. "We sort of told her that he had a stroke because of the stress from the legal case with Jenna Tate."

"What? We settled that case a few weeks ago." I gaped at them.

She handed me a piece of paper. "He had me write out this script to read to her last night."

I glanced down at the chicken scratch and rolled my eyes. "So, you basically blamed me for your stroke? That's fucked up, Lionel. Even for you."

"I didn't blame you," he slurred.

I glanced down at the paper and read a few lines. "River was his attorney, but unfortunately, he wasn't able to get a grip on the case, and the stress was just too much for your father." I used my best imitation of Doreen's voice, which was one of a middle-aged woman who'd smoked heavily for most of her life. She glared at me, but I saw the corners of her lips turn up with amusement. "You fully blamed me."

"What were we supposed to tell her? That her father can't get it up enough for his current lady friend, so he tripled his dose of medication?" Doreen crossed her arms over her chest.

"For fuck's sake. I thought you doubled it. You tripled it? What were you thinking, Lionel?" I hissed. It pissed me off because I loved the asshole, even if I wouldn't admit it. And mixing his old-man dick medication with booze and his poor current cardiovascular condition had been a recipe for disaster. "And, yeah, that's what you were supposed to tell her. Because it's the fucking truth. Instead, you threw me under the bus. But if Ruby's as smart as you claim she is, I doubt she'd buy that bullshit story anyway. People don't just have strokes because someone sues them for a workplace accident. You weren't facing prison time, for fuck's sake."

"Hey. I played Juliet in our high school play. I'm a theatrical genius. Trust me, she bought it."

I leaned back in my chair and shook my head. I'd represented Lionel in this ridiculous case, even though he was completely in the wrong and should have just paid Jenna Tate's medical bills right when the accident occurred. But his cheap ass tried to save a dime, which cost him three times what it should have in the end.

"Listen, you and your limp dick better pull your shit together. Stop dating women who are half your age and maybe you'll be able to keep up. Have you ever thought of that?"

Lionel shrugged, the right side of his mouth drooping. "Stella's hot."

"And you're a stubborn ass. I'll go along with your ridiculous charade, but I don't think Doreen is that good of an actress, and if Ruby buys this shit, then she isn't the genius that you claim she is."

"Ahhh . . . I see the whole gang is here," a voice said from behind me, and I glanced over my shoulder.

Ruby fucking Rose had grown up since I'd last seen her.

She had long dark waves falling down her back, red plump lips, and hazel eyes that looked more gold at the moment with the sunlight coming in through the windows and illuminating her pretty face.

Fuck me.

Lionel's daughter was hot as hell.

She sure as shit didn't look like this when I'd seen her last. Obviously, it had been a while, and she was no longer a teenager.

She was a sexy-as-sin woman.

I raised a brow because she was glaring at me like my mere presence offended her.

"Long time no see, Ruby." It had been years since I'd seen her. Lionel went to visit her most of the time, and when she came home, she never stayed long. Lionel's ex-wife, Ruby's mother, Wendy, was a real piece of work, so from where I was sitting, Ruby appeared to be avoiding Magnolia Falls.

"Oh, how observant of you," she hissed, her words pure venom. What the fuck was her deal? She hardly knew me. "Is it your brilliant ability to recall that you haven't seen me in a long time that makes you such an amazing attorney?"

"Ruby," Lionel said, his voice much softer when he spoke to his daughter than when he spoke to anyone else.

She held her finger up as if to silence him. "No. Don't you *Ruby* me right now, Daddy dearest. I'll get to you next."

Doreen chuckled, and Ruby shot her a look. Lionel's feisty daughter was small in stature, but fierce in presence. I was six foot two, and she couldn't be more than five foot four inches, and she was wearing black military boots that probably gave her an extra inch. Her dark skinny jeans hugged her curves, and I tried hard not to let my eyes roam from her head to her toes the way they were dying to. Her black leather coat stood out like a sore thumb, considering it was the end of May. The sun was shining, birds were fucking chirping, and Magnolia Falls was all sunshine and unicorns this time of year.

This girl looks like she's just returned from the bowels of hell.

I recognized that kind of anger, because it lived and breathed in me as well.

"Doreen, I thought you being my father's oldest and dearest friend, and him choosing you as my godmother shortly after I was born meant that you had some sort of loyalty to me?" She crossed her arms over her chest.

Jesus. She was pissed at everyone.

I normally focused my anger on one individual at a time. I reached for the baggy with apple slices on Lionel's tray, grabbed a slice, and popped it into my mouth while I enjoyed the show.

"You know I love you, baby girl. My loyalty is always to you and your father." Doreen glanced between Lionel and Ruby, and I reached for another slice of apple, which earned me another glare from the queen of darkness.

"Is that so?" Ruby moved closer to Lionel's bed and plopped down on the end as she glanced at each of us. "Well, we must have different interpretations of loyalty. Lying to me, when you've all but begged me to come home to take care of the bar—I don't know. It seems a little . . . disingenuous, no?"

Damn. She was smooth.

Confident and condescending and terrifying all at the same time.

I reached for another apple slice, and she moved so fast that she caught me off guard. She slapped my hand, sending the wedge of apple to the floor.

"Stop eating his goddamn apples. How about you focus on the law and do your job."

And that was my limit. I was on my feet and towering over her within seconds. "I do my job very well. Not that I need your approval. But I'll let your little attitude slide because I know you love your father, and I'm guessing you're having some sort of internal meltdown and pointing the finger in every direction you can."

I expected her to cower, but instead, she smirked. Like she welcomed the challenge.

She pushed to her feet and tipped her chin up, eyes gold and blazing with pops of blue and green.

Damn, she was an evil queen, and I'd be lying if I didn't say it was turning me the hell on.

"I was standing outside the door, and I overheard you agreeing to their ridiculous plan to lie to me. Doesn't seem very *lawyerly* of you, or is that the way you run your practice? My father ended up paying quite a bit more to Jenna Tate than he should have. Or are you playing both sides? Maybe getting a little kickback from the ole horndog Jenna?"

"Ahhh . . . I don't know if I'm more offended for my moral compass or the fact that you think I need to work a deal to get laid. Clearly, you underestimate my abilities."

"Ruby," Lionel said, reaching for her hand and she raised a brow as she looked at her father. "I asked them to lie. I didn't want to embarrass myself."

"Really, Dad? You thought I bought that dumbass story about your legal woes? I pulled those records weeks ago to see what you paid her. One of us has to make sure you stay afloat." She let out a long breath and squeezed her eyes shut. "I already talked to Dr. Peters while I was in the car, heading home yesterday. I knew about the medication. I expected more from you. And from you too, Doreen."

"I'm sorry. He was desperate." Doreen shrugged, her eyes watering, and even I felt slightly bad for her when she started coughing profusely and shaking her head.

"Save it." Ruby held her hand up abruptly, and I'd be damned if Doreen didn't immediately stop hacking up a lung dramatically. Maybe her theatrical abilities were better than I'd given her credit for, because Ruby was definitely not buying it. "I get it. He's very persuasive when he's backed into a corner."

"Thank you," Doreen said, moving closer and wrapping her in a hug. "I missed you."

"Sure," Ruby said, as she stepped out of the embrace, completely unaffected. "Anyway, the lies stop now. I will not run Whiskey Falls for you while you go to inpatient physical therapy if you lie to me even once more. Do you hear me?" She stared down at her father. "We've always agreed to be honest with one another."

"I do. And I'm sorry that I missed your graduation." I heard the disappointment in Lionel's voice. Ruby was the most important person in his life, and everyone in Magnolia Falls knew it.

"You're fine. You know I don't care about that kind of stuff." She glanced down at her phone when it vibrated, and she groaned. "I've been home for less than twenty-four hours, and what do you know . . . Mom just had a fight with Jimbo. Shocker. And Rico thinks his girlfriend is pregnant."

Jimbo Slaughter was married to Ruby's mother. She'd been married so many times, it was hard to keep up on that woman's shit. But she had two sons, Zane and Rico, who were both always hanging out at the bar and using Ruby's name to get free shit from Lionel.

"I'm sorry you have to deal with that," Lionel slurred, and Ruby's gaze softened for the first time since she'd walked into the room.

"Don't worry about it. I've got it handled. Right now, my priority is you. Dr. Peters said he talked to you about going right into an inpatient physical therapy program. You've got a long road ahead of you. And you aren't getting out of this. I will cover the bar, and you're going to do the work to get yourself back on track. Got it?"

Lionel reached for her hand, and this time, she took it. "Thank you. Love you, Rubes."

She sighed. "Love you, too."

And this time, her smile was genuine.

The evil queen definitely had a weakness, and it was her father.

2

Ruby

We finished the meeting with Dr. Peters, and thankfully, my dad had agreed to everything the doctor had suggested. My father could be a stubborn ass when he wanted to be, but he was humbled at the moment, and he'd stopped fighting me on everything once the truth had been exposed.

Was I surprised that he had taken not one, not two, but three doses of medication to give him an endless erection?

Not even a little.

This was very on-brand for him.

He was an impulsive guy, and we'd always joked about it.

He was the life of the party, and I was the adult in our relationship.

At eight years old, I was meal prepping for the two of us and organizing the bills.

But we'd always been open and honest with each other, and I hated that he'd lied to me. I understood why he'd done it, but it didn't mean I had to like it.

My father was the one person in my life that I trusted.

He always had been.

My mother was an entirely different story.

Wendy Rose-Dane-Holt-Smith-Slaughter was a brand all her own.

Most short-term apartment leases lasted longer than her marriages did. So yes, I made it a point to call her by *all of her married names*—absolutely.

I was petty that way.

My mother was a very skilled woman when it came to her control over men. Unfortunately, she just didn't pick very good ones.

At least, not after she'd devastated my dad.

My father was a good man. Beneath all the bad decisions and alcohol-fueled nights, he was good to his core.

It was painful how much I loved him.

Even when I was angry, which was sort of my love language. He'd mess up, and I'd complain about it—it was our shtick.

My mother—well, it didn't matter how many layers I peeled back with her . . . there was just nothing substantial when you got to the core.

Wendy Rose-Dane-Holt-Smith-Slaughter was beautiful, but she was selfish and thoughtless and calculated.

I pulled into the driveway of her trailer and put my piece-of-shit white Honda in park before climbing out of the car. My stomach churned, but I held my head high and marched up to the door, swinging it open and finding exactly what I always found.

At least she is consistent.

Dirty dishes and garbage littered the countertop and floors.

The strong scent of cigarette smoke and weed filtered through the air around me.

Beer bottles stuffed with cigarette butts sat on the small table, and I shook my head with disgust. "Hello. I'm here."

"I'm not feeling well. Grab me a Coke and come to my room," my mother called out.

When I opened the refrigerator, I covered my nose to stop

11

myself from gagging as the overpowering smell of something sour flooded my senses.

Nothing ever changes.

I'd lived with my father after their breakup when I was four years old. And by breakup, we're talking an epic, explosive, disastrous ending of a union that should have probably never happened. However, I was grateful that one thing came out of their time together—me.

But the ending had been soul-crushing for my father and just another day at the office for my mother.

She'd been caught having an affair with my father's childhood best friend, Rico Dane. My younger brother, Rico Dane Junior—don't even get me started on the fact that there should be rules about naming a child *Junior* when Rico Dane Senior had accomplished nothing more than being a sperm donor and the champion beer pong player at Whiskey Falls bar—had been the result of that union, and he was a hot mess just like our mother.

"Sis!" A voice came from behind me, and I startled before turning around just as Rico came flying through the door.

He was a big, lovable dufus.

He'd dropped out of high school because he wanted to start growing marijuana long before it was legal, and he named his company Kingpin Weed.

That's not going to draw any attention to law enforcement, am I right?

The business never took off, and Rico spent his days getting high and called it research. Now he worked at The Daily Market for Oscar Daily. At least he was holding down a job.

Was he ready to take on fatherhood? Absolutely not.

But that had never stopped any member of my family from going there.

I let him pick me up off the floor and shake me, because I

loved the hell out of him, even if I didn't always understand him.

There was nothing fair about being born the offspring of Wendy and Rico Dumbass Senior. So, I'd always tried to have his back. Keep him out of trouble when I could.

"Hey. You can put me down now." I chuckled, which was something I made a point not to do often, because I didn't find life to be all that humorous. But I was a bit of a softy for my younger brothers, Rico and Zane.

"So, what are you? A real doctor now, Dr. Rose?" he asked. As he whistled, a wide grin spread across his face.

He had my mother's dark eyes and blond hair. I looked more like my father, and I'd never minded that. But my brother was adorable, and he knew it.

"If you call me Dr. Rose again, I'll shave your eyebrows off in your sleep." I shot him a warning look.

I was officially Dr. Rose in the academic world that I lived in—a faraway place from Magnolia Falls, the life I'd always wanted to run from. But being called "doctor" in my mother's home would be the equivalent of committing a crime. My mother hated that I'd pursued my education.

Hell, I'd always had an endless thirst when it came to psychology. Learning what made people tick. Maybe because I'd been pretty much solving problems for all the people in my life since . . . birth.

Or at least it felt that way.

I liked learning about what made people do the things that they did, the motivation behind both positive and negative choices, and the potential to forgive those who hurt you.

I hadn't quite practiced forgiveness much in my life, and maybe that was because no one was apologizing for anything most of the time. For the bad situations my mother had put me in as a child. For the way she'd relied on me to take care of my brothers when I was only a little older than both of them.

So, I learned how to take my skills and make them useful.

I'd graduated magna cum laude from one of the most prestigious universities in California, and apparently, the world was my oyster now.

Well, it will be in eight weeks after I finish running Whiskey Falls and wait for my father to make a full recovery.

But I still had to figure out what my oyster was.

The University of Western California offered me a teaching position. I'd be a professor teaching two different introductory psychology courses, which should be the goal after all the schooling I'd gone through. I just wasn't certain if teaching was in my future. I hadn't had the time to think about my options, because I'd graduated on a Saturday morning and my father had had a stroke the night before. He'd been getting ready to get in the car to come attend my graduation ceremony when it happened.

It was fitting for the story of my life, really.

I couldn't seem to leave this place behind. The only person I'd be willing to ditch graduation for was my father, and that was exactly what I'd done.

There wasn't anything that I wouldn't do for him.

"You already shaved off Zane's eyebrows in middle school. I won't challenge you there because I know you'll do it."

"Damn straight. Tell me what's happening with Panda." Yes, my brother's girlfriend since middle school was named Panda. She'd been named Sally once, but she'd hated the name and changed it to Panda when she was fifteen years old, and no one questioned it, aside from the endless snide comments I'd made over the years.

He cracked open a beer and took a long pull. "She's not preggers. She was fucking with me."

I nodded. This was Rico's and Panda's love language.

Cheat. Lie. Fuck with one another. Repeat.

"You do know that if you use protection, you won't have to worry so much every time she *messes with you*."

This wasn't the first time she'd done it, nor did I think it would be the last. They were the epitome of toxic, and he'd grown so used to it that I didn't see him ever walking away.

"I use protection sometimes. But sometimes I just want to put a baby in her."

"Do you know how demeaning that is to say: *Put a baby in her*. Like she's an object. Or a baby-making machine. It's really offensive, Rico. And you know I'm not Panda's biggest fan, so that's saying a lot that I'm defending her."

"Of course, you're going to go all women's rights on me. Are you still mad at Panda for stealing your navy sweater before you left for college?" He had a big, goofy grin on his face that made me want to hug him and throat-punch him all at the same time.

"No. The reasons that I don't care for Panda are: A. Her name is ridiculous, and B. She encouraged you to drop out of high school when you were doing well." I crossed my arms over my chest.

"Kingpin Weed was her idea, and it was a brilliant one. But now that pot's legal, everyone's doing it."

"Yeah. It's much easier to get a business loan when you're selling products that are legal. It's a wiser path." Yes. I was fluent in sarcasm, and I made no attempt to hide it.

"I've never been as smart as you, you know that."

I hated when he said that. Both of my brothers tossed that one out there every time when they'd mess up and ask me for help. I despised it.

Was it true? Probably.

But was it their fault? No.

They were lacking the tools needed to pull themselves out of the shit life they were born into.

"Are you two just going to stand out there and gab while

15

I'm under distress in here?" my mother shouted from the room, and Rico chuckled.

"The big, bad Jimbo gambled all the money in their savings account, so they're not speaking at the moment."

"How much money did he lose?"

"I don't know. A couple hundred bucks, maybe. But Mama is real pissed about it." I grabbed her drink and followed my brother the short distance to my mother's smoke-filled oasis. I glanced around the room, taking in the red and gold bedding, the half-filled ashtrays on the dresser and the end table, and the large, nearly nude photo of my mother framed over her bed. It was giving desperation vibes with a side of *I'm over the hill, and I'm not happy about it.*

I moved to the window and opened it, allowing the fresh air to at least offer a reprieve from this hellish cancer-causing cave.

"My god, Wendy. No one should be breathing this in," I said.

"Of course, you call me Wendy when you know I'm down and out."

She was always down and out—otherwise, she would be missing. She never called or made herself available when she wasn't in a bad place.

So, bad was all I knew of this woman.

"I've called you Wendy since I was a kid. Don't find another reason to stay bedbound. Get up. Breathe in some fresh air. Maybe drink some milk or eat something that doesn't come pre-packaged. You don't look well."

Her skin was pale and tinged slightly gray. If she didn't spend most of her days in bed sleeping, I would have believed she was a vampire back when I was a sucker for the *Twilight* series. After all, the woman had a real gift for sucking the life out of the people around her.

She sat forward and held out her hand for her drink. I didn't give it to her. Instead, I reached for her hand and pulled her up on her feet.

"You get the Coke after you take a shower. Go." I pointed to the bathroom, and she glared at me before storming the few feet away and slamming the door.

"Damn, Sis. You're the only one who can get her up and moving when she's in a slump," Rico said.

I took the beer from his hand and raised a brow. "How about you don't drink when it's not even noon? How's the job going?"

"You know Oscar likes to ride my ass, but at least it's a paying job."

I set my mother's glass on the dresser and shouted through the door that it was waiting for her there.

Rico followed me back out to the kitchen, where I poured what little bit was left of his beer down the drain and found a trash bag beneath the sink. I started dumping all the empty bottles into the bag before heading to the refrigerator to clean out the rotten food.

The door to the trailer swung open, and Zane stepped inside. He was a year younger than Rico and three years younger than me. My two brothers resembled one another, while I didn't look like either of them.

It was fitting in a way. I'd never felt like I fit in here.

My father was the only one I'd ever felt like I belonged with.

But I loved my brothers fiercely, and I tolerated my mother because they couldn't seem to escape her orbit.

"Well, if it isn't the professor!" Zane scooped me up and spun me around. They were both big guys. Tall, broad, and muscular.

"Put me down and help me clean this place up. You guys shouldn't be living like this."

Yes. They both still lived at home.

Zane moved to the sink and started washing dishes. "I, uh, was kind of hoping you could help me with something."

17

Here we go.

"What did you do?" I asked, whipping around to face him.

"I sort of made a dumb bet on a horse, and Sam White is threatening to take my car if I don't pay him by Friday." He scratched the back of his neck, and I squeezed my eyes shut.

"How much do you owe him?" I asked.

"Three hundred bucks."

"And you leveraged your car for a stupid horse bet?" I hissed before turning back to the refrigerator and questioning the fact that I'd willingly returned home.

In the name of my father, of course.

But this was the reason that I hated coming back.

I could feel myself being pulled under.

Even my breathing felt more constricted when I was home.

I felt trapped here.

I'd wanted a different life, and that was why I'd left.

I loved my brothers; I just didn't know if I could save them and save myself at the same time.

Zane gave me that sad, pathetic look that he always used when he fucked up.

I let out a long breath. "Come by the bar later in the week and I'll get you the money."

He wrapped his arms around me from behind, and I shook him off.

I was enabling him, and I knew it. But I didn't know how else to help him. I'd tried getting them both jobs. I'd bailed them out of endless shit. Talked ad nauseam about them moving away and changing their lives. Coming to stay with me in California. About going back to school to get their GEDs.

But it never went anywhere.

And I was more than aware that the definition of insanity was doing the same thing over and over again and expecting a different outcome.

So, I just tried to bandage things the best I could.

"Damn. Ruby always knows how to fix things," Rico said.

I turned around to face them.

"Yeah. I'm the Ray Donovan of this shit show," I grumped as I tied the garbage bag and moved to the door to set it outside. I sucked in the fresh air and waited until the queasy feeling I had from the rotten food was out of my system.

"Who the hell is Ray Donovan?" Zane asked.

"It's a TV show." I shook my head.

"Oh, yeah, with that actor, Liev Schreiber?" Rico nodded, like he knew exactly what I was talking about. "He's a fix-it guy, right?"

"Yes. People make endless bad choices, and he cleans up their shit. Sort of like me with you two."

"You are the Ray Donovan of the family," Zane said, hooking an arm around my shoulder and kissing the top of my head.

"Lucky me." I rolled my eyes and thought about it.

It had been this way since I was a little kid.

Moving away hadn't really changed much.

They still called.

I still answered.

Maybe this was just my purpose.

But I'd be lying if I didn't admit that it was exhausting.

3

River

I walked into Whiskey Falls bar, and Romeo held up his hand and waved me over. My boy had won his fight a few weeks ago, and we were all relieved to have that behind him now. He'd officially made a statement that he was retiring from boxing, and he would be focusing his energy on the gym that he owned, the house he'd just bought, and of course, his girl, Demi, who was one of us now.

My brother, Kingston, was sitting beside him, and Hayes and Nash were on the other side of the table. The five of us had been the best of friends since we were kids, and our bond ran deep. I glanced over to see Demi standing at the bar, talking to Ruby.

I made my way over and leaned down to kiss Demi on the cheek, and she smiled up at me. "Hey, River. Glad you're here. Everyone is getting hungry."

My eyes landed on Ruby.

Dark hair fell all around her shoulders.

Red lips.

Cat eyes that looked more green than blue or gold today.

She wore a black concert tee that outlined her perky tits perfectly, and my mouth watered at the sight.

There was just something about her.

She was Lionel's daughter, which meant she was off-limits, not to mention the fact that she appeared to hate me, but a man could appreciate a fine woman without acting on it.

"I got hung up at work." I turned my attention to Ruby, who stood on the other side of the bar. "Hello, Evil Queen. I'll take a beer."

She raised a brow. "That's original. I hope you didn't lose any brain cells coming up with that one."

She reached for a glass and pulled the tap as Demi covered her mouth with her hand to hide her laughter.

"First, you didn't think I knew how to do my job, and now you're worrying about my brain cells. You sure are worried about me. Maybe you're sweeter than you let on." I smirked when she set the glass down and glared at me.

"Romeo's waving me over." Demi looked between us like this was too much tension for her. "Just let Ruby know what you want to eat. I gave her everyone's food order just now."

I nodded as she hurried away, and I turned my attention back to the little vixen on the other side of the bar.

Her tongue moved along her bottom lip, and she raised a brow. "Don't mistake my concern with how you assist my father as anything more than that."

I nodded. Damn. She could dish out the shit, and I fucking loved it.

"Such an angry, evil queen. Trust me, I don't need your concern. I do just fine on my own."

"I don't doubt that for a minute. That's my concern. Were you looking out for yourself or my father with that lawsuit?"

Now that shit pissed me off once again. I was a lot of things, but I wasn't a shitty friend. I was loyal to my core, and Lionel was one of the few people I would walk through fire for.

I took a pull from my beer before leaning forward and moving just a few inches from her face. "Your father is my friend. I advised

21

him from the start that he should have just paid the fucking medical bill for Jenna, and none of this would have happened. He paid more than he should have because he's a stubborn ass. And for the record, she could have gotten a lot more out of him if I hadn't talked some fucking sense into her and convinced her to let it go. So be careful who you point the finger at."

She didn't even flinch. "How very lawyerly of you, but unlike my father, I don't trust you."

"Good. Then you're as smart as your father says you are." I moved closer, those red lips beckoning me. I'd never felt a pull toward a woman like this.

Or maybe she was just hot as hell, and I hadn't stopped thinking about her since the run-in at the hospital.

She pulled back, mouth in a straight line, completely unaffected. Cool as a motherfucking cat. "Don't go getting any ideas. I know a wild River when I see one."

I chuckled. "Takes one to know one."

"No. It takes one who's dealt with many to know one."

"All right. Then how about you lose the attitude and realize I'm not the enemy? Your dad is important to me, and I'll do whatever I can to help him. Always."

She tucked her hair behind her ear. "We'll see about that. What do you want to eat?"

"I'll take a burger. Medium."

"Got it. You can go now." She turned away, and I chuckled. I grabbed my beer and made my way to the table.

"That looked a little heated," Romeo said, glancing from me back over to where Ruby stood behind the bar.

"I told you guys that they were extremely tense with one another." Demi sipped her wine and smiled up at me.

"She thinks I screwed over her father. She's mad that he lied to her about why he had the stroke. That shit has nothing to do with me. She's just an angry woman," I said, taking another long pull from my glass.

"But damn, she's hot." Kingston waggled his brows. The dude had a one-track mind, but for whatever reason, hearing him talk about Ruby pissed me off.

"For fuck's sake, she's Lionel's daughter. Keep your dick in your pants." The words were out of my mouth before I could stop them.

Hayes whistled while Nash barked out a laugh.

"Take it down a notch, brother. I'm just stating the obvious. No need to piss on your turf," Kingston said with a big, dopey grin on his face.

I swear, our only genetic similarity was that we had the same birth parents. The dude was too fucking happy for his own good.

"No one is pissing on anyone's turf. I'm just saying . . . be fucking respectful, you dickweiner."

"You know, I think that's a new favorite. I'm a big fan of both." My brother winked at me.

"You're a fan of both?" Demi asked.

"Did you really just ask that, baby? He's going to enjoy this." Romeo wrapped an arm around her and kissed her cheek.

"Well, I have an extraordinary dick, and I'm proud of it. And . . . I like hot dogs, also known as wieners. I think they should have their own food group."

Everyone laughed, and I rolled my eyes just as Ruby came by with a ton of plates balanced on her arms. She set the food down in front of us, and everyone thanked her.

"Are you a fan of wieners, Ruby?" Kingston asked her, and I squeezed my eyes shut because it was like watching a kitten play with a scorpion.

"I'm a fan of silence." She stared him down, and he rubbed his hands together excitedly, because the fucker didn't know when he was annoying someone.

"You'd never be able to be quiet with me." He waggled his brows.

23

Demi was looking between Kingston and Ruby, probably wondering if he'd gone too far, which happened often with my brother.

"That's probably true." Her lips turned up in the corners the slightest bit as she leaned closer to him. I doubted anyone else noticed, but I found this woman fascinating, so I was noticing all sorts of shit now. "Because I'd be telling you to get the hell away from me."

"Shots fired," he said, placing both hands on his heart. "Just giving you shit. It's nice of you to be covering for your dad right now. I went by to see him today."

"Yeah? Thank you. He'll be moved to another floor in the hospital for inpatient physical therapy soon. But he's got a long road ahead of him, so I appreciate all of you being so good to him." Her gaze softened, and my chest fucking squeezed, which freaked me the hell out. I'd never seen the softer side of her, and for whatever reason, I liked that, too. But then she turned to me, eyes hard once again, but I saw the humor there. "Even if you give him shit legal advice."

"You know, as a doctor of psychology, I'd think you could come up with something better than that. If all you've got on me is my bad legal advice, I'd call it a win. I don't give a shit if I'm a good lawyer."

That wasn't true, but I preferred people to think I didn't care when they insulted me. The truth was, I cared more than most people thought I did.

"How the hell do you know I'm a doctor of psychology?"

Everyone's eyes were ping-ponging back and forth between us now.

I popped a tater tot into my mouth and groaned because they were the best tots in town. I glanced up at her as she sat there, giving me her death glare and waiting for an answer. "Remember. I'm an attorney. I have my ways of finding shit out. Even if I'm not very good at my job, right?"

Lionel and I were close, so he'd told me. But I wouldn't tell her that.

Demi's eyes were wide, and Romeo had a ridiculous smile on his face as if he were enjoying this.

"Why don't you focus on keeping my father out of trouble and stay out of my business?" Her words were ice, and then she turned and stormed off.

"Did you really research her?" Demi asked, after the evil queen had made her way back around the bar.

"Of course not. Lionel told me. But I like getting under her skin." I tossed another tot into my mouth.

"For the first time in his life, I actually think King was right about this," Nash said, holding his hands up and laughing when my brother feigned being offended. "I just mean that you were right about River pissing on his turf. You like this girl."

"I hate to say it, but I agree," Hayes added.

"Are you fucking kidding me right now? That's what you got out of that exchange? I like her about as much as I'd like being poked in the eye with a sharp stick."

"Are you saying you don't find her attractive?" Demi asked, raising a brow as if she dared me to deny it.

"Oh, my sweet, naïve Beans," I said, referencing the nickname we all called her. "I didn't say that. Hell, anyone with eyeballs can see she's fucking gorgeous. But I can find someone attractive and still despise them."

"So, you despise her?" Romeo smirked. "You sure about that, brother? You keep looking over there and watching her."

"Agreed. I think you fucking like that she hates you." It was Kingston's turn to add on, because God forbid that fucker didn't have something to say.

"I don't know, River. We watched Romeo fall not that long ago. Maybe it's your turn next." Hayes looked proud of himself for coming up with that one, and I flipped him the bird.

"Give me a fucking break. This guy was pussy-whipped from the minute he got that pumpkin magic our girl puts in her cups over at Magnolia Beans." I barked out a laugh at the memory of how crazy Romeo was about her from the very beginning.

"I don't know, brother. You seem a little defensive," Romeo said over his laughter.

"Hey. Maybe that's your love language," Demi said.

"I don't have a love language." I took a generous bite of my burger.

"What exactly is a love language?" Kingston asked her.

"It's the way you respond to love. Maybe you like the fact that she hates you, but in a sort of weird, tension-filled attraction that is impossible to miss," she said proudly, and Romeo looked at her like she'd just invented the cure to a deadly disease.

Kingston was nodding at her proudly.

These motherfuckers were a bunch of crazy saps.

"That's the most ridiculous shit I've heard. I can't stand most people. I like to get laid. And I tolerate you guys. That's my love language." I reached for my beer.

"Now I know where this is coming from," Nash said. "Cutler was talking all sorts of shit about his love language."

"That's Beefcake to you," I said, because Nash's son, Cutler, was more like all of ours. The four of us were his godfathers, and Demi fell just as in love with him as the rest of us were. He was quirky as shit, and we were all crazy about him. He'd recently changed his name to Beefcake, and we'd all respected it, even if it annoyed the hell out of Nash.

More laughter.

"Yes," Demi said. "Beefcake's love language is physical touch. He loves to hug and hold hands. He's got a tender heart."

"Just like his dad." Kingston's head fell back in laughter as he slapped Nash on the shoulder.

Nash flashed him the bird, and I glanced over as the door swung open and a group of guys walked in.

I recognized one of them as Ruby's brother, Zane. He was a bit of a fuck-up. The dude was always in here asking for free shit from Lionel.

There were a few locals here as well, and I didn't miss the shift in energy when Sam White moved to his feet and made his way toward the group.

I'd learned at a young age to read the room.

To recognize when shit was about to go down and to prepare for it. I'd been on the wrong side of that equation once, and it wouldn't happen again.

And shit was definitely about to go down.

Romeo's eyes found mine. Kingston, Hayes, and Nash noticed, and they all stopped eating. Demi was clueless, and she continued telling us about how sweet and tenderhearted Cutler was, but none of us were responding anymore.

She gazed over her shoulder and whispered something to Romeo.

Sam moved into Zane's space and pulled him to his feet, just as he sat down at a table. I slipped off my barstool and started to head that way with my boys right behind me.

Out of my peripheral, I saw a flash of movement.

Ruby fucking Rose came sailing over the bar like a motherfucking ninja. She didn't miss a beat as she landed on her Dr. Marten-clad feet.

"Do not fucking think about it," she hissed at Sam, who slowly turned toward her.

I was already moving. There was no fucking way this was going down on my watch.

This was Lionel's daughter, after all.

I needed to make sure she was okay.

It was the least I could do while she was home, covering the bar.

But her hand shot up, and she turned toward me. "I've got this. Go back to your table."

You could hear a pin drop in the bar, and I didn't take another step in either direction. If Sam so much as sneezed, I'd be on top of him. He was a piece-of-shit loan shark who thought he was a tough guy.

He wasn't.

He intimidated weak dudes like Zane, but he was all bark and no bite.

Ruby reached into her back pocket and slapped what looked like a wad of cash in his hand. "This shit ends now. Now go finish your beer and stay the hell away from my brother."

Sam looked down at his hand and quickly assessed that whatever she'd given him was what he'd wanted, and he gave her a curt nod.

"You're too sexy to be cleaning up your baby brother's mess, Ruby," he said, and my hands fisted at my sides.

"And you're too stupid to realize that I don't give a shit what you think of me. Go drink your beer, Sam."

Damn.

Ruby Rose was even more of a badass than I'd thought.

Maybe I was pissing on my turf, after all.

4

Ruby

I spent the morning scouring my father's house, which was the home I'd grown up in. It wasn't large, but it sat on a quiet street right on the water. It was my favorite place in the world, if I was being honest. Minus all the stress that came with being back in Magnolia Falls.

But when I tuned out all the noise and just let myself be . . . this was where I found the most peace. In this little cottage on the lake that had two bedrooms, a small kitchen, and a whole lot of love.

My father had always been my safe place.

Yes, he drank too much. Yes, he got himself into a shit ton of trouble without even trying.

But he loved me, and I'd always known it.

Felt it.

So, I'd cleaned the place up, stripped the beds, and stocked the refrigerator with food, as there'd only been a case of beer and a bag of shredded cheese in there when I'd arrived.

I slipped into my jean shorts and a tank top, as it was a gorgeous day outside and I wanted to take the kayak out. I remembered the day my dad had brought it home for me on my sixteenth birthday. He'd had my name painted on the side: Ruby Rose.

I hadn't been out on the water in years.

When I left for school, I'd been desperate for a fresh start.

I'd needed to get away from this place.

My mother had just divorced husband number three, and she was spiraling. My brothers were both out of control, and I was putting out fire after fire.

And as much as I loved my father, I couldn't be what he needed. I'd had to pick him up from the bar night after night, because he was drinking even heavier than usual during that time—and it all just got to be too much.

So, I'd reached for a lifeline and saved myself, because the fear of not leaving had started seeping in. The fear of staying sedentary like the rest of my family.

I wanted more out of life.

But my father was my weakness. It had always been the two of us against the world.

He'd cut way back on his drinking over the last few years and I'd appreciated it. He liked to say that he was a work in progress, and I'd tell him that as long as he was working on himself, that was what mattered.

I needed him to take better care of himself because he was important to me.

I made my way down to the dock, noting how worn it looked now.

I'd always been the one to keep up the house. Dad ran the bar, and I ran the household.

I trailed my fingers along the chipped paint on the dock and bent down to untie the rope attached to the kayak, which looked just as dingy as the dock. I climbed in and found the paddle, tipping my head back and letting the morning sun shine its warmth on my face.

The mountains surrounded me, and the smell of pine flooded my senses.

I'd missed this. Living in the city meant that I was always rushing. I didn't spend a lot of time outside because I was always studying or working. Balancing school and work had been difficult, especially while writing my dissertation.

But I'd done it.

I made my way down the narrow path, maneuvering my kayak the way I'd done hundreds, if not thousands, of times over the years. Our home sat on a little alcove on the lake, and the turquoise water had a way of settling me, no matter what was going on in my life. The flowers were in bloom, and the birds were chirping. It looked like something straight out of a Disney movie. If only it were this peaceful when I wasn't out on the water.

I let my paddle steer to the left as I turned toward my favorite spot where I used to go and let myself dream about a life outside of all the drama.

A life where I could make a difference in the world, and not just in the confines of my inner circle.

But when I pulled into the little cove where I'd always found serenity, there was another canoe already parked there.

My eyes widened as I took in River Pierce, who stood out in great contrast amongst the scenery. There was nothing peaceful about this man or his presence.

He wore a black fitted tee, and his muscled arms were covered in colorful ink. His dark hair was wavy and unruly, and his eyes were shielded by a pair of gold aviators. His head turned slowly as I came to a stop a few feet from him.

"I didn't think evil queens liked sunshine and water?" He insulted me without missing a beat.

"Where do you think we plot the demise of our enemies?" I purred, and he chuckled.

"All right. That explains it." He was lying back with his

denim-covered legs crossed at the ankles as if he didn't have a care in the world.

My instinct was to leave, because I sure as hell didn't come out here to make small talk with a man who irritated the hell out of me, and the feeling appeared to be mutual. But I hadn't missed the way he'd quickly moved to his feet when Sam and Zane were getting ready to fight the other night, before I'd jumped in.

I wasn't used to anyone ever having my back outside of my dad, and even he'd grown comfortable letting me handle things as I'd grown older.

I wrapped my hands around the paddle, ready to move in a different direction.

"Don't leave on my account. I'll be heading out soon."

I paused. "How do you know about this place? It's sort of a hidden spot on the water. I used to come here all the time. I've never seen anyone else here before."

He sat forward and raised his gold aviators, and his dark brown eyes looked jet black with the light shining down on him.

"I bought a house right around the turn, at the end of this cove, a few years ago. Never thought I'd be into boating, but I like coming out here on my own and chilling. Gives me time to think about other career opportunities, you know, since I'm not good at being lawyerly." He smirked, flashing me this wicked grin that had my lady parts reacting.

What the hell was that about?

I couldn't stand this guy, yet my body was quick to betray me every time he was around.

It made me dislike him even more.

He was unpredictable, combative, aggravating, and too good-looking for his own good.

A wild river.

He got under my skin, and that was never okay with me.

I'd learned at a very young age that being in control was the only way to survive this world.

Unpredictable people were red flags, and I avoided them at all costs.

I set my paddle in the kayak and lay back, acting as if he didn't affect me at all. "I wouldn't have guessed you to be so sensitive. Does my opinion of how you do your job really matter?"

The water splashed against the shore, and I tried to relax, even though my heart raced every time this man was near.

Maybe it was my instincts warning me to stay away from him.

Maybe it was just the fact that I was wildly attracted to him.

Of course, I was . . . because why not be attracted to someone dangerous? Someone who would cause you grief.

It was all I knew.

I'd studied psychology for more than half of my life.

I knew how to read the signs.

And River Pierce was full of warning signs.

"What matters to me is when someone judges me unfairly. I dealt with that enough as a fucking kid. As an adult, it pisses me the fuck off."

I hadn't expected that answer, so I shot forward, sitting up and tearing my sunglasses off my face to meet his angry gaze. "So, let me get this straight. You're offended that I've misjudged you?"

"Did I stutter?"

"Why do you care what I think of you?" I hissed. "I'm an evil queen, remember?"

His lips turned up in the corners. This man was all over the place. I couldn't tell if he was angry or joking half the time.

"Ahhh . . . is someone sensitive about being called an evil queen? Have I misjudged *you*, Ruby?" His voice was gravelly and sexy as hell.

"First off, I don't care what you think of me. I care what *I* think of myself," I huffed. "And for the record, calling me an evil queen is not an insult to me. It means my work here is done."

"You've got it all figured out, don't you? You think your big, fancy degree makes you an expert on people?"

A sarcastic laugh escaped my lips.

It was very evil queen of me, and I liked it.

"Well, yes, genius. I have a Ph.D. in psychology. That, by definition, makes me fairly skilled at reading people."

"So, tell me, *Doctor* . . . who am I? You seem to think you know me so well. I'm curious how skilled you are."

I loved this part of the game. When someone lets me assess them and call them out for just how easily I'd been able to read them.

"Sure. It would be my pleasure. I'll even do it pro bono because I'll enjoy it." I raised a brow and thought it over. "You had a rocky past. I don't know what exactly happened in your childhood, obviously, but it left you with trust issues. You don't do relationships or anything where commitment is involved. You're smarter than most of the people you interact with," I said, and he barked out a laugh as if I'd just said he was the smartest guy in the room. "Don't get cocky. You aren't even the smartest person in this cove."

"I see. So, I'm smarter than most, but not smarter than you."

"It's my opinion. But I make it a point to be more knowledgeable than my opponents, so don't take offense." I shrugged.

"Do you really believe that your assessment about how I don't do relationships makes you some sort of brilliant doctor of psychology? It's not a secret. Hell, everyone in this town knows I don't do relationships. Get in line, Evil Queen. You haven't told me anything I haven't heard a million times."

Now it was my turn to chuckle. "Yeah, but they don't know why you're so closed off. They don't know that if you took away all the layers, it would come down to fear."

"I see. I'm afraid of women. Is that it?" I could tell he was enjoying himself.

"You're afraid of being hurt. You're afraid of loss. You're afraid of allowing yourself to feel joy. You're afraid of trusting anyone outside of your circle."

He was quiet now as his gaze studied mine. "Wow. All this time, I thought I just enjoyed fucking different women because I get bored easily. Thank you, Dr. Rose. I feel like I can breathe now."

"Laugh all you want. You're a classic textbook case. Hard on the outside and damaged on the inside." I knew this because I was the same way; I just wouldn't admit that to him.

This draw that lived between us was most likely the recognition of one damaged soul to another.

"All right. I'm not going to argue with the fact that I'm damaged. I'll be the first one to admit that. I guess you really are the expert," he said, but I didn't miss the sarcastic tone.

I'd always made a point of knowing things about the people in town when I was young. Like who to avoid.

River and his friends were on that list.

Hell, I'd gotten into a street fight with his friend Romeo back when we were young. He hadn't even put up a fight. I'd been forced to fight him because a few kids had jumped me on my way home after school, and he'd come to my rescue to help me.

I couldn't have that.

Couldn't look weak.

So, I'd punched him in the gut and told him that I could take care of myself.

He hadn't done a thing in response. He'd just nodded as if he understood why I had to do it.

But unlike River and his friends, I'd always preferred to fly solo. I didn't want to rely on anyone outside of my father. The few times I'd done it, it had bitten me in the ass.

My dad had been the only person who hadn't completely failed me.

We'd taken care of one another the best we could.

River was scowling at me now, and I knew I'd pissed him off, even if he was trying to act like I hadn't told him anything he didn't already know.

"You asked me to tell you what I thought of you, and I did. Don't shoot the messenger," I said, reaching for my paddle.

"What's it like, sitting up on your high horse judging the world? I'm guessing it's pretty lonely up there, Ruby. Unlike you, I've found people that I trust. Yes, I had a fucked-up childhood. So the fuck have millions of other people. But I did something about it. I didn't like what happened to me, and I chose a profession that would help me make a difference in the world. So I could stop that shit from happening to others. But *you,* you chose a profession that allows you to make assumptions about everyone. I may not have a degree in psychology, but I think you've just found a way to keep everyone at bay. It's probably a form of protection. Decide everyone is bad and then stay the fuck away from them. But unlike you, I'm living every day. Enjoying my life. You've run away and buried yourself in books so that you don't have to deal with real life. Who's the fucking phony now?"

Motherfucker.

This guy had just psychoanalyzed me?

And he'd been somewhat right about a few things.

The thing he didn't understand, was that I wasn't in denial about who I was.

So I did what any intelligent woman would do in this situation.

I took my paddle, plunged it into the lake, and used force as I shot it forward and doused him in the face with water.

He didn't even flinch. He just smiled, like he'd won some big challenge.

I flipped him the bird and got the hell out of there.

River Pierce was more than a red flag.

He was too smart for his own good.

Dangerously good-looking.

And he'd just summed me up in a nutshell without any formal training.

That just made me hate him a little more than I already did.

5

River

I pulled up to the hospital and parked my car.

Fuck.

Ruby had gotten under my skin earlier, out on the water. Why was I so drawn to a woman who insulted me every time I saw her?

Yeah, I'd dished it back, because you shouldn't talk shit if you can't take it in return.

But the way her hazel eyes had shown her hand was something I hadn't expected.

I'd hurt her feelings.

Hell, I didn't even know she had feelings.

And her bullshit about me being afraid. Sure, there was some truth there. I didn't trust many people. I kept my circle small.

But at least I had a fucking circle.

She'd run away from everyone.

At least I dealt with my shit.

I got out of the car and made my way into the hospital to visit Lionel. He'd just started inpatient physical therapy, and he'd been grumpy and annoyed about being there, so I knew the visits helped him.

But damn, did I hate being here.

I took the elevator up to the sixth floor. When I stepped off, I came to a stop at the sound of her voice.

"I want to know why my father is sitting in his own urine. It's completely unacceptable." Ruby was on a tirade, which I'd come to learn was the norm for her.

I moved beside her, because for whatever fucking reason, I felt the need to make sure she was okay.

She glanced over at me, but for the first time since we'd met, she didn't seem annoyed by my presence.

"We didn't know he needed to use the restroom," the older woman on the other side of the desk said. She crossed her arms over her chest, but I could tell she was nervous, even if she was trying to act like she hadn't done anything wrong.

"That's interesting, *Betty*." Ruby said her name with complete disdain. "My father said he rang the bell four times. Four goddamn times. And he isn't allowed to get up and walk on his own, per your rules. So, you just let him pee himself like he's a child? Do you know how demeaning that is?"

"I must have missed the bell. We have other patients here. He isn't the only one who needs us."

"Got it. So, there's no apology or attempt to make things better for him?" Ruby's voice cracked as the words left her mouth, and it startled me. I'd never seen a vulnerable side to her before this morning, and now it seemed like she was ready to lose it.

But she raised her chin, shoulders squared—almost like she was gathering herself and getting into fight mode.

Damn, did I recognize that move.

I'd always been able to shift quickly when I needed to.

Fight or flight? I'd always fucking fight.

"Betty," I said, and the woman turned toward me, eyes hard. "Have you ever had a family member have a stroke, leaving them unable to take care of themselves?"

"I don't know why that's your business."

"I'm just making a point. How about a little empathy for Ruby? Seeing her dad in this state is tough. She left her home and her job to come here and support him. I'm sure you can understand why it's difficult for her to see her father like this, yeah?"

I thought Ruby would yell at me for interfering, but she didn't. Her shoulders sagged a little, as if she didn't have the energy to fight me at the moment.

Damn. When was the last time someone had her back?

"I know it's difficult to see a family member struggle. I'm sorry that we didn't get there fast enough. How about I go and check on him, and I'll get him cleaned up. I'll try to keep a better eye on the monitors moving forward."

Ruby nodded. "I appreciate it. I'll just wait out here until you're through."

Betty nodded, her gaze more sympathetic now. "It'll take a bit. I'll get him showered now, if you want to go grab some food or coffee. Give me about thirty minutes."

She stepped away, and Ruby turned to look at me. I thought she was going to rip me a new one for getting involved, but she surprised me. "Thank you."

"That was painful for you to say, wasn't it?" I smirked.

"You have no idea." She sank her teeth into her juicy bottom lip.

"You want to go grab a cup of coffee or some food in the cafeteria while we wait to see him?"

She nodded and walked beside me toward the elevators. We stepped on, and when the doors closed, it was quiet. Being in this small space with just her was almost overwhelming.

The smell of jasmine and orange filled the air around me, and I shoved my hands into my pockets to distract myself. But then the most shocking thing of all happened.

A tear ran down her pretty face, and my eyes widened as her shoulders started to shake.

A sob escaped her throat, and she lost it.

Ruby fucking Rose was crying.

Hard.

On instinct, I moved toward the panel of buttons and stopped the elevator.

"Hey. It's all right." I stepped closer, not sure if I should touch her for fear she might throat-punch me.

The woman was completely unpredictable.

But I couldn't stand there, watching her break down and not do something. Normally, I ran away from this type of shit, but for some reason, seeing Ruby Rose like this felt more like I'd won something.

Like I was the only one to see the moon during an eclipse.

I moved closer, wrapping my arms around her slowly.

Cautiously.

Like she was a cat who might whip around and scratch my eyes out.

But she didn't. She buried her face in my shirt and cried.

It wasn't loud or hysterical. It was controlled, just as I would expect it to be with her.

Just pure sadness.

Little whimpers she was trying hard to hold in.

My hand moved up and down her back, and my thumb traced the skin along the collar of her tee. It was soft and smooth.

Her scent was invading the air around me, and I warned my dick not to react.

Getting an erection while the strongest woman I'd ever met was having a meltdown seemed like an act of war.

Her little sobs slowed, and her hands, currently fisted in the cotton of my shirt, relaxed. She kept her head down for a minute, wiping her face.

And when she looked up at me, it was like catching a rainbow right after a storm.

Her hazel eyes were a soft blue with sage green rings around them and a bit of gold right in the center.

Soft.

Vulnerable.

Wounded.

"You okay?" I asked, keeping my voice low.

"Yes. Let's go get something to eat." She stepped back, face completely void of emotion now, and she stared straight ahead.

I hit the button on the elevator, and we rode down to the ground floor in silence.

I held the door when it opened, and she stepped off, walking slightly ahead of me toward the cafeteria. We each grabbed a cup of coffee, and Ruby reached for a blueberry muffin.

Once we took our seats, she broke off a piece of the muffin and popped it into her mouth before looking up at me. "If you tell anyone what happened in that elevator, I will use all of my evil queen powers to torture you until the end of time."

"Don't worry about it. I won't say anything. You're dealing with a lot, and it's normal to cry sometimes."

"Oh, yeah? When was the last time you cried?" She raised a brow.

"It's been a while." I chuckled. "How about you?"

"I haven't cried since I was six years old, and my puppy ran away."

I raised a brow. "You haven't cried in over twenty years?"

"That's the first thing that came to mind after that statement?" she said, shaking her head in disbelief.

"Yeah. What else would I ask?"

"If we found the puppy." She reached for her coffee.

"Did you?"

"We did. I made my dad take me out every single day after school, and we finally found him."

"Where was he?"

"It's funny you should ask. I found Bullet walking with

42

Midge freaking Longhorn," she said, as if this were the most scandalous thing she'd ever shared.

Midge Longhorn owned The Golden Goose, the diner in town, which was one of my favorite places to eat. But she was about as grumpy as they came, and I wouldn't have guessed her to be a puppy snatcher. I figured small children and animals ran for cover in her presence.

"You named your puppy Bullet when you were only six years old?" I barked out a laugh. "That's so fucking you to do that."

She rolled her eyes. "Again, I tell you that Midge Longhorn stole my puppy, and you focus on the name of the dog."

"So, what did she say when you confronted her? Because there's no fucking doubt in my mind that you confronted her."

"Of course I did. It had been the first time in my life I'd ever cried other than when I was a baby. And the last time, up until now. So clearly, I was attached to Bullet. And Midge acted like she'd just found him a few minutes before in the park. He'd been missing for a week. Trust me—she's shady. And she's been uncomfortable when I've been at The Golden Goose ever since. She won't even make eye contact with me. *She knows* that I know she stole that puppy from a child."

I sipped my coffee and studied her. "You do realize Midge doesn't look at anyone. She's in a perpetual bad mood."

"Trust me. She knows. But she has the best tomato soup and grilled cheese in town, so it doesn't stop me from eating there when I'm home. Plus, I get a special kind of pleasure staring her down and watching her squirm."

"Damn. I've got to give you credit if you can make Midge Longhorn squirm."

"I'm a woman of many talents."

"I don't doubt that. You might have nailed a few things about me in your assessment this morning. Not the part about being fearful, though. That's not the reason that I don't connect with many people."

She looked surprised that I'd brought it up. But I didn't mind talking about it. She'd been right about a lot of what she'd said. No doubt, I was damaged. I'd had a tough childhood—a lot of loss at a young age.

"If it's not fear, what is it?" she asked, leaning forward like she was genuinely interested.

"It's a choice. I don't trust easily, and I'm okay with that. I'm not afraid of being let down by people because I don't give them the option. I take care of myself. I take care of my grandmother. And I can trust my boys without question. It's enough for me. I'm not longing for some fucked-up fairy tale. Not because I'm afraid of it, but because I don't want it. I don't need it."

She nodded and raised a brow. "That's very intuitive of you. Maybe you just haven't met anyone worth taking the risk on. It seems like you've all grown close to Demi. She was an outsider, right?"

"Exactly my point. I was willing to let her in because she's Romeo's girl, and I respect that. But not everyone wants what they have." Why was I telling her all of this? "How about you? I don't see a ring on your finger. I don't take you as someone who trusts easily, nor would I guess that you're seeking the white picket fence."

"Gee. What gave me away? My bubbly demeanor?" She oozed sarcasm.

"Something like that. Answer the question."

"Why are you so interested in my personal life?" And this time, when the corners of her lips turned up, my fucking chest squeezed like I was a kid watching a goddamn unrealistic, bullshit Disney movie.

I hated Disney movies.

I hated happy endings.

Give me a thriller with a few kidnappings and murders and a healthy dose of torture, and I'll grab the popcorn.

"I am. You're Lionel's daughter. You just had your first breakdown in more than two decades in front of me since dear, sweet Bullet was kidnapped by Midge fucking Longhorn. So that bonds us in a dark, serial killer kind of way, right?"

She chuckled, looking away briefly before her gaze found mine again. "I was dating the professor I worked with for a few months, but I ended it shortly before I came home."

"The professor. How very rebellious of you. Why'd you end it?"

"You know that saying that your strengths are often your weaknesses?" She broke off another piece of her muffin and popped it into her mouth, red lips taunting me as she did so.

"Yes."

"Well, it's similar with relationships. I pick men who I don't have to worry will catch feelings. The professor was fifteen years older than me. A real intellect. He'd been a bachelor his whole life, so it was a safe bet that he wouldn't want anything serious. But, just like the last guy I dated, he suddenly dropped the L-word out of nowhere. He started talking about forever. I picked him because I didn't want forever. Yet he pulled a one-eighty on me."

"Maybe you're just that impossible not to fall for."

"It's a curse," she said, as she popped her thumb into her mouth and sucked the blueberry muffin crumb off without any awareness of how fucking sexy the move was.

"So, what happened to the boring professor?" I said, trying to act unfazed.

"Nothing. He understands that we don't want the same things. I was honest from the beginning. We were friends, and it wasn't anything serious for me. I'm not some damsel in distress looking to be saved. I've been saving myself for as long as I can remember. And the timing helped because I left to come home shortly after our breakup. But if I take the job I've been offered at the university, we'd be working together."

"Do you want to teach?"

"Not really. But I don't know for certain what I want to do with my degree. I'd like to maybe work with kids. I'd have loved to have someone to talk to when I was young and struggling, you know?"

There was an earnestness in her voice. In her eyes.

It hit me in that moment.

Ruby Rose is not an evil queen at all.

She was guarded and cautious and fierce.

She was the epitome of a queen.

Nothing evil about it.

6

Ruby

I glanced down at my phone and noticed the time. I couldn't believe the way the morning had gone.

I'd cried in front of River Pierce.

And talked to him like we were friends.

I guess I'd hit my breaking point today. We all had one, and apparently, I wasn't immune to it either.

"Well, this has been enough show-and-tell for one day, don't you think? We should probably get back upstairs."

"One more question."

"I wouldn't have guessed you to be a guy who likes this much small talk," I groaned.

"How would you have guessed me to be?"

I didn't hesitate because I'd assessed who he was the moment I'd met him. "A wild river."

He laughed. "Touché. Tell me why you were upset in the elevator."

I let out a long breath. I'd already shared too much. But for whatever reason, I didn't feel panicked about opening up to this man. My father clearly loved him, and he didn't strike me as someone who would tell your secrets. His dark eyes burned into mine, letting me know he wasn't leaving this table without an answer.

"Being home exhausts me sometimes. I had to pay off Zane's debt to Sam, which took my tip money for the week. My mother just told me she couldn't make rent. Again. So next week's tips will be gone, as well. It's such a vicious cycle with them, and I can't seem to get away from it. And then I think you hit a nerve this morning, because a lot of what you said was true." I held my hands up to stop him from gloating. "Not everything. I'm definitely not in denial about who I am. But I was surprised that you read me so well. I did run away from here because I was drowning. But distance didn't make it stop. It's a lot sometimes. And the one really good thing in my life is my father. Seeing him embarrassed about not making it to the bathroom put me over the edge. I'm paying off bookies for my brother and cleaning up my mom's shitty trailer, and I couldn't even make it to the hospital in time to help my dad. He should have been my first priority."

"Jesus. You can't save the world, Ruby. No wonder you're so fucking exhausted."

"Have you met my family? Lionel's the easy one." I forced a smile.

"It's not your job to take care of everyone. And Lionel is fine. Shit happens. Well, hopefully not literally for him."

A loud laugh escaped my lips. I didn't laugh often, but it felt good. This day was full of surprises.

"Let's hope not."

"My point is . . . he had a stroke. He wet himself. They'll clean him up, and he'll get better with time. It's okay. You can't be everything to everyone."

"Wow. That was deep. Sounds like you speak from experience."

"Nah. I'm all about boundaries. I choose who I'm willing to go out on a limb for. Not everyone deserves that, you know? But Lionel does. Let's go check on him."

I nodded and pushed to my feet. "Thanks for the chat. And I meant what I said earlier: If you tell anyone I cried, I'll kill you slowly and painfully."

"Maybe I'll surprise you by keeping my mouth shut. Not everyone is going to let you down."

His words hit, and a lump formed in my throat.

I was used to being let down, wasn't I?

We stepped onto the elevator, and I glanced over at him, my eyes scanning the colorful ink on his forearms. "Well, thanks for that. Do we go back to hating each other now?"

"Seems like the natural thing to do." His lips turned up the slightest bit in the corners. Dark scruff peppered his jaw, and his thick, wavy hair curled at the ends above his ears. "But I'll know the truth."

The doors opened, and he held out a hand for me to step off. I looked over my shoulder. "I can't wait to hear what you think the truth is."

He walked beside me and leaned in. His lips grazed the lobe of my ear, and goose bumps covered my arms. "I think you like me, Ruby Rose."

I forced myself to act unaffected. "Keep dreaming."

"Funny you should mention that. You did appear in my dream last night," he said, as we approached my father's room.

I wrapped my fingers around his wrist to stop him from walking in. "What was I wearing? An evil queen dress?"

"No. You weren't wearing anything. And you looked fucking beautiful. No wonder the professor wanted to keep you." He winked and stepped into the room, and I stood there, gaping at his back.

This man was definitely a wild card.

I shook it off and made my way over to my father, who was sitting up in his bed. He was dressed and had his sneakers on, looking like he was ready to go. He shook River's hand and looked up at me.

"What did you say to nurse Betty? She was a lot nicer to me this time." He chuckled.

"I didn't say anything," I said, bending down to fix one of his shoes that wasn't tied.

"My daughter always makes sure I'm okay," Dad said.

"Yeah. I'm getting that. Seems like she likes to make sure everyone is okay," River said, and I refused to look up at him.

I pushed to stand. "Okay. Time for physical therapy, right?"

"Yes. Jesse is coming to get me. You don't need to stay for that."

Jesse walked into the room and introduced himself to us. He went over the plan to get my father up and moving on his own soon. I listened and asked a few questions, and every time I looked over, I found River's eyes on me.

I hated how much I liked it.

I'd never wanted that kind of attention from a man.

But there was something different about him.

I knew it wasn't a good idea, so I forced myself to look away.

I was here to focus on my father, not flirt with a wrecking ball.

That was exactly what he was. He would destroy me if I let him in. I knew better.

"Is it fine if I come with?" I asked. "I'd like to learn the exercises that you're doing so that when we bring him home, I can continue them."

"Absolutely," Jesse said with a smile. He was about my age, a few inches shorter than River, and muscular.

River's phone vibrated, and he looked down at his screen before turning his attention to my father. "All right. I've got some issues at the office. I'll stop by after work."

"Thanks, River. I'll see you later," Dad said, moving to stand and placing his hands on the walker.

River nodded, giving me a forced smile before glaring at

Jesse, which had me covering my mouth with my hand to keep from laughing.

He was so broody and gruff on the outside.

But I'd seen a softer side.

A kinder side.

I followed my father and Jesse down to the workout room and took one final glance over my shoulder as I watched River turn the corner toward the elevators.

I spent the next few hours watching my father fight his way back to reclaim his life.

When we got back to his room, they brought his lunch in.

"How are things going at the bar?" he asked as he took a sip of water.

"Everything is running smoothly. You have nothing to worry about."

"I know. But I worry about you. I'm sorry you had to come back here and clean up my mess."

"Yours is the only mess I don't mind cleaning up." I shrugged. It was the truth.

"Yeah? How are things going with your mother? I'm sure she swarmed you once she found out you were home."

"She and Jimbo are fighting, so you know how she is. Same story, different day."

"You've got to draw the line, Rubes. She'll just keep taking until you have nothing left to give."

I nodded. He was the only person who really understood the toxic relationship that I shared with Wendy. Because he'd been there. And he hadn't drawn the line in the sand either. She'd left him. He'd given her everything, and she'd replaced him.

I knew who she was.

But she was also tied to my brothers.

"She can't make rent. Zane and Rico live in that trailer. How does one draw the line when it means their family will be out on the streets? She'll show up at your front door and want to move in."

"And I'd tell her no," he said, as he forked some of the noodles and popped them into his mouth.

"And the boys?"

"The boys are grown men, Rubes. They need to get their shit together. You're telling me between the three of them, they can't cover rent on that trailer? Come on now. They're taking advantage of you. And you feel guilty because you're doing well and they're struggling. But they make their own choices, just as you do."

I shook my head. He wasn't telling me anything that I didn't know.

With success came guilt. I felt it all the time, but much more now. I'd worked really hard to get to where I was, but I would be making good money now. And knowing how they were living—it bothered me.

"Let's focus on getting you better, okay?"

"Yes. I'd like to be one less person for you to worry about. So, tell me about this job at the university you've been offered."

I sat down in the chair beside his bed as he started eating. "It's a good offer. The money is really good. Great benefits. Everything I should be jumping at. I just don't know that I see myself teaching college kids, you know? I never planned to use this degree to teach others about psychology. I thought I'd be doing something where I applied what I'd learned to help others."

He finished chewing. "I get that. Then what would be the ideal job for you?"

"Well, originally, I got into this so that I could figure out how to read the people in my own life. How to help them help themselves." I chuckled because it was crazy that my original drive brought me this far. "I'd love to do something that actually helps people to have better lives. You know what I mean?"

"I think so. But tell me."

"Well, people repeat their mistakes over and over. Take Mom, for example. Or even Rico and Zane. They do the same things over and over, and they don't accept the consequences of their actions. They want others to fix the mess. Bandage the choices that they made, instead of digging deeper. Wouldn't it be nice to understand what you're doing and why you're doing it, so that you can make positive changes for yourself?"

"I could ask you the same thing, couldn't I?"

"Meaning?" I grumped as I folded my arms across my chest.

"You keep cleaning up the messes they make. You keep doing the same thing over and over, and nothing changes. You're completely enabling them. So, maybe you need to be taking a deeper look at why you keep doing it."

Those words hit hard.

"I know. I made the decision to move away, hoping that would help. And in some ways, it did. It was easier to focus on what I wanted to accomplish, and I could only help so much from a distance."

"But isn't that the whole point? You shouldn't have to leave to solve your problems, because you aren't really solving anything by doing that. You're just running away and dealing with the same shit from there; you just aren't here to see it. But from where I'm sitting, it's the same damn thing. And it's going to eat you alive if you don't start protecting yourself."

"When did you get so smart?" I teased.

"Hey, my daughter is a doctor. It must run in the family."

"I guess it does," I said, letting his words sink in.

Maybe it was time I practiced what I preached.

7

River

"How come your name is River and Uncle King's name is Kingston?" Cutler asked, over a mouthful of noodles.

I'd picked him up from summer camp, and we'd taken the canoe out for a bit before heading to The Golden Goose for dinner. Nash was working late on a project, as he and Kingston owned Ride or Die Construction, and they were busier than ever lately. This town was booming, and the tourists were starting to buy up properties. Apparently, small-town life wasn't such a bad thing.

We all pitched in with Cutler, as he really was all of ours, in a way. We'd been there the day he was born and every day since.

"Well, I guess that's what our parents wanted to name us. Sort of like your parents naming you Cutler."

"But I go by Beefcake now, so I don't think they did a very good job picking that name." He shrugged before taking a big swig of milk, leaving a white mustache above his lip.

I leaned forward with my napkin and wiped his face. "Yeah. Your handle is Beefcake, I get it. But you have a pretty cool name. You know that, right?"

"Pops says that Tara picked the name Cutler when I asked him about it." Tara was Cutler's mother, and she wasn't around a whole lot, but I'd never heard him call her by her first name before today.

"Ah . . . I didn't realize that. I think your dad liked the name Cutler too, though."

He shrugged. "Maybe. But Tara thought of it first."

"What's with you calling your mom Tara?"

"Joey Bindle goes to summer camp with me, and he said that moms are supposed to take you to camp and make you breakfast and do all the things that my dad does. Things that you and Uncle Ro and Uncle King and Uncle Hayes do. So, I don't think Tara should be called Mom."

Damn. Beefcake was a straight shooter.

That was the fucking beauty of kids. They didn't spend a lot of time analyzing shit. They said what they thought. I was down with that.

I ran a hand along my jaw. "All right. I get that."

The bell on the door rang, and I turned to see Ruby walk in. Midge approached her, and I'll be damned if Midge fucking Longhorn didn't look uncharacteristically nervous. Her posture stiffened, and she kept clearing her throat.

She obviously snatched that fucking dog.

I barked out a laugh, and Cutler turned to follow my gaze.

"What's funny, Uncle River?"

"That lady over there is Lionel's daughter, and she told me something funny."

"She's real pretty, isn't she?" he asked, and I nodded.

"She is."

Ruby's shoulders were back, chin up, as if she were about to confront a fucking mob boss, as she stared at the older woman with a brow raised. Midge turned away quickly and led her in our direction, and Ruby's gaze locked with mine. They stopped at the table beside our booth, and she dropped the menu down for Ruby.

Ruby shot her a death glare, and Midge hurried off.

"Didn't I tell you she stole that dog?" she said, keeping her voice low as her gaze moved from me to Cutler. "Oh, hey. I'm Ruby."

"I'm Cutler, but you can call me Beefcake."

"Beefcake, huh?" Ruby dropped to sit on the chair. "Good name. I like it."

She paused to place her order with Letty, one of the servers, and Cutler was practically bouncing in the booth now. "Why don't you sit with us? We just got our food."

I could tell Ruby was uncomfortable about how to answer him because apparently, her hostility didn't extend to children. "He just told you his handle. The least you could do is sit with him."

She fidgeted with her napkin before moving to her feet and sliding into the booth beside Cutler. "You don't have to wait for me to finish eating, though."

"We aren't in a hurry. Uncle River is watching me until my pops finishes work."

She nodded, and Letty smiled at her before setting down her soda.

"Okay." Ruby took a sip from the straw and peeked up at me. Damn, she was pretty, and I was glad she was sitting with us. "So, tell me why you go by Beefcake."

"Well, I was just telling Uncle River that Tara picked my real name, Cutler. And I don't like it."

"Who's Tara?" Ruby asked, as Cutler finished chewing and smiled up at her. I wasn't surprised Ruby didn't know about Tara. Tara hadn't been from here, and her relationship with Nash was short-lived.

"She's my mom, but she doesn't come to see me much, so I'm calling her Tara now."

"Ah, I see," she said, as Letty set her food down in front of her. "My mom was kind of like that, too. I get it. I call her Wendy instead of Mom."

Cutler's eyes widened as she bit off the top of a french fry. "Really?"

"Yeah. But I have a great dad, and I'm happy about that."

"I like Lionel." Cutler mimicked her by dipping his fry into the ketchup and then waggled his brows before biting off the top.

Why am I so fucking fascinated watching these two interact?

"I like Lionel, too." She chuckled. "And that's all you really need, right? It seems like you've got a great dad, and it's obvious that all your uncles love you, too."

"Joey Bindle says that it's weird that I don't have a mom who brings me to camp."

Kids could be little fuckers when they wanted to be.

"Who is Joey Bindle?" Ruby asked when she set her grilled cheese back down on her plate and finished chewing.

"He's in my class at school, and he goes to summer camp with me."

"Well, I think he's weird." She shrugged.

"You do?" Cutler asked, eyes wide.

"Yeah. Why does he care who drops you off at camp? Do both of his parents drop him off every day?"

"No. I've never seen his dad. Just his mom."

"Well, why does Joey make the rules? Why can't a dad drop you off? Or a grandparent? Everyone's families are different, and that's what makes them special. You tell Joey that you feel lucky to have a great dad who shows up for you every day. But you don't have to make him feel bad that his dad isn't there; just let him know that you're okay with having a parent who comes to get you. Not everyone has that."

Cutler's lips turned up in the corners. "Sometimes my uncles pick me up. Like today, Uncle River picked me up."

"I'll bet Joey wishes he had cool uncles like you. Sometimes people say things to make you feel bad, because they feel sad about something, too."

"You think Joey feels sad that his dad doesn't pick him up?"

God, I love this fucking kid.

"I don't really know, because I don't know Joey. But I know that if someone is pointing out something that you don't have, it's usually because they aren't happy on the inside."

"Are you happy on the inside, Ruby?" Cutler asked, and I chuckled because, damn, the kid didn't hold back.

Ruby surprised me when she wiped her hands on her napkin and smiled at him. "Most of the time I am. Sometimes I'm sad inside too, though."

"Why?"

She thought about it. "Well, sometimes I get sad when my brothers do things that aren't good for them, and I don't know how to help them. How about you? Are you happy on the inside, Beefcake?"

"I'm happy on the inside." He looked up and then reached for her hand, and she startled a bit. Cutler wouldn't notice, but I did. "I'm sorry your brothers make you sad sometimes."

A wide smile spread across her pretty face. I'd never seen her smile like that before. "You know what?"

"What?" he asked, as he dipped another french fry into his ketchup.

"Talking to you makes me happy on the inside, Beefcake."

These two.

Who'd have guessed it?

The woman despised almost everyone, but Cutler fucking Heart was a closer. He'd won her over without even trying.

"Talking to you makes me happy on the inside, too." He looked over at me. "Are you happy on the inside, Uncle River?"

I rolled my eyes, acting annoyed, even though I wasn't annoyed at all. "Right now, I am."

The little dude barely missed a beat. "Hey, Ruby. Do you know Demi?"

"I do know Demi. I used to work at her family's ranch when I was a teenager, and she and I would ride together when I finished my shift."

"Oh, man, really? Demi's my girl, but you can be my other girl. We ride horses on Saturdays together. You want to come ride with us?"

"I haven't been on a horse in a few years, so I'm probably a little rusty."

"You going to say no and break Beefcake's heart?" I said, my voice all tease.

She raised a brow before narrowing her gaze at me. "I promised to stop by Demi's coffee shop tomorrow and I'll mention it to her."

"I know Demi will want you to come with us."

"He's a persuasive kid, huh?" I said, as I rumpled the top of his head.

"He sure is." She smirked and reached for the other half of her sandwich, and we spent the next half hour listening to Cutler tell us all about his plans for the summer.

I insisted that her meal be added to my bill. Even though she put up a huge fight, she finally conceded, and we made our way to the door. She shot Midge a final glare, which made me laugh.

"All right, well, thank you for letting me crash your dinner," she said, bending down to get eye level with Cutler. "I'm glad we got to chat."

"I'm glad we got to chat, too." He kissed her cheek, the little Casanova, and damn if a little part of me wasn't fucking jealous.

She pushed back to stand.

"Do you need a ride home?" I asked.

"Nope. I'm heading to the bar to close. I just left so I could grab dinner." She held up her hand and waved before walking away.

"I like her, Uncle River."
You and me both, little dude.

* * *

The office had been a shitshow today, and I'd made it over to Magnolia Haven just before the sun went down.

"Oh, my boy, those are beautiful. You always were the best at picking out which blooms I'd plant next," Grammie said.

Pearl Arabella Pierce was the epitome of everything good. The woman who'd never given up on me. My North Star. My home.

She'd put up with a lot of shit from me, but she'd never turned her back on me.

"I just know what you like," I said, brushing my hands together to get rid of the dirt that settled there. "These will be easy to see from your window now. And I'll come back and fill the flowerbed beneath that tree next week."

"Let me feel the dirt, please," she whispered, as she smiled up at me from her wheelchair, which I'd parked outside in the garden while I got these flowers planted. I reached into the bag of soil that I'd brought with me, and I grabbed a little in my palm before kneeling in front of her and placing the soil in her dainty hand. She closed her eyes and rubbed her thumb along the dirt. "I always loved getting my hands dirty in the summer and spring."

My grandmother was an avid gardener. It had always been her happy place. So, when she could no longer live on her own, Kingston and I found her the best place we could. A room of her own with a west-facing view of the mountains and a little garden area that I could fill for her.

"You sure did. But you didn't like when I made you those mud pies very much." I chuckled.

She sifted the dirt through her fingers and decorated the

grass beside her, before brushing off her hands. "You loved to turn on the hose and make a mess, didn't you? And King just liked to roll in it and laugh. Gramps always got a kick out of what little rascals you two were."

My grandfather had passed away two years ago, and Grammie's health had declined after that. She and I had spent hours in the hospital at his bedside as the cancer ate away at him, day after day. Kingston found reasons to stay away. He'd never been good at dealing with the heavy stuff. Maybe he was the smart one, because I thought it had taken a toll on me and Grammie, watching him disappear before our eyes each day. Grammie had never been the same.

"We did put you two through it, didn't we?" I asked as I wheeled her back inside. She waved and greeted everyone we passed in the hallway.

"You two gave us the greatest joy in our lives," she said, as we stopped at the sink to wash our hands before I parked her chair beside the window. She smiled when she took in the pink and white blooms I'd just planted.

She was being kind. I was a hellion, but they'd embraced me all the same. Kingston was a whole lot easier than me, and I was grateful they'd had him to balance things out with my moody ass.

"So, tell me what's going on with you? Any new lady friends in your life you want to tell me about?"

She wasn't a fan of my dating life, nor my brother's. If Grammie had her choice, we'd both settle down and have a couple of kids—but she knew that wasn't happening.

"I haven't been out much this last week. Nothing new to report." I'd been tired of my routine, and as much as I enjoyed having a beautiful woman in my bed as much as the next guy—lately, I'd just been keeping to myself.

I was a moody bastard. I wouldn't deny it.

"When are you going to bring little Cutler by to see me?"

she asked. "I can't believe he's moving on to first grade after the summer. I feel like Nash just brought him home from the hospital not that long ago."

I chuckled. "Yeah. He's growing up fast. I told you he goes by Beefcake now. The kid is hilarious. I'll bring him by next week."

"Thank you. King brought him by not that long ago, and he asked me to call him Beefcake, so it sounds like the new name is sticking, huh?" She chuckled.

"Yep. At least for now. Have you had any other visitors this week?"

"Romeo and Demi came by to see me yesterday, and she brought me the most delicious sun tea from her coffee shop. I'm so glad Romeo found himself such a special girl and finally gave his heart away."

Here we go.

"Yep. She's great for him." I raised a brow. "He has a rough exterior, but you know he's a big softy beneath it."

"I know someone else who is just like that." She winked.

God, I loved this woman.

"All right. Enough of the birds and the bees talk. We're way past that. Let's go play some gin rummy with the girls. It's that time. Kingston's probably already in there flirting with all the ladies."

Yes. I came here several days a week, but Wednesday was gin rummy night at the nursing home, and Kingston and I always spent an hour playing with Grammie and her friends.

It was the least we could do.

This woman had done everything for us.

So, in a way, I'd already away given my heart when I was a young boy.

The woman who owned my heart just happened to be an eighty-three-year-old saint whom I called Grammie.

8

Ruby

I had some time before I had to be at the bar, so I walked the short distance to Demi's coffee shop, Magnolia Beans. When I pulled the door open, I was happy to see that it wasn't very busy. Romeo was behind the counter, talking to Demi, and he tipped her back and kissed her.

Oscar Daily was there, and he made a gasping sound, as if the move was completely inappropriate. Romeo laughed as Demi's cheeks tinted pink.

"What can I say, Oscar? I'm just a guy who's crazy about his girl," Romeo said as he walked toward me.

"This is a place of business, Golden Boy. I don't want to see that kind of smut when I'm paying too much for a cup of coffee," Oscar grumped.

"You get your coffee for half price. You're hardly paying too much." Demi laughed. "And don't knock the smut until you've tried it."

"That's what I like to hear," Romeo said as he winked at her and then turned his attention to me. "Hey, Ruby. How's your dad doing? I'm going to try to get over there this week to see him."

"Rehab is going well. I'm sure he'd love to see you."

He nodded and made his way out the door, and I walked toward the counter as Oscar pushed to his feet from where he'd been sitting at the table. "All right, Demi, I need to get to work. Thanks for the coffee."

"I'll see you tomorrow," she said.

"Hey, Ruby. Your brother no-showed to work this morning, and I had to call in my son to cover his shift."

My brother, who needed the money to cover rent, no-showed to his shift.

Shocker.

The apple did not fall far from the tree. My mother could never hold a job down for very long either.

"I'm sorry about that. I'll talk to him."

He shook his head and shrugged. "Not your problem. But it might not be my problem for much longer either, if he pulls this one more time. He's a good worker when he shows up, but I can't have him not showing up for his shifts."

"Yep. I understand that." I sighed. "But if you could give him one more chance, I'd sure appreciate it. I know he loves working there."

"I wish that brother of yours had your work ethic. Then I'd be a lucky man." He held up a hand and waved before making his way out the door. I'd worked for Oscar in the summers during high school. Hell, I'd always been hungry to make my own money. To be independent. I'd started a dog walking business when I was ten years old, and I'd realized no business would hire me because I was too young. I'd had a long list of clients by the time I was eleven and had been able to tuck away more money than most teenagers could make at a summer job.

"He shouldn't hound you about Rico. He's not your responsibility; he's a grown man," Demi said.

"It's fine. My brother's a flake, and it's frustrating. I get it."

She poured each of us a glass of sun tea, grabbed two lemon bars, and motioned for me to sit at the little table in the corner. "Things are finally slow. Let's sit and visit for a little bit."

"Thanks," I said as I took a sip and groaned at the sugary goodness. "This is so good."

"I make it fresh each day."

"I'm impressed. You're doing exactly what you always wanted to do."

She nodded. "I do feel lucky that it all came together. But I didn't go off and get my Ph.D. like you did, so don't give me too much credit."

"Well, a fancy degree is one thing. Figuring out what you want to do with it is another."

"I get that. What are you thinking you want to do? Any chance you'll stay here permanently?" she asked. I'd always liked Demi. We were from two very different worlds. I'd never had many girlfriends when I was growing up, but she was genuine and down to earth, and we'd just clicked all those years ago. She was a bit younger than me, but you wouldn't know it. She'd always known who she was and what she wanted, and I admired that.

"That's a hard no. You saw Oscar a few minutes ago. I can't get pulled back into all that drama. I'm here for my dad. I'll stay as long as he needs me. But if I stay any longer, I'll just be bombarded with all the family drama, you know?"

She nodded. "You know that I've been through a lot with Slade and his drug addiction. He's doing really well for the first time in a long time, and he'll move back when he proves he can remain clean for three months post-rehab. Romeo's going to hire him at the gym, and Slade will rent the little apartment across the alley."

"Good for him. I know how much you love him, so I'm happy that he's doing the work." She and I had always bonded over our family dramas. We may have come from two very different socioeconomic backgrounds, but addiction and family issues existed everywhere.

"Well, if Slade can get better, anyone can. It's been a long road, but honestly, I think him facing a lot of his issues has made a huge difference. My family is still pretty broken, but guess what?"

"What?" I asked.

"I'm still standing. We're all still standing, Ruby. I know what you're going through with your mama and your brothers, but you don't have to carry that on your own. Lean on me. Remember the times we used to just ride out as far as we could along the water, and we'd vent and let it all out? I miss that."

My head fell back on a chuckle. "You miss losing our shit as teenagers?"

"I miss you." She reached for my hand on the table and squeezed it. "You helped me through a really dark time, and I want to be there for you, too."

I nodded, and she pulled her hand away, and we both broke off a piece of our lemon bars and popped them into our mouths. "Damn, girl. I missed you, too. But these . . . these are life-changing."

She smiled. "It's a new recipe. All organic."

"They're so good."

"So, tell me . . . you don't know where you're going, but you don't want to stay here. Let's start with what you want to do. If you could dream up a position, what would it be?"

This was so Demi to do this. To tell you to make it up in your head and go with it. So, I thought it over. "I've been offered a really great position at the university, but if I could have my choice and there were other options, I honestly don't think I want to teach college kids."

"All right. We know what you don't want to do. How about what you do want to do? Close your eyes and think up what you would do if you could choose anything in the world."

66

I laughed and closed my eyes as I finished chewing. When my lids opened, she was smiling at me and all excited about what I was going to say. "Well, I'd really like to work with kids. I've felt that way for a while, and then I got to have dinner with Cutler Heart last night. And just talking to him about his mom and feeling like our little chat helped—it sealed the deal, I guess."

"Oh, trust me, I heard all about it. I'm going to convince you to join us on Saturday to ride together. He can't stop talking about you."

"He's really sweet."

"He is. So, what would that look like? Would you open a practice? Work at a school?"

"I don't like the idea of having my own practice because there are limitations. That would mean that parents would have to bring their kids to see me. If the parent is the issue, it's doubtful they are going to offer resources to their kid, right? Plus, therapy can be pricey, and they may not be able to afford it."

"So maybe a school would be a good idea?"

I nodded. "That could be an avenue to explore."

"Oh, hi there. I didn't know you were here, Ruby. I just finished cleaning up the back," Peyton said, as she came around the corner and hugged me. I didn't know her well, but we knew of one another from growing up in the same small town. She'd been by the bar a few times since I'd been home, and I liked her.

"Yeah. It's good to see you. I just stopped by for a little catch-up."

"Hey, I just thought of something," Demi said.

"No." Peyton held her hands up. "Do not start thinking again. Every time my girl thinks of something, it means I have to walk a 5k or go pick up trash at the park with her. I'm not in the mood to do a good deed. I'm tired from work and school. I've hit my limit."

Demi was laughing now, and I couldn't help but smile. "I'm not asking you to do any good deeds. At least not today. But you're getting your master's in education, and Ruby just graduated with her doctorate in psychology."

"Ummm . . . those are not the same thing. You know that, right? She's like . . . way smarter than me."

"I am not. I'm older, and I've been in school longer than you," I said, shaking my head.

"That isn't what I was saying. Ruby is interested in working with kids—you know, like a therapist. I thought maybe you would have some insight since you've student-taught at the school district, and you know how all of that works. I'm just trying to think of options for her to work her magic with children."

"Oh, okay. Got it. So, they don't hire therapists at the school district." She chuckled. "But they do hire counselors, which I think you are probably way overqualified for. There is also the path of an educational psychologist, which would be having your own practice. But they are so needed. Kids' needs are just not being met these days. At the end of the day, there are children struggling all over the place who would benefit from your expertise."

I thought it over. "Thank you. I'll definitely research these options."

"What age group would you like to work with?" she asked.

"I actually think I'd like to focus on middle school and high school kids. That's when I feel like I struggled the most with all the pressures of life."

"I think you'd be amazing at it. You're so . . . cool. I think kids would find it easy to talk to you." Demi beamed at me.

"Well, I know *I* like talking to you." Peyton reached for my phone and typed in her phone number, and Demi laughed at her boldness. But it reminded me that Demi and I still had one another's numbers, even though we hadn't kept in touch when I'd left for school all those years ago. Our friendship had consisted of our time out on the horses when we were younger.

"Good. Now you've got my number, too," Peyton said as she handed me my phone back. "And I just texted myself from your phone, so I've got yours, too. Basically, you're stuck with us now."

"I can live with that," I said, clearing my throat and glancing down at the time. "All right. I need to get to the bar."

"Hey, what night are you off this week?" Demi asked.

"Um, only Sundays when Doreen covers. I work the other six nights. I can take breaks, but I'm sort of running the place right now, and my dad does not have the most reliable people working there."

"That's ridiculous. You need more than one night off." Peyton gasped like this was the most insane thing she'd ever heard. "Pick a night, and we'll have a girls' night out. I think we could all use one," Peyton said, as she pushed to her feet and hugged me.

I wasn't big on girls' nights out. Hell, I didn't even know what that meant. I'd never had one.

"Yes. And if you can't completely leave the bar, you can get someone to cover, and we'll come there so you can still keep an eye on things. But we can dance and drink and have a good time."

I guess girls' night didn't sound so terrible.

"Okay. Sounds good. I'll text you."

Now it was Demi's turn to hug me.

I didn't know what I'd gotten myself into, but oddly enough, I didn't mind it.

I was going to be here for a few months, so I may as well have a little fun.

If I even remembered how to do that.

9

River

"Will Goldy is here, and he's insisting on seeing you immediately," Cassie said. "You have about ten minutes before your next client."

"I thought we talked about this. They can't just show up without an appointment."

I leaned back in my chair and pinched the bridge of my nose. My receptionist, Cassie Windfield, was the daughter of Samantha Windfield, the woman who ran Magnolia Haven and had pulled some strings to get Grammie the room she had.

The best room in the place because of the views.

Kingston and I owed her more than a favor, so hiring her daughter, who was fresh out of college, seemed like a fair enough exchange.

But Cassie probably shit rainbows and unicorns and didn't have a serious bone in her body. Ever since I'd hired her a few weeks ago, locals were showing up unannounced because word had gotten out that she wouldn't turn anyone away.

Which meant I was working my ass off and never got a break between clients.

"Right. But Will was my eighth-grade science teacher. He is the reason that I majored in Bio Chem."

Which didn't really pan out, seeing as you work as a receptionist at a goddamn law office now.

I knew Will Goldy. He was one of the biggest pains in the ass in Magnolia Falls. The man complained about everything and everyone.

I let out a long breath, trying to keep from losing my shit. "When I have ten minutes between clients, Cassie, it's my time to take a piss or a shit if so needed and grab some coffee."

"Oh. I totally get that," she said, all wide-eyed and hopeful, completely incapable of reading the room. "I'll get your coffee, and I can . . ."

"You can . . . what? Take a piss for me?" I pushed to my feet and walked toward the door.

"I do need to use the restroom, and then I will most definitely grab your coffee, boss."

"I told you not to call me boss. My name is River." For the love of God . . . why couldn't she follow one rule that I'd put in place? If she were anyone else, I'd have fired her by now. She hadn't been here that long, but we were certainly not off to an impressive start.

So maybe I went through assistants faster than most people stopped for gas. I didn't have a lot of patience, and you either did your job or you didn't. I wasn't a goddamn babysitter.

Will Goldy was standing and pacing in my front office when I cleared my throat. "Will, you don't have an appointment, and I have a client coming in less than ten minutes. You'll have to make it quick, or you'll have to make an appointment like every other client that comes here."

"I don't need longer than that. This is quick. Trust me, you don't want to wait to hear what I'm going to tell you."

Yes, I actually would prefer to wait.

I had zero interest in what he was going to say. The man

was an alarmist. He got worked up over nothing most of the time, and I was the exact opposite.

I didn't get worked up over much.

If something pissed me off, I did something about it.

I didn't need to run it by anyone.

He moved toward my office when I motioned him inside, and he took the seat across from me.

"What can I do for you?"

"I'm guessing you haven't heard the news?"

"You've guessed correctly." I glanced down at my phone. "And we've got six minutes left."

"I only need three."

Then spit it the fuck out, man.

"I'm listening."

"The Magnolia Falls board has voted, and they are expanding the size of the dog park. That means that with the expansion, the dogs have the added space on First Street. It's unacceptable."

"Yes, I actually did hear about that. It will give the dogs an extra area to stretch their legs. No one uses that space. It's city land. It's literally right next to the current dog park. Why do you have a problem with that?"

"Because I go to Benny's Barber. And I don't want to see dogs taking a shit when I'm getting a fresh cut."

"Benny's Barber is on Third Street."

"Correct. But I have to walk by First Street on my way."

This fucking guy.

I pushed to my feet when I glanced down at my phone and realized his time was up. "Will, the original dog park is also on First Street. You've always had to walk by the dog park to get your hair cut."

"But now it's larger, and that is unlawful."

"No. It's actually not unlawful. The land is owned by the city. The people that live in this town love their dogs, and they want to expand the space, and the land is there to do so. They voted. It got approved. And it's done. The people have spoken. Perhaps you should park somewhere else and walk a different route to get your hair cut." I stared down at him and waited for him to stand.

"This doesn't enrage you? You don't feel the need to join our voices and stop this madness?"

At the moment, I feel like buying a dog just so I can have it take a shit on your front porch.

"No. I have no issue with the expansion. You have no case. Next time, please call ahead and make an appointment."

He was barely out of my office, and I let the door shut before moving back to my desk and getting my notes together for my next meeting.

The door flew open, and my annoyingly bubbly assistant came hurrying inside. "Isn't Will so hot?"

"I hadn't noticed," I grumped, staring down at my notes.

"Well, I made your coffee just the way you like it. Extra cream and two sugars."

I squeezed my eyes closed and repeated the same words I'd said more than a dozen times *this week*. "It's no cream and one sugar."

"Oh, no. I did it again."

You sure the fuck did.

She went to leave, but I knew Mary Swan would be here any minute. "It's fine. Just leave the coffee and then bring Mary in when she arrives."

Cassie turned quickly and held out the mug before losing her footing and tripping toward the desk, the piping hot coffee landing in my lap.

Also known as covering my denim-clad dick in motherfucking hot lava.

"Oh, no!" she screamed, like someone who had *their* family jewels set on fucking fire.

"Fuck." I pushed to my feet and grabbed some tissues off my desk, wiping as much of the liquid away as I could.

"Should I call 9-1-1?" she asked, her voice shaky now, probably because I may try to murder her in the next two minutes.

"Why would you call 9-1-1?"

"Because you might be hurt." She winced. "Or how about an ice pack?"

Yeah . . . first, you burned off my balls, now let's cover them in ice. That sounds peachy.

"Cassie. I need a minute. Go see if Mary's here and get her a water. I'll clean this up. Close the door and give me five minutes."

"You got it, boss. I mean Mr. River." She hurried out the door, and I wiped down my desk and chair and assessed my coffee-stained groin.

Well, I'd be sitting for the next few meetings, so I'd at least be able to hide the stain until I could change clothing after work.

I picked up my phone and got on the Ride or Die group chat that was going at all times.

> Remind me why I can't fire Cassie Windfield.

KINGSTON

> Because her mother got Grammie in that great room at Magnolia Haven. Your flowers are looking good. I went by this morning. You've got a real green thumb.

> Well, I've also got a dick that probably has third-degree burns. Cassie is driving me fucking crazy.

NASH

She set your dick on fire? Should we call Hayes?

HAYES

Those aren't the kind of fires that we put out. What happened?

She continues to let locals come in with no appointment, and she just spilled a hot cup of coffee in my lap. She's completely incompetent.

KINGSTON

She's sweet, and she's hot. That's a win.

ROMEO

Sweet and hot is not going to help a dick that's been burned.

KINGSTON

I think he's being a bit dramatic. Cassie's great.

Then why don't you and Nash hire her at the construction company?

NASH

Hell no. I ran into her last week at The Golden Goose, and she went on and on about how babysitting Cutler last week was the highlight of her year.

ROMEO

You let Cassie babysit Cutler?

NASH

Nope. In the end, she realized she'd been confused. It was someone else who'd been the highlight of her year.

HAYES

Now I kind of want to know who she mixed up with Beefcake. He's kind of a unique kid.

NASH

Funny you should ask. It was actually Midge Longhorn's border collie. She mixed up my fucking kid with a dog.

KINGSTON

I didn't know Midge had a dog.

NASH

I tell you that Cassie mixed my kid up with a dog, and that's your response?

I immediately thought of Ruby, and I couldn't wait to tell her that Midge apparently had a dog now.

ROMEO

Fuck her for mixing up our boy with Midge's mutt, which, by the way, is weird in itself. Demi told me that Oscar is missing his border collie, Boone, and Midge suddenly has the same type of dog? Aren't they neighbors?

Holy fuck. I think Midge Longhorn is a dog thief. This isn't the first time she's done this.

HAYES

What the fuck is happening here?

NASH

My sentiment exactly. My kid was mixed up with a dog by a woman who just burned off River's dick.

KINGSTON

His dick is fine. He's been grumpier than usual lately. I think it's been a while since he's been laid.

ROMEO

He's in a slump. Let him be.

I'm done with this ridiculous conversation. I have a client waiting for me, my crotch is soaking wet, and my dick is probably blistering beneath the denim. Go fuck yourselves.

KINGSTON

Good chat.

ROMEO

Put some ice on it.

HAYES

I can grab you some ointment from the firehouse if you need it.

NASH

Now he's definitely not getting laid any time soon.

I turned off my phone and slipped it onto my desk when Cassie opened the door.

"Mary is here," she said, with a big smile on her face as she guided the older woman to the chair across from me. "Oh, and, boss, Geneva Springs is here. She doesn't have an appointment, but she just needs a quick minute when you're finished."

This was my life now.

I just had to accept it.

I narrowed my gaze at her, trying hard to keep my anger contained. "Close the door, please."

I turned my attention to Mary and forced myself to get through the rest of the day.

I had no break, as my receptionist allowed not one, but three more clients without appointments to be seen.

The only thing that hadn't been seen today was my cock.

I had no idea what kind of shape he was in. When I left the office, I was in a foul mood. I should go straight home, change my pants, and check my dick out.

But instead, I took a hard right toward Whiskey Falls because a cold beer sounded good about now.

And the woman behind the bar was the best thing I'd seen all day.

10

Ruby

I had just finished drying off a few cocktail glasses when the light from the open door flooded the space, and River walked inside. There was no one here at the moment, as it was country music night, and the bar would be packed in a couple of hours.

This is the calm before the storm.

He looked all broody and pissed off, and it worked for him.

He wore a black collared button-up, dark hair a bit more tamed than usual, and—*Oh.*

His jeans had a clearly obvious stain covering his entire groin area.

"Wow. You've been here for thirty seconds, and you already lost control from my mere presence?" I smirked.

Couldn't help myself.

His lips turned up in the corners as he pulled out the barstool and sat down. "One can wish. That's a title I'd wear proudly."

I rolled my eyes and poured him a beer and slid it across the wood bar top. "I'm guessing you could use one of these."

He took a long pull before setting the glass down. "Thanks."

"Do you want to unload your problems on your bartender?"

I leaned against the edge of the bar and batted my lashes. "Evil queens are good listeners."

"Fuck. That has to get old, listening to everyone's shit. I feel like a damn therapist myself lately. I don't know when attorneys became sounding boards for everything going wrong in their clients' lives."

"Let me guess. You were so busy listening to a client that you couldn't make it to the restroom?" I bit down on my bottom lip to keep from laughing.

"I didn't piss my pants, but odd that the first place you looked when I walked through the door was at my dick."

My heart raced faster than normal, but I acted completely unfazed by his words.

"It comes with the territory. First sign of a guy needing to be cut off from the booze is if he wets himself." That was completely made up, but it did seem logical enough.

"I see. So, it's not my dick in particular that you can't take your eyes off of."

"Correct." I raised a brow.

"I'll tell you what. I'm not big on sharing my shit, but I'll trade you. One shitty thing for another. I tell you something, you tell me something."

"I thought you were tired of being a therapist."

"I'm tired of listening to meaningless shit from people I'm not interested in," he said, reaching for his glass and taking another pull.

"Fine. Tell me why you have a giant stain on your crotch, and maybe I'll tell you a fun fact about my day."

"My receptionist is a complete train wreck. She can't follow the simplest of directions. She also can't walk for shit, and she tripped over her own feet and poured a scalding-hot cup of coffee on my dick."

"Are you sure it wasn't intentional?" I smirked. "You seem like you'd be a tough boss to work for."

He looked flattered by what I'd said, as if it were a compliment. "Thanks. But no, she doesn't have a manipulative bone in her body. She's just too bubbly for her own damn good. It was an accident."

"And your dick? How's it going down there?"

His tongue slid along his bottom lip, and I squeezed my thighs together in response. "Seems to be fine. You want to check it out for me just to be safe?"

"I told you. I don't play in wild rivers."

"Yeah, that's right. You like boring professors."

"Don't deflect. Why don't you just fire her?"

"It's Cassie Windfield." He reached for the bowl of nuts before grabbing a handful.

"Samantha Windfield's daughter? Yes, I remember her. She is a bubbly ball of joy, isn't she?"

"Yep. That's the one."

"So, why can't you just tell her it isn't working out?"

"Samantha runs Magnolia Haven, and she pulled some strings to get my grandma a room where she could have a little garden area. She lives for her flowers."

"Ah, that was nice of her. I always liked your grandmother. She worked at the library. I remember her talking about her flowers even back then. Is she still able to work in the garden?"

"No. King and I keep the garden up. Well, I do most of the planting. King just shows up and entertains her most of the time."

This was unexpected. I couldn't picture River Pierce planting flowers. Although I guessed this man liked to get dirty. I just didn't imagine there were flowers involved.

"You're sweeter than I would have guessed."

"Don't get excited. It's only for her."

I nodded. I understood that. I felt the same way about my father.

"So, you owe Samantha a favor, and employing Cassie is the way to repay her?"

"Correct."

"Then you just have to try to make it work. Suck it up, buttercup. Maybe praise her for the things she does right and try not to focus on everything she's doing wrong."

His heated gaze locked with mine. "You like praise, Queenie?"

I cleared my throat. "Not particularly, but I think most people do."

"All right. I'll think about it. But let's get back to business. I told you something. You tell me something now."

"You didn't get enough at the hospital when I had my meltdown? How about we focus on you today. I'm sure there's more to commiserate about than your bubbly receptionist being a pain in the ass."

He took the last swig of his beer, slapped down a ten-dollar bill, and pushed to his feet. "All right, then. I'll just head out."

I rolled my eyes. "That's a bit dramatic. Stop being a baby."

"I don't think I'm the one being a baby. If you want more out of me, then you need to give me something."

"I'm certainly not desperate to get more out of you. If you don't want to share anything else, why should I care?" I raised a brow.

"I see the way your breathing has accelerated. You're enjoying this. So stop fucking denying it, and have a goddamn conversation with me."

"Has anyone ever told you that you're extremely bossy? And rude?"

"Daily." He fixed his gaze on me and stared, letting me know that he was waiting.

"Fine. Let's see . . . I went to the hospital, and my father is making progress, so that was great. I then met my mother at the property management company and paid her rent. Then she called me a piece of shit because I paid them directly, and that pissed her off. And then I came to work where fifty locals will be coming in a few hours to get their *giddy up* on and dance to country music, and Demi and Peyton want me to line dance with them and make it a girls' night out, and I'd rather stick myself in the eye with a hot poker. Is that enough sharing for you?"

A loud laugh bellowed from his sexy mouth, and I couldn't help but stare. He really was a beautiful man. All hard lines and muscled shoulders and dark eyes as he dropped back down on the barstool.

"Fuck your mom. She should be kissing your ass. I take it she wanted you to give her the money directly?"

"Correct. But we've been down that road one too many times. And she would have taken the money and paid half toward rent and kept the rest for God knows what. Then she'd hit me up in another week."

He nodded. "She's a real piece of work. So, what's your problem with line dancing?"

"I'm just not a big joiner, you know? I don't care much for group activities. But I like Demi and Peyton."

"I'm not a joiner either. I hate that shit. But I'll go out with the guys and sit on the sidelines. There's nothing wrong with that."

"So, he plants flowers for his grandmother and sits on the sidelines while people are having fun. Inquiring minds want to know, Wild River, what do you do for fun?"

He asked for a water when I offered to refill his beer, and I set the water glass down in front of him.

"I don't really care about having fun. I just do what I want to do, which means I work a lot, spend time with my grandmother, hang out with the guys, and I have my time with Cutler, which is usually the highlight of my week."

This man was full of surprises.

"All work and no play?"

Why was I asking? Why did I care?

"Well, if you're asking what I think you're asking . . . Yes. I like to have a good time with a woman. Apparently, I'm a really good fuck. So, sure, sex is my outlet, I guess."

Did it just get hot in here?

I cleared my throat and tried to play it cool, but I hadn't expected that answer. Even if it was what I'd wanted to know.

"Well, we've already established that you aren't very lawyerly, so you'd have to be good at something, I guess."

Is my voice shaking?

He ran the tip of his pointer finger around the rim of his glass, and for whatever reason, it was the sexiest move I'd ever seen. "How about you? Do you enjoy sex? I wouldn't guess the boring professor could keep you satisfied."

The man could have his Ph.D. in psychology. He was really good at reading people. Maybe that was why I was so drawn to him. We were both guarded and always assessing everyone around us.

"I've never relied on a man to satisfy me. I've always been the only one who could get the job done."

Yeah. I just went there. And it's true. I have no shame in my game.

His tongue dipped out to wet his lips again. "No man has ever made you come? That's a shame, Queenie. You're missing out."

"I don't particularly find men to be all that skilled. So why would I rely on someone to do something I could take care of myself as often as I want to?" I waggled my brows, attempting to be playful.

But his eyes were jet-black now, as they bore into mine. "Sixty seconds and I could get you there."

"So cocky," I said, trying to keep my voice steady when I was anything but.

Have I ever been this turned on before?

"Not cocky. Because I wouldn't even need my *cock* to get the job done."

"Really?" I leaned forward, elbows propped on the bar, closing the distance between us. "You're that sure of yourself, huh?"

"Oh, yeah. I could do it a few different ways, but I think I'd prefer my mouth. I've got a magical tongue, Queenie. I'd enjoy tasting you and making you fall apart with a few flicks."

Oh. My. God.

What was happening right now?

And why was I enjoying it so much?

"I mean, I've never seen a man pull that off in sixty seconds. Hell, I haven't been with one who could pull it off in twenty minutes. But I like the confidence."

"Well, you seem pretty confident in your own abilities as well," he said, his voice gruff as he shifted forward.

His lips were so close to mine; his warm breath tickled my cheek.

"Oh, no doubt about it. I'm not the only one I please. I've never had a problem pleasing a man either. I guess I have a magical mouth, too."

"Yeah? Yet they don't get you off?"

"Nope. But I can take care of myself just fine."

"It's a lot better with a partner."

"I guess I'll never know," I teased.

"Give me sixty seconds. I'll make you come so hard you'll never want to touch yourself again because you'll be begging me for more."

A burst of light flooded the space, and I pulled back just as Doreen strolled through the door. "Hey there, Ruby girl. You ready for country music night?"

She paused and looked between us. I was certain there was a layer of sweat across my forehead, and I made an effort to steady my features. "I'm as ready as I'm going to be."

"Hey, River. Good to see you." She waved at him.

"Yeah, you, too," he said, as he reached for his water.

Doreen walked behind the bar and put the back of her hand to my forehead. "You okay? You look a little flushed. I think you're working too hard."

I shook her off and started unloading glasses from the dishwasher, when I looked up to see River smirking at me. The bastard.

"I'm fine. It's just warm outside today," I said.

"All right. Well, we're going to be busy tonight. I just need to go put my purse in the back and grab a bite to eat in the kitchen."

I nodded, and she disappeared into the back just as River pushed to his feet. "Thanks for the interesting conversation. Think about my offer."

"I think I'm going to stick with my usual plan. It's been working out just fine for me. You best head home and make sure all your parts aren't burned off."

He leaned forward, pushing the cash toward me. "Oh, there's no doubt that everything is working just fine down south. I can't remember a time I've ever been this hard. I guess I'll need to take a quick shower and take care of my own needs, too."

"All right, then. I'd say this was enough sharing for one day." I cleared my throat and forced a smile.

"You know the best way to shut me up, don't you?"

I raised a brow. "Oh, I can't wait to hear this."

"You could just sit on my face, and then you'll be the only one making noise." He tapped on the bar twice, winked, and strolled right out the door.

I just stood there with my mouth hanging open as the door closed behind him.

And I wasn't a girl who was easily surprised.

But River Pierce was full of surprises.

11

River

Country music night was the equivalent of hell for me most of the time. It was too much peopling and excitement. I preferred a few beers with the boys over a bunch of people nagging me to get on the dance floor.

I didn't dance.

It wasn't my thing.

But there was a bonus tonight . . . and she was standing behind the bar, serving drinks.

"Okay, Ruby gets to stop working in twenty minutes, so we're all going to get out on the dance floor. Got it?" Demi asked.

"Baby, I like watching you dance. I don't like doing it myself." Romeo attempted to turn her down, but she smiled up at him, and I could see the shift. "But I can make an exception for you."

"I love dancing. I swear I was born with all the moves," Kingston said, and everyone laughed. The dude was right. He did have moves. He'd been dancing his way through life since the day he came into the fucking world.

I'd always found it so interesting that we'd been raised in

the same house, but we were so completely different, yet so connected at the same time.

I think the age difference played a huge role in that. Kingston barely remembered our parents. And he hadn't been in the car the day of the accident.

Or maybe he was just a happier dude.

"I love ya, Demi, but I'm going to sit here and enjoy my beer. Dancing is not my thing." Hayes winked at her.

He was a grumpy son of a bitch most of the time, so no one messed with him when he didn't want to do something.

Demi smiled as if she understood him. Hell, the girl understood all of us, and she hadn't even been around that long. She'd just fit right in from day one.

Nash wasn't out tonight, as he was home with Cutler.

"When do you think we can get Beefcake a fake ID so he and Nash can be out with us?" I asked, taking a pull from my beer glass, my gaze moving to see Ruby walking our way.

"I think you've got a while before that happens," Peyton said over her laughter.

"Yeah. And we'll be too old to be out by the time he can come here," Hayes said.

Ruby paused at the table, her gaze avoiding mine. It didn't surprise me. We'd had a pretty heated conversation earlier, so I knew she'd retreat after that.

It was what I normally did, but for whatever reason, I couldn't take my eyes off her tonight. I wanted to pick up where we'd left off.

"Are you officially off the clock?" Demi asked.

"I am. At least until we close, and then I'll need to cash out and lock up. But I've got the next two hours to have some fun," Ruby said. She was wearing a Whiskey Falls tee that was cut and cropped, showing off her flat stomach and feminine curves. She wore a short black skirt and her typical military boots. She was sexy as hell. Her legs were long and lean, and I had a strong vision of them being wrapped around my shoulders as I buried my face between her thighs.

What the fuck was wrong with me?

I didn't fantasize about unattainable women.

I hooked up with women who knew the score.

Women who were down with the same thing as I was.

A one-and-done.

A good time.

No strings.

Ruby Rose was complicated. She was Lionel's daughter, for starters. She was probably the only person I'd ever met who was more guarded than me. Hell, she didn't even trust another person long enough to get her off.

A new song started blaring through the speakers, and Demi and Peyton both squealed. I didn't miss the way Ruby's eyes widened as she took them in. They reached for her hands and dragged her out to the dance floor.

"Thank God I don't have to go out there yet," Romeo said, his eyes on his girl like they always were.

"You're so pussy-whipped you can't see straight," Kingston said over his laughter.

I took another pull from my beer and watched as Ruby tucked the hair behind her ear, and I'll be damned if she wasn't a fucking natural out there.

Her hips swayed perfectly to the beat, and I didn't miss the way several dudes around her were taking notice.

"Dance with me, King," Sophie said as she approached the table. She was a local who had been after my brother since grade school, like every other girl in this town. The guy was a magnet.

You didn't have to ask him twice to do anything. He was always down for a good time.

He waggled his brows as she led him out to the dance floor.

Claire and Evie approached, and they both said hello. Country music night was always popular with the locals, so I wasn't surprised to see them here. Romeo left to go get us another round of drinks, and Claire settled onto the chair beside Hayes and started chatting.

"You want to dance with me, River?" Evie slurred. She was already well past buzzed.

"I think you know I'm not much of a dancer," I said, but my eyes were still on the sexy-ass woman who was drawing all the attention on the dance floor. A guy had moved in right behind her, a little too close for comfort. I was ready to jump in if I needed to.

"Well, you're staring at the dance floor, so I thought maybe tonight you'd want to give it a try."

Evie and I had hooked up once about a year ago. She got a little clingy after that, even though I'd been very honest about what I was willing to give the night I'd gone home with her. So, I'd kept things platonic ever since. She was hot and sexy and everything that normally held my attention. But lately, I wasn't feeling it with anyone.

Well, with anyone I could actually have.

"Thanks for asking, but I'm just going to chill here." I kept my eyes on Ruby.

Evie wasn't taking the rejection well, which was somewhat on par for her. She leaned close to my ear. "How about you take me into the bathroom then and fuck me senseless?"

Normally, a bar quickie, though not my favorite, would be right up my alley.

Tonight, I had zero interest.

I turned my gaze to her for the first time since she'd walked over. "How about we just keep things friendly like we've been doing, huh?"

"You're seriously turning me down?" she said with a sarcastic chuckle, as if she were stunned. It wasn't the first time I'd turned her down. Hell, it wasn't even the first time I'd turned her down this month.

But she was drunk, so she was going to make things awkward.

"I think we're better off as friends. We've talked about this."

"Do you know how many guys in this bar want to take me home? Do you have any fucking clue?"

"I'm sure there are many. I'm just not one of them." I wasn't going to argue with her about it.

"Fuck you."

"Have a good night." I took the beer from Romeo when he came back to the table.

"That looked—heated." He laughed.

"She's drunk. I'm not interested. Not a good mix."

"What's up with you? You've been staring at that dance floor like you're ready to go out there and beat the shit out of someone," he said.

"I don't like how close to Ruby that dude is getting. I told Lionel I'd keep an eye on her."

Romeo barked out a laugh. "Sure, you did."

The song changed, and the girls came walking over to the table, and I was relieved that the clingy asshole had taken the hint and gone back to his own table.

Romeo passed out drinks, and Demi hugged him because they couldn't keep their hands to themselves.

"Thanks for the beer," Ruby said to Romeo, as she settled onto the barstool beside me.

She glanced over at me before putting the bottle against her lips and tipping her head back. I watched the way the liquid slid down her throat. Peyton was deep in conversation with some friends at the next table, and Hayes was chatting with Claire. Well, Claire was chatting, and Hayes was just listening and nodding the way he usually did.

"It looked like Evie was pretty pissed off at you," Ruby said.

Yeah, Ruby had been watching me just the way I'd been watching her.

"She wanted to dance. She's drunk. She'll get over it."

"That's right. You aren't a joiner, are you?" Her voice was all smooth and sexy.

"I thought you weren't either."

Her teeth sank into her bottom lip. "I didn't think I was. But that was actually fun."

"Look at you, out there, trying new things."

One of my favorite Luke Bryan songs came through the speakers, and Demi pulled Romeo out to the dance floor. It was a slower song, and couples were heading out there now.

"I'm full of surprises." She shrugged and took another pull from her bottle.

"Well, my offer still stands, if you want to try something else."

Her gaze locked with mine. "And you just get to call all the shots? How about you try something new first?"

That was all I needed. I was on my feet and tugging her off her stool, leading her to the dance floor. I pulled her against me and wrapped my arms around her as we swayed to the music.

Slow and sexy.

Her head tipped back, and she raised a brow. "You could have asked first."

"You want to dance?" I said against her ear.

Her body shook a little, and I knew she was laughing, but she tucked her head beneath my chin, and we continued moving together. The scent of jasmine and orange flooded my senses.

I'd never wanted a woman more than I wanted Ruby right now.

In this moment.

My hand moved to the nape of her neck, and I ran my fingers through her silky, long hair. The other hand rested on her lower back, fingers grazing the exposed skin there. I tugged her closer. My dick was threatening to break through the denim of my jeans, and I wanted her to know the way she affected me. Her head tipped back again, and she looked up at me, eyes wide. "You really are happy to see me."

"I am."

"Why?" she asked, her hips moving right in sync with mine.

"I don't have a fucking clue."

"I'm not going to have sex with you, if that's what this is about."

"Who said anything about sex? All I asked for was sixty seconds. And I promise you, Queenie, if you and I ever have sex, it would be for a hell of a lot longer than sixty seconds."

"I have to close tonight, and I'm not going home with you." Her chest was rising and falling again, I could feel the excitement coming off her in waves.

She was actually considering this.

"I never said anything about going home with me. If you did that, it would be a whole different story. You wouldn't know what to do with yourself. I'd make you feel so good."

She raised a brow, tongue swiping out to wet her bottom lip. "So, what? You're going to make me orgasm right here on the dance floor in sixty seconds? Tell me how you plan to pull this off."

I leaned down close to her ear. "No fucking way. I wouldn't let any of these fuckers see you fall apart. It would be just for you and me."

She cleared her throat. "Go on."

"If you're only giving me sixty seconds, I'll walk you straight to the bathroom. I'll lock the door, drop to my knees, and hike this skirt up to your waist. I'll slide your panties to the side and spread your legs wide before I bury my face there.

And I can promise you, I'll enjoy every goddamn second that I'm there."

"Impressive answer. Those are some steep goals you're setting, seeing as no one's ever pulled that off before. I'd hate for you to be setting yourself up for failure," she said against my ear, her lips grazing along the bottom of my earlobe.

I leaned back down; we were taking turns whispering to one another. "You've gotten yourself there. You've just been with the wrong guys."

"You're awfully sure of yourself. You know this would be a one-time thing, right?" She pulled her head back to study my gaze.

I chuckled. "I'm good with whatever you want. It's no secret I don't do relationships. But I would consider bending the rules to give you a little pleasure while you're home."

"One. Time. That's the deal."

"One time. Sixty seconds. I can live with that."

The song came to an end, and I waited for her to make the next move. She found my hand and led me through the crowd, into the back hallway, and down the stairs. I guess we weren't going to the bathroom.

She pushed open the door to the office and led me inside before locking it behind her. "I'm not going into that bathroom where everyone is waiting in line. This is no one's business. It stays between us."

"I'll do it wherever you want me to." I pressed her up against the wall, my hand finding the side of her neck.

"Aside from the dance floor, right?" She chuckled before pulling her phone from her back pocket and setting the timer to one minute.

"Damn straight. No one else gets to see this."

"What's in it for you?"

"I get to feel you come against my lips. Doesn't get any better, Queenie."

"Holy shit," she whispered. "You have a filthy mouth."

"My mind is even filthier." I took the phone from her hand. "Are you ready?"

"I guess so. Sixty seconds. Have your way with me."

God damn, was I ready.

I hit start on the timer and tossed her phone onto the chair beside us.

12

Ruby

My head was spinning, my legs shaking, and I didn't know how I'd ended up here.

How I'd agreed to this.

But it was all I'd been thinking about since I saw him a few hours ago.

One time. Sixty seconds.

What could possibly go wrong?

He'd most likely fail, and then I could tease him about it forever.

But he surprised me when his mouth found mine, my lips parting as his tongue slipped in. I hadn't expected a kiss, but I wasn't going to push him away. It was by far the best kiss I'd ever had, but I'd never cared much for kissing.

His hand trailed down the front of my body before it settled on my waist. The other hand tilted my head back as his tongue explored my mouth in the most erotic kiss of my life.

It was sensual and heated and sexy all at the same time.

The way he groaned against my lips.

Rocked his hips against mine, letting me know just how much he wanted me.

His lips moved down my jaw and my neck, trailing kisses along my skin.

Licking and nipping in between.

My body was on fire.

And before I could process what was happening, he dropped to his knees, kissing his way down my stomach before tipping his head back to look up at me.

"You don't have a fucking clue how beautiful you are," he said. "If I wasn't on the clock, I'd take my time."

"Sixty seconds. That's it," I said, my words completely breathless. I needed to stay in control. Keep my wits about me, even when all I wanted was to get pulled under by this man.

I'd never felt so out of control.

Wild.

I wanted to give in to it.

He found the hem of my skirt and pushed it up before burying his face right over the lace of my panties and breathing me in like a man taking his last breath.

Holy shit, this was hot.

"I'd tear these fucking panties off if I didn't have to worry about you walking back out there without anything beneath this little skirt." He slipped them to the side and tugged them down my legs, pulling my thighs over his shoulders as he supported my weight.

I couldn't breathe.

Couldn't think straight.

I swear I was on the verge of blacking out when his fingers swiped along my most sensitive area.

"Just as I thought. You're fucking soaked, Queenie."

I whimpered as he leaned forward and teased me with his tongue.

My legs were shaking out of control, and I was grateful that he was holding on to me. My hands reached down and tangled in his hair.

It's too much and not enough all at the same time.

I moaned when his tongue slipped inside me, thrusting in and out.

Nothing had ever felt so good.

I tugged at his hair as my hips bucked against him.

Wanting more.

Needing more.

His mouth was a fucking magical thing, the way it worked me over.

His thumb moved to my clit, and he applied just enough pressure to make me gasp as his tongue continued to slide in and out in the most erotic way.

My mouth fell open, eyes squeezing shut as the most powerful feeling moved through my body. Bright lights exploded behind my eyes as my hands fisted in his thick hair, and I cried out his name in a voice I didn't even recognize.

I went right over the edge, my body shaking as I gasped and rode out every last bit of pleasure.

When my breathing calmed and my hips stopped rocking against him, I released my grip on his hair, and he tilted his head back to look at me.

"That was fucking amazing. You're much sweeter between your legs than you are in real life."

I was too sated to laugh as hard as I wanted to, but a raspy chuckle escaped my lips as he slowly placed my feet on the floor and fixed my panties and then my skirt.

Just as the timer sounded on my phone.

He'd done it in less than sixty seconds.

Taken me somewhere no man had ever taken me.

He pushed to his feet and grabbed my phone to turn off the timer before shifting his attention back to me.

"Was it better than what you've been doing all on your own?"

"Yes," I conceded. "It was fan-fucking-tastic. Best sixty seconds of my life, so thank you."

His lips turned up in the corners, and it was this sexy, confident grin that had me squeezing my thighs together to stop the ache that was building again.

My god.

What was wrong with me?

"Happy to prove you wrong. And now that we know how quickly I can do it, you just give me a call if you need to take the edge off again."

"Well, don't go saying it like it's so outrageous. I could do the same to you in sixty seconds. We're clearly just two horny people."

"I can't say that anyone has ever gotten me off in one minute. I have some pride, Queenie. I'm not a thirteen-year-old, inexperienced kid. But I guess you know that now, don't you?"

Maybe it was all part of his plan to get me to return the favor.

It didn't really matter.

Because I wanted to make him feel good, the way he'd done for me.

River and I may not be friends, but we understood one another.

We respected one another.

My hand moved between us, and I covered his erection, which was currently threatening to tear through the denim of his jeans. "How's it feeling down here? All healed up from coffeegate?"

"Don't tease me, Ruby. I'm already rock-hard, so if you aren't going to do anything about it, I'm going to need you to leave this office and give me a few minutes alone. Or you can stay and watch if you want." His voice was gravelly, eyes on me, as I continued sliding my palm up and down over the bulge behind the denim.

"I can't have you gloating about your skills, now can I?" I

stopped touching him and reached for my phone and held it up. "Sixty seconds on the clock."

He nodded, eyes hooded, as I started the timer and tossed it onto the chair. I leaned forward and kissed him hard, my hands working the button and zipper on his jeans at the same time. I shoved the denim down as our tongues tangled once again.

Hungrier now.

Needier than ever.

Almost like we'd had a taste, and now we were insatiable.

My hands plunged into his briefs, desperate to feel him.

He groaned into my mouth, and I pulled back and nipped at his bottom lip before dropping to my knees.

I'd never been so desperate to give someone a blow job. To wrap my lips around him and take him as deep as I could.

I shoved his briefs down his legs, near his jeans that sat at his ankles.

He was long and thick and rock-hard. I wrapped my hand around him and pumped a few times as he hissed out a guttural sound, and his head fell back. My tongue swirled around the tip of his dick, tasting the pre-cum that was already there. River Pierce could own me if I wasn't careful.

I continued teasing him as I tipped my head back to find his eyes on me.

"You going to let me fuck that sweet mouth of yours, Queenie?"

My god. The mouth on this man.

I was here for it.

I leaned forward and took him in. Inch by glorious inch. He didn't move; he waited for me to set the pace. I started slowly, sliding my lips up and down, and each time, I tried to take him further.

Faster.

My hands moved around his backside and gripped his ass.

And that was when his hands tangled in my hair, and his hips started bucking in rhythm with my mouth.

"Fuck," he hissed, as I took him deeper, feeling him in the back of my throat.

I didn't gag.

Didn't slow down.

I fucking loved it.

Loved the way I was affecting him.

"Reach beneath that little skirt and touch yourself. I want you to come with me."

I did exactly what he said because I was so turned on, it wouldn't take much.

My fingers moved between my legs, pressing little circles against my clit as he fucked my mouth.

Harder and faster.

He tugged at my hair in warning.

"Ruby." His voice was gritty.

But I stayed right there.

Wanted all of it.

And my body started tingling just as he unleashed into my mouth, and I followed him into oblivion. A guttural sound left his lips, and I loved hearing him lose control.

I continued moving up and down his shaft until he slowed.

I wiped my mouth with the back of my hand and looked up at him just as the timer went off.

My lips turned up in the corners, and he laughed.

I turned off the alarm and pushed to my feet as he pulled up his briefs and his jeans and tucked himself in.

"Well, that was—eventful."

"I'll take my glory now. Sixty seconds was all I needed." I pumped my arm into the sky in celebration. "Turned you into a prepubescent teenage boy with no control whatsoever."

"Says the woman who just came twice in two minutes."

"Hey, you only got me there once."

"I beg to differ. I think having my dick in your mouth got you there the second time."

"Touché. Either way, it was a win for me." I stepped back, unsure how to act now. So I did the most awkward thing possible and held out my hand. "It was a pleasure doing business with you, River Pierce."

He took my hand and held it there, staring down at me with a wicked grin on his face. "I don't know that this deal is done. I think you've had a taste of the wild side, and you'll be back."

"How very unlawyerly of you to say that. We had a deal. You're already willing to break the contract?" My voice was all tease as I pulled my hand back from his grasp.

"I told you that I'm not a very good lawyer. But I am a good fuck, and I have a feeling you're going to want to find out for yourself."

"I thought you were Mr. One-and-Done?" I patted my skirt in place because I didn't know what to do with my hands.

"I've never had a sixty-second deal with a woman, so I don't really have a set rule on how that works. I'd normally spend an evening with someone, not a minute. So I think the rules could be bent."

"I don't think so. I just got everything I need. There's nothing more to explore."

He nodded, a cocky smile on his face. "We'll see about that."

"Don't hold your breath."

And then he did the most surprising thing of all. He stepped forward and wrapped his hand around the back of my head, and he kissed me.

Hard.

When he pulled back, I was breathless. "See you later, Queenie."

And he walked right out the door.

And what do you know? I was turned on all over again.

This man was dangerous, just as I'd suspected.

I needed to take the gift he'd given me and run as far away from him as I could.

13

River

I'd just gotten to Knockout Gym to meet the guys. Romeo owned the place, and ever since he'd won his fight, the gym had been packed. He planned to expand on the building, and I'd just helped him file the paperwork with the city to get the permits in place.

Everyone was there, and I dropped down to sit on the chair where I sat every week when we met.

"What's up? You look pissed off," Romeo said, tossing me a bag with my sandwich in it.

"Fucking Cassie, man. She's got to be advertising free consulting or something, because everyone is coming in now, and it's completely out of control. Wendy fucking Slaughter showed up with no appointment, telling me she wanted to sue her husband for gambling a couple hundred bucks. And then Jimbo blows through the door, screaming at her for getting an attorney. The fucker thought I was a divorce attorney and started throwing things around the office."

"What the fuck? What did you do?" Hayes asked, leaning forward and dropping his sandwich as he waited for an answer.

"I came over the desk and pinned him to the fucking wall until he calmed his ass down." I reached for my soda and took a sip. "And then fucking Cassie comes in, flailing her arms around and screaming about calling the police, which had Wendy freaking out, and they got into it. I kid you not. It was a complete shit show."

"Well, did she call the police?" Kingston asked, and the asshole had a smile on his face like he was enjoying himself.

"No. Wendy knocked the cell phone out of her hand, and now Cassie wants to file an assault charge against her." I shook my head because you couldn't make this shit up. "But I calmed them all down. Told Jimbo to pay her the money he owed her. Told Wendy to pull her shit together and go home. And I told Cassie that if she'd stop taking clients without appointments, none of this would have happened."

"Damn. Look at you, brother. Taking the bull by the horns." Nash reached for his sandwich and started eating again.

"Does Ruby know her mom came down there? I'm guessing she wouldn't be a fan of her making a scene like that," Romeo said. "She's been hanging out with Demi a bit, and apparently, she doesn't like to talk about Wendy."

"Ruby's a boss babe, and her mom is a train wreck, so I'm guessing that's the issue. But speaking of the lovely Ruby . . . I noticed you two on the dance floor the other night." Kingston smirked.

"Yeah? Why are you saying it like you're some sort of fucking rocket scientist? We danced. Big deal."

"But then you two disappeared for a little bit, didn't you?" My brother made no effort to hide the humor from his voice.

I paused mid-bite and raised a brow. "What are you . . . a fucking stalker? I went to take a piss."

Romeo barked out a laugh now. "It's not a big deal if you like her. Hell, we all like her. Even if we're a little scared of her."

"The dude who just won the belt in a nationally televised boxing match is afraid of a girl who's half his size," Hayes said with a laugh.

"Hey, she had a good left hook that time she dropped me when we were kids." Romeo glanced down at his phone when it vibrated, before turning his attention back to us. "But I think she's all bark and no bite. She's riding with Demi and Cutler this weekend out at Demi's parents' ranch."

I was glad she'd agreed to ride. I'd seen that look in her eyes when Cutler had brought it up, and I could tell she wanted to go too.

"So, what's going on there?" Nash asked as he studied me.

"Nothing's going on there. She's Lionel's daughter. She hates me most of the time. And she's just here until Lionel gets out of the hospital." I shrugged. It was kind of true, minus the two best fucking minutes of my life. I needed a subject change before they figured that shit out. I wasn't about to share what happened, because if Ruby found out that I told a soul, she'd probably cut my dick off. "How's Saylor? Is she back for a while?"

Saylor Woodson was Hayes's little sister. She'd just graduated from college and had gotten home last night, and he was already worrying about what she was going to do. He'd always been ridiculously protective over her, which I understood. We were all that way with the people we loved.

"Yeah. She's staying with me for now, and she's having lunch with Demi this week to talk about some business ideas." Hayes ran a hand through his hair, which was always a tell that he was worried.

"That's good she's staying with you. You haven't mentioned your mom in a while, and I haven't seen her around. She doing all right?" Romeo asked.

"She's back with Barry, so I want nothing to do with her.

And I sure as hell don't want Saylor being pulled into her shit, you know?"

"You know we're here if you need us. If Saylor needs a place to stay or anything at all, we've got you," Kingston said. The dude was rarely serious, but we all knew the shit Hayes and Saylor had been through, and there was no joking about that.

"I know you do. A part of me hoped she wouldn't come back here, even though I miss the hell out of her, but I just need her to be fucking smart, you know?"

"She's smart, brother. She'll be fine. We'll all be watching out for her," Nash said, and Romeo, Kingston, and I nodded.

"Ride or die. Brothers till the end. Loyalty always. Forever my friend," I said. It was our motto. The words we'd lived by since we were kids.

"Always." Kingston balled up the paper from his sandwich and shot the basket into the trash can across the room, sinking it easily. "And I'm glad Saylor is home. I missed her."

"Yeah? Well, she's all grown up now, so keep your filthy paws off her." Hayes raised a brow, and we all laughed.

Sisters were off-limits. It was an unspoken rule. It had never been a problem because only Romeo and Hayes had one sister each. Romeo's sister, Tia, was far too young for anyone in the group, as she'd just left for college this year. And Saylor was Romeo's age, so not much younger than the rest of us, but she'd always been shy, and we'd all looked at her like a little sister. Not to mention the fact that she'd come to live at our house when some shit had gone down with her family. I was gone at Fresh Start, but she and Kingston had grown close during that time. I was grateful they'd had one another to lean on when they were both going through tough times.

"Hey now, don't go looking at me. I'm not the settling-down type." Kingston waggled his brows.

"Exactly my point. She dated that fucker in college that I

couldn't stand, and that's the one good thing about her moving back here. So, keep your eyes on her for me, but *don't keep your eyes on her,* if you know what I mean." Hayes raised a brow and focused most of his attention on Kingston.

My younger brother was the biggest player in the group. He loved women, and they loved him, but he had the attention span of a toddler on a sugar high, so he certainly wasn't kidding when he said he wasn't the settling-down type.

And he and Saylor shared a bond that he'd never risk fucking up by crossing the line.

"Dude. You know me better than that." Kingston placed a hand on his chest. "I'd never go there."

Hayes nodded. "I know that. I'm just fucking with you. What else is going on?"

"You still going to hire Demi's brother when he comes back to town?" Nash asked, directing his question to Romeo.

"Yeah. Slade's checking in every day and putting in the work. I'm willing to give him a chance, but it's up to him if he can stay clean."

Demi's brother, Slade, had once been our enemy, letting Romeo and me take the fall for something that he'd done. Something that changed the course of our lives. But life had a way of coming around full circle, and the Crawfords were no longer the enemy. There wasn't a lot of love between Romeo and Demi's father, but the rest of her family embraced him like he was one of their own.

Hell, they'd embraced all of us.

"Well, for Demi's sake, I hope he does. She loves him, and I know it would make her happy to see him turn his life around," I said, and everyone gaped at me.

"Damn. Never thought I'd see the day River went soft," Romeo said.

"Nothing soft here, brother." I laughed. "I can't really hate the dude now that you're with Demi."

"Just admit that there's a tender heart buried under all that grumpiness," Kingston said as he pushed to his feet. "All right, Nash and I have to get back to work. I suggest you fuckers do the same."

"I need to go make sure Cassie isn't still sitting in the corner, crying," I groaned as I walked toward the door.

"She was crying in the corner when you left?" Nash asked as he shook his head.

"Dude. She was the reason all that shit went down in the first place. She lets them all in, and then she's crying because Jimbo the dickhead was making a scene. I'm not a fucking therapist. I don't have time for this shit."

"Remember that her mom is the reason Grammie has the garden view," Kingston reminded me, as if I hadn't already reminded myself a dozen times today. That was the reason the girl still had a job.

"Thanks, Genius. I'm more than aware. I still think you should hire her at RoD Construction. I've done my time." I crossed my arms over my chest. Kingston and Nash owned Ride or Die Construction, which was what we'd named our group of friends when we were just kids.

"Absolutely not," Nash interrupted and flung his thumb at Kingston. "This guy keeps hiring people, and we have more employees than we need. It's ridiculous."

"I'm sorry that Mrs. Pinkerton asked for a job. Gladys is a good friend of Grammie's, and personally, I think she's doing a fantastic job," Kingston said defensively.

"She's eighty-fucking-five years old, and you hired her to be a foreman." Nash shook his head in disbelief, and I tried not to laugh.

"She's got a good eye," Kingston argued.

"She's practically fucking blind, asshole. I took her to the job site at the Smiths' house, and she was facing the wrong direction when she told me how everything looked—" he paused to use two fingers on each hand to make air quotes "—peachy."

"Ahhh . . . Gladys is my girl. Heart of gold. And she makes the best peach cobbler." Kingston clapped him on the shoulder.

Nash turned to look at me, pointing a finger in my direction. "You're keeping Cassie. No more strays for your brother."

We laughed, and I gave a fist bump to each of them before I made my way back to the office.

I'd needed the break. I was still pissed, but I'd simmered down.

When I pushed the door open at the office, it was quiet, and I was thankful there were no surprises waiting for me. Cassie was sitting behind her desk, and she looked up and winced.

Never a good sign.

"What now?" I hissed.

"Don't get mad, boss. But Ruby Rose is in your office. I told her I was not allowing anyone to step foot in here without an appointment," she said proudly, chin up, shoulders back.

"Yet you let her in?"

"She said she just needed sixty seconds. One minute. She said you'd understand. She was very specific." She shrugged.

Now, it was my turn to laugh.

Fuck me.

I would have been pissed if she'd turned Ruby away.

I held up my hand when she started talking again, and I made my way to my office. I pushed the door open, and there she was, sitting behind my desk, looking like a badass. Long, tan legs crossed at the ankles where her black military boots were propped on my desk. She was wearing a white sundress of sorts, showing off all that golden skin.

My mouth watered at the sight of her, and my day suddenly turned around.

"Hey there, Queenie. I hear you need sixty seconds of my time," I said, waggling my brows playfully at her.

"You're so predictable. Of course, you fell for that." She pushed upright, her legs falling beneath the desk, and I immediately missed them. Although she leaned forward, elbows on my desk, giving me a perfect view of her modest cleavage. "Did you seriously offer to represent my mother?"

She was pissed.

This woman was so hot and cold I couldn't keep it straight. Now she hated me again?

"Excuse me? Are you seriously barging into my office to reprimand me for something you know nothing about?"

She pushed to her feet and stormed toward me, her finger poking me in the chest hard. "What I know is that my mother has no money. She said that you've agreed to help her fight Jimbo, who, by the way, did nothing legally wrong, in case you don't know the law. He took money out of a joint account. Just like she does all the time. She's batshit crazy, and if you represent her, you will lose, and then I'll get slammed with a bullshit bill. Not happening."

I snatched her finger and wrapped my hand around it. "So what is it you're worried about? Me losing the case, or you getting stuck with a bill?"

She narrowed her gaze and tried to pull her finger away, but I held it still. "Both. It's ridiculous for you to take her on as a client."

I leaned forward, my chest brushing against hers. "We finally agree on something."

"So why did you agree to be her lawyer?"

"I didn't. I kicked her and her lunatic husband out of the office. There is no case. But I would have told you that, if you hadn't come in here with both guns blazing."

"Oh."

"Oh? That's all you have to say? You poked me in the chest, and once again, you tell me that I don't know how to do my job."

Her tongue peeked out and moved along her bottom lip, and my dick jerked to life.

This woman got under my skin like no other.

"No. I said that if you'd taken her on as a client, that it wouldn't be very lawyerly," she said, the corners of her lips turning up.

And goddamn, when Ruby Rose smiled, it was like catching the last glimpse of the sun before it set.

It was rare.

And sweet.

I leaned down and wrapped my lips around her finger, and she gasped before I released it. "Either way, I think an apology is in order."

"Is that your legal opinion?" she teased.

"It is."

"Fine. Sorry. I should have asked first before I accused you."

"Or maybe you just wanted an excuse to come here after what happened the other night? I told you that you wouldn't be able to stay away," I whispered as I nipped at her ear.

"Don't flatter yourself." She pushed me back and gave me this devilish smile. "I haven't thought about it once."

"Is that why your nipples look like they could cut glass at the moment?" I asked. My fingers grazed over the fabric of her dress, where two hard peaks were clearly excited to see me.

She sucked in a breath before her hand moved between us, and she gripped my dick in her hand. "I think you're the one who's struggling. I'm doing just fine."

I chuckled, and my hand moved over hers, guiding her up and down my shaft, right over the denim of my jeans.

"You aren't ready for seconds?"

My desk phone rang, and she startled, pulling her hand back and shaking her head the slightest bit.

I leaned back and picked up the phone, unable to hide my irritation. "What is it, Cassie? I'm with a client."

"Sorry, boss. But your first scheduled client has arrived, and I thought you'd want to know."

I didn't. Sure, I'd instructed her to always let me know when an appointment arrived, but she'd never followed any rules before.

Why the fuck start now?

"I'm leaving anyway." Ruby smirked. "Take care, *boss*."

She sauntered out the door, and I groaned.

This day had been a disaster.

Very on par to now be suffering from a bad case of blue balls.

And the only person who could help had just walked out the door.

14

Ruby

I'd ignored my mother's texts over the last few days, and I was actually enjoying setting these new boundaries with her.

The rent was paid, they had a roof over their heads, and my work was done there.

At least for the time being.

She'd come to the bar all high and mighty, telling me she'd hired River to represent her, and it had all been bullshit.

But I hadn't minded going to his office at all. Hell, I couldn't stop thinking about the jackass ever since he'd given me the best two minutes of my life.

Damn him.

Damn his sexy ass.

His handsome face.

His badass tattoos.

And his filthy mouth.

Especially his filthy mouth.

I'd always been turned off by men who thought dirty talk would impress me.

Dereck Hamilton, aka Professor Hamilton, had tried it once. He'd failed epically, but he'd taken his shot.

He'd smacked my ass with his perfectly manicured hand and told me he wanted to fuck me.

It was a hard no.

And by hard, I wasn't referring to the professor's penis. He took a while to warm up, and then once he was ready, everything was fast and uneventful on my end.

But River Pierce was a whole different story.

The man got me going the minute I saw him, and the bastard took me to euphoria on steroids in less than sixty seconds. Hell, I couldn't even get myself there that quickly.

I hadn't seen him since I left his office a few days ago, and I'd be lying if I didn't admit that I was disappointed every day that he didn't stop by the bar.

I'd never been big on flirty banter, but everything was different with him.

I walked the short distance to The Golden Goose because Demi and Peyton had me on some sort of group text that they'd added Saylor Woodson to, and we were meeting for lunch.

I pulled the door open to the diner, and when Midge looked up, I saw the panic when her gaze locked with mine.

Apparently, the dog-snatching devil had a conscience, and I was a reminder of what she'd done.

I raised a brow. "Midge."

"Ruby," she said, grabbing a menu. "The others are already here. They said they were expecting you."

"I heard you got a new dog," I said from behind her, because when I'd gone to the Daily Market yesterday, Oscar had told me his dog was missing. He was certain Midge had snatched him, as she lived two houses down from him.

"I have a rescue dog," she snapped over her shoulder.

When she paused in front of the table, Demi, Peyton, and Saylor all stopped talking at the same time and looked up at her.

"It's interesting that Oscar's dog, Boone, went missing, and you suddenly have a rescue dog that's the same breed as his? Does this not strike you as a bit too coincidental?"

She cleared her throat. "My dog was sitting on my front porch when I came home. He claimed me."

"Or you lured him into your yard with beef sticks." I raised a brow. "Just know that Oscar is pursuing legal action. It's a felony to steal someone's dog. And Boone has a chip in him, so if animal control comes to your house and checks the chip on that dog and it's Boone, you're going away for a very long time, Midge."

This was complete bullshit. Oscar hadn't considered legal action as far as I knew, and I highly doubted Boone was microchipped, but the look on her face was priceless.

If Casper the Friendly Ghost had a cousin, her name would be Midge Longhorn, dog snatcher extraordinaire.

All the color had left her face.

The three women at the table were looking back and forth between us, and I was enjoying myself.

Stealing someone's fur baby was evil. I wasn't going to stand for it.

"Is that so?" She lifted her chin.

I leaned forward. "Do the right thing. Put Boone back in his yard and go get your own damn dog."

She shocked the shit out of me when she did a curt nod and then stormed away.

Holy shit. This was as much of an admission as I could have hoped for.

That was far too easy. I dropped down to sit in the booth and smiled.

"Whatever that was, it was impressive. You had Midge quaking in her Crocs." Saylor laughed. "Good to see you, Ruby. It's been a long time."

I didn't know Saylor Woodson well, but we'd grown up in

the same small town, and though she was a few years younger than me, we'd always been friendly. I'd run into her a few summers down at the lake when we were kids, and she'd always seemed a little shy but very nice.

"That was just me catching Midge with her hand in the cookie jar." I shrugged before turning my attention back to Saylor. "Good to see you, too. Are you home for good?"

"That's what we're talking about," Demi said. "Saylor wants to start a business, and we just came up with the best idea."

Letty approached the table to take our orders, and we all quickly told her what we wanted before she walked away.

"I can't wait to hear it," I said.

"I want to open a romance bookstore." Saylor waggled her brows like this was the most devious thing she'd ever said aloud.

"I am so here for it," Peyton said, as Letty set our drinks down in front of us.

"So, we have that space next to the coffee shop, and we're thinking that she could put a bookstore in there. What goes better with coffee and muffins than a book?"

"I'll tell you what goes better with coffee and muffins than a book. Coffee, muffins, and a book with lots of sex in it. A swoony man who loves his heroine fiercely and throws her down on the dining room table and has his way with her." Peyton reached for her soda and took a sip.

Saylor and Demi both laughed as I gaped at them. "I've not read for pleasure in forever. I've been in school for so long that I haven't gotten to read anything that wasn't academic. Clearly, I'm missing out."

"Oh, you are so missing out." Saylor shook her head and smiled. "Romance is the best escape ever. I read a few books a week, and I think owning a bookstore would be the best way to spend my days. I'd be tying my passion to my career."

"Damn straight," Peyton said. "I am here for the passion. I love a dirty-talking asshole, and I'm guessing most of this town will be all over a romance bookstore. Even if some of the uptight locals act like they wouldn't dream of reading swoony fiction. They'll be there. Trust me."

Demi was laughing now, and Letty set our plates down in front of us. "I think it'll be brilliant. They can get their drinks and treats and then grab a book and read."

"And then after they've had their fill, they can come on down to the bar to have a cocktail and find themselves a book-worthy man." I reached for my burger, and they all nodded in agreement, like I hadn't been joking.

Damn. Maybe I need to start reading romance.

"My brother will probably have a meltdown when I tell him I'm staying and investing in a business, but he'll get over it."

"Why wouldn't he want you to stay?" I asked, as I set my burger back down on my plate.

"My mom is back with Barry Leonard, and let's just say, there's no love there with Hayes and me and our evil stepfather. He doesn't want me around Barry, but I love our mom, and I'm not going to stay away from my home just because she has a crappy husband, you know?"

"Well, coming from someone who has a very complicated relationship with her mother, I get it. I've stayed away for a long time just to avoid it."

"But then they win. That's not really fair, right? Why should I be run out of a place that I love? The place where I grew up. Where my brother lives and I have friends. No. I'm not running away because someone is an asshole." She reached for her drink and took a sip.

"I never thought of it as running away, because that's not really my style. But I get what you're saying. I guess it just depends on how toxic things are. If you can avoid being pulled under," I said.

Saylor's gaze softened as she took me in. "But you love your dad. You two have always been so close, from what I remember. I used to see you and Lionel everywhere together when we were young. So why shouldn't you be able to be here? I get it. Sometimes being away is freeing. Being removed from the drama. But at the end of the day, this is home. I like it here. And where else can I open a romance bookstore next to the world's cutest coffee shop?"

"Yes to that, girl!" Peyton said, loud enough that several heads turned in our direction.

"Do you like being here?" Demi asked, turning her attention to me. "I mean, outside of the drama with your mom and brothers."

"I don't know. I never stop long enough to think about it, because there's always something going on with one of them, and I usually can't wait to get out of here. And the jobs that I'm applying for are not here in Magnolia Falls. I don't know what I'd do here, and I certainly don't want to run the bar forever. My life is just not here anymore." It was the truth, but there was a peacefulness here that I hadn't felt anywhere else. When I was out on the water, tuning out all the noise, it was actually my favorite place in the whole world. I'd applied for a therapist position in the city, as well as a high school counselor position in Arizona. I was open to anything at this point. But from a professional standpoint, the collegiate teaching position would be the wisest move for me in my career.

"Well, maybe you should just enjoy this time while you're here. Cutler is counting on you to ride with us every week now, so hopefully, we can convince you that this place isn't all bad." Demi reached for her water and took a sip.

"How's your dad doing?" Saylor asked.

"He's doing so much better. He still has a way to go, but I spent the morning over at the hospital, and he's working hard in physical therapy every day."

"I took him some pastries yesterday, and I guess I'd just missed you, but he was going on and on about how proud he was of you," Demi said. "I think he loves having you home."

My chest squeezed the slightest bit, and I nodded. "Yeah. It's been nice spending all this time with him again. I didn't even realize how much I'd missed him."

"Well, I'm glad you're here, even if it's just temporary. We've got a fun group to go out with now," Saylor said as she lifted her glass to clink with ours.

"Cheers to a badass girl group." Peyton waggled her brows.

I shook my head and acted like they were ridiculous, but the truth was, I was enjoying myself. It was nice to feel like part of something.

I'd been solo for so long that I didn't realize how alone I'd felt over the last few years.

We finished up lunch, and I made my way back to the bar. Doreen was unloading inventory downstairs, and I checked on the kitchen staff to make sure all the orders had arrived.

Things were running smoothly here.

My father had let things go a bit, but the books were getting cleaned up, and the bills were all paid. If he'd stop loaning money to his friends, he'd be making a good living. I'd had to turn away a few of his buddies with outstanding tabs that hadn't been paid in years.

It was funny how quickly they'd come up with the money once they'd realized they weren't going to be served until they'd paid it off.

I had just unloaded the dishwasher and cleaned up behind the bar when the door was pulled open, and River walked in.

"Hey, I thought you were avoiding me. It's been a few days," I said, as my heart pounded in my ears, which pissed me off for obvious reasons.

I wasn't a girl whose heart fluttered or whose stomach had butterflies.

But my body was clearly responding to the man who'd managed to give me an epic orgasm and made it look as easy as taking his next breath.

"Ahhh, did you miss me, Queenie?" He pulled up a barstool and sat down. "Just a Dr. Pepper today, and how about a turkey club?"

"You got it," I said as I filled his glass with ice and soda before sliding it over to him. "How's the office going today?"

"Hmmm . . . funny you should ask. Cassie brought her cousin to the office. Yeah. She brought an actual human to work with her and acted like she'd brought a plant or a picture to set on her desk." He paused to take a sip of his drink. "She just looked at me and said, 'Hey, boss, I hope you don't mind that I brought my cousin to work today.'"

I leaned forward and chuckled. "What is her cousin doing there?"

"They talk non-fucking-stop. And then Cassie peeks her head in every twenty minutes or so to tell me that she's still working while visiting." He shook his head with pure disgust on his face.

"So, it's exactly like bringing a plant to the office, then?"

His lips turned up in the corners, and he nodded. "How's it going over here?"

"Good. It's been busy. My dad said you were there early this morning. I must have just missed you." I heard Calvin, our short-order cook, call out that the sandwich was ready, and I walked the few short steps to the window leading into the kitchen and grabbed his order. "Here you go."

"You think I can eat this in sixty seconds?" He smirked, and damn if it wasn't the sexiest thing I'd ever seen.

"I don't know why you'd want to."

"I think there's only one thing that I'd want to eat that quickly." His tongue swiped out along his bottom lip, and his gaze locked with mine. "And I'm looking right at her."

I did my best to act unaffected. "That was a one-and-done, remember?"

"Sure, it was." His head turned when the light came in from the door that had just opened, and I sighed as Rico strode toward me.

"Hey, sis. I've texted you twice today, and you haven't responded." He sat in the seat beside River and turned to give him a quick nod. "I'll take a beer as long as I'm here."

I'd ignored his texts because I'd already answered the question he was asking, and he knew that.

"We've already talked about it. There's nothing more to say."

River sat there eating his sandwich as Rico started to unravel. My brother was charming and sweet, but he had a habit of behaving like a child when he didn't get his way. I was used to it.

Rico took a long pull from his beer and then flailed his hands around. "We didn't talk about it. I asked for a goddamn job, and you just shut me down. That's not talking about it."

I leaned forward, making no effort to hide my irritation. "You had a job. You chose to no-show to said job multiple times, and you lost it. Oscar said you failed to come to work three times over the last week. You think that makes you appealing to hire? No thanks."

"You're being such a bitch," he hissed, and before I could put him in his place, River moved so fast I startled.

He grabbed Rico by the collar of his shirt and yanked him off his seat so they were both standing. "Watch your fucking mouth when you're talking to her."

"What the fuck?" Rico yelped, and River towered over him. "She's my sister. Why is it any of your fucking business?"

"She's my fucking business. You got me? Call her a bitch again, and I will beat your ass so bad you won't walk for days."

123

Holy shit. This was equal parts annoying and hot as hell all at the same time.

My inner feminist was shouting at me to stop this madness, but I stood there, watching with my heart pounding like my goddamn knight in shining armor had just rescued me from the big bad wolf.

Apparently, I liked having someone stand up for me.

And I liked that it was River doing it.

15

River

This motherfucker let her cover his rent, while the other asshole let her pay off his gambling debts, and he thought he could come in here and talk to her like that?

Not on my fucking watch.

Ruby's voice broke through my anger. "Let him go, River."

I glared at him for a few more seconds before letting the fabric of his shirt slip through my fingers, and he ran his hands along his chest as if he were trying to iron out the wrinkles on his shirt.

I sat back down, and he did the same.

"Are you going to let him treat me like that?" His voice was so whiny, I wanted to slap him just to knock some fucking sense into him.

"I am. My only complaint is that I didn't get to do it first." Ruby rested her elbows on the bar, looking from me to him. "I'm not hiring you because you aren't reliable, and I'm trying to run a business. This is my father's livelihood, and you claim to care about Lionel, yet I haven't seen you stop by to see him once since he's been in the hospital. He's been really decent to you, Rico."

"Panda's been sick, and I've had so much going on with Mom and Jimbo, I just haven't had a chance to get there. So that's why you won't hire me?"

"Come on, Rico. You don't get to just drink for free and ask for a job because I'm your sister. You need to grow the hell up. You got fired from the Daily Market because you didn't go to work. Why would I hire you?" she asked.

I had to give it to the guy . . . he made no attempt to hide how puzzled he was. He scratched his head and looked at her like he genuinely couldn't figure out for the life of him why she wouldn't want to hire him.

"Because I'm your brother."

"Yeah, you are. And I'm your sister. So I could make an argument that it's not my job to keep saving you. How about you help me out for once and save yourself?"

"And how do I do that when I have no job?"

Jesus. Grow the fuck up, man.

I had to look away because this dude was pathetic. I couldn't watch it without stepping in, which I knew wouldn't go over well. So, I let Ruby do her thing and put him in his place.

"You find one. You beg for it, and you show up and prove that you're worth keeping around."

"But if I can't get you to hire me, why would anyone else hire me?"

"For fuck's sake," I groaned, because I couldn't take it any longer. "Stop whining. Everyone works. Everyone has to pay their bills. You aren't the only one. Your sister works her ass off, and she's here helping her father because she's a good fucking person. And you're taking advantage of her. You need to figure your shit out."

His eyes widened, and he nodded. Damn. That was easier than I'd expected it to be.

"I don't know where to start."

I turned in my chair and faced him. "Start by being a fucking man. Tell your sister that you're sorry for calling her a bitch when she's done nothing but help you. Tell her that you're sorry for taking her money all these years and that you'll stop doing it. Right fucking now. Let's see if you can do that first, and then maybe, *maybe,* I'll fucking help you."

He blinked a few times before turning to look at Ruby, who was staring at me with her mouth hanging open.

"I'm sorry, sis. I shouldn't have called you a bitch. You know I love you, right?" he asked, and then glanced at me.

"And . . ." I said, rolling my eyes.

"I'm sorry for taking your money and for being a pain in the ass all the time."

I reached for the pen sitting on the bar near Ruby, and I wrote my number on a cocktail napkin and raised an eyebrow. "Do you have five bucks on you?"

"Yeah." He reached into his wallet and counted out five singles.

"Pay her for the beer."

His eyes widened, but he dropped the cash onto the bar.

I handed him the napkin with my phone number. "If you call her for one more thing, and I'm talking anything—like a free beer or rent money or even to fucking complain about your bullshit—the offer is off the table. This is my number. I won't be as nice as Oscar. You get one fucking chance with me, and I will have zero problem firing you. Call me, and we'll figure something out."

He glanced at his beer and then back at me. "Can I finish my drink, or . . ."

I shook my head with irritation because what the fuck was I even doing helping this prick out?

But I wasn't doing it for him.

I was doing it for her.

I didn't know why, but I knew that I wanted to help her.

"You bought it. Why do I care if you drink it?"

He nodded and slammed the rest of it down before wiping off his mouth with the back of his hand and slipping off the barstool. "Thank you. I'll call you as soon as I get home. But I'm not a lawyer, so I'm not sure what work you've got for me."

No shit, Sherlock.

"Don't worry about it. If you're willing to work, I'll help you out. But I told you before, you get one chance with me."

"All right. Bye, Rubes." He held up his hand, and she had a forced smile on her face when she said goodbye as he walked out the door.

When I turned my attention back to her, she had her arms folded over her chest, watching me. "What was that for?"

"That was for you, Queenie." I wiped off my hands and set my napkin on my plate before dropping a twenty-dollar bill on the bar and pushing to my feet.

"What are you going to have him do?" she asked, anger radiating from her hot little body.

"I don't know yet. Let's see if he even calls first. If he's willing to work, I'll find him something. It's up to him."

"I don't need you to give him a handout. I've got it covered."

"Yeah, you've got everyone covered, don't you?" I asked as I stood there, staring at her. I couldn't get this fucking woman out of my mind. Out of my thoughts.

I was horny as hell, and I didn't want anyone else.

This had never happened to me before, and I didn't know how the fuck to handle it.

I'd tried avoiding her for a few days, but that hadn't eased my discomfort at all.

So here I was, helping out her misfit fucking brother.

Because I just wanted to be around her. Be within a few feet of her. Hear her voice. Watch her work.

I just wanted to be in Ruby fucking Rose's orbit.

It calmed me in the strangest way. Even if she was pissed or irritated, I liked it.

"I do. And we're all fine."

"Let me get this straight. Your asshole brother calls you a bitch and begs for a job, and you turn him down. I tell him to apologize to you, and I offer to help him out, and you're pissed at me?"

"Correct. What even is this? You saw me break down in an elevator one time, and you think I need saving now? I'm not some damsel in distress, River. I don't need your help."

"You are one fucking stubborn woman, aren't you?"

"You don't know anything about me." She raised a brow.

"I know more than you think I do. But one thing is for certain: You sure do get pissed off at the wrong fucking people. I'm not the bad guy here."

She glared at me. "Who do you think you are? Some sort of expert on my life? Please. And who is it that you think I should be pissed off at?"

"How about the people who treat you like shit? Your mother. Your brothers. The people who use you and just keep coming back for more. But by all means, get pissed off at the dude who tried to help you. That makes a fuck ton of sense."

"You have no idea what you're talking about!" she shouted. "I don't need your help. I don't need anything from you."

Her reaction was completely irrational, and I expected nothing less.

The woman didn't know how to let anyone in.

And I understood it, because I didn't trust most people either.

But I trusted some.

My boys. My grandmother.

Everyone needed someone.

And Lionel couldn't be that person for her right now, and we both knew it.

So, I did what I do best—I acted like I didn't give a shit.

"Yeah. Just sixty seconds with me on my knees, right, Queenie?"

She moved so fast that I barely reacted in time, as she chucked the bar towel at me. "Fuck you, River."

"I think you'd like that, wouldn't you? Maybe that's why you're so pissed off all the time. You've never been fucked properly. That has to be pretty frustrating for you."

"You're an asshole." She flipped me the bird. "Don't let the door hit you in the butt."

I couldn't help but smile, because I liked seeing her all pissed off and worked up. She was sexy as hell and full of fire, and I'd never wanted to slam someone against a wall and cover their mouth with mine just to shut them up as much as I did her.

Just to taste her.

To hear those little moans that she makes when she's about to come undone.

Hell, maybe I was the one who was frustrated.

This woman was so far under my skin I couldn't think straight.

I held up my hand and walked out the door.

When I got back to the office, Cassie and her cousin were busy chatting about their plans to go to the lake later, and I told her not to interrupt me until my next client arrived in thirty minutes.

My phone rang, and it was from an unknown number.

"This is River," I grumped.

"Hey, dude. It's Rico. Are you still willing to help me out?"

"I wasn't kidding about the one shot. You flake, and you're gone."

"I got it."

"Be at my office tomorrow at 8:00 a.m. sharp. Don't make me regret this," I hissed.

"I won't," he said, and I ended the call.

I dropped to sit behind my desk and saw that the RoD group chat was going off, so I took a minute to catch up.

KINGSTON

Just left the Daily Market, and Oscar's dog, Boone, had been returned to his yard.

HAYES

And I give a fuck about this because?

NASH

My thoughts exactly.

KINGSTON

Because Oscar was reunited with his best friend, you dickwads.

ROMEO

Holy shit. Demi said that Ruby called Midge out at the diner for stealing Boone and basically told her she'd be arrested if she didn't return him.

KINGSTON

Ruby is such a badass. Have you made a move yet, brother?

I told you, there's nothing going on. But she's convinced Midge is a dog snatcher, and clearly, she was right.

NASH

Why the fuck doesn't Midge just go to the pound and adopt a dog like everyone else?

KINGSTON

The pound makes me sad. I don't like it there.

ROMEO

Why? Bad childhood dog experience? I don't ever remember you guys having a dog.

No. We never had a dog. He's just a sappy fucker. Remember how he cried over that Super Bowl commercial?

HAYES

How could I forget? We were at Whiskey Falls, and the bastard sobbed on my shoulder like a fucking pussy.

KINGSTON

Hey now! Any time you put two animals together who can't function without one another, I'm done for.

NASH

There were two animals in that

commercial? I thought it was an ad for beer?

KINGSTON

How did you watch that commercial and not see the horse and the dog? #adorbs

HAYES

Maybe because you were crying so loud, we were watching you instead of the TV.

If you ever say #adorbs again, I will twist your balls so hard that you'll see double.

KINGSTON

My balls are like my nipples. They're very sensitive. Even talking about you harming them makes me uncomfortable. 😉

Do you have a mirror near you, King?

KINGSTON

Yes. Why? You want me to look at my handsome face to remind me how good-looking I am?

No. I want you to hold it between your legs and check and see if you still have balls there, you sappy motherfucker.

ROMEO

HAYES

NASH

Too fucking good. I think he lost them a long time ago.

KINGSTON

I assure you . . . they are firmly in place, and the ladies love them. 😊

Anyway . . . I need a favor. Are any of you in need of some help around the house? Yard work? Handyman type of shit?

NASH

I told you that we aren't hiring Cassie. She's all yours, brother.

I'm more than aware. It's not Cassie.

ROMEO

Why am I nervous? This is usually a question we'd get from King, not you. Who the hell are you helping out?

KINGSTON

Oh, I cannot wait to hear who it is.

It's not a big deal. Rico Dane is looking for work. Oscar fired him.

HAYES

Rico Dane Junior? Because Rico Dane Senior was so fucking memorable?

NASH

I hate when people think they're so important that they need a title at the end of their name. Everyone should be given their own fucking name and own it.

ROMEO

Like Beefcake Heart the first?

NASH

He's definitely the one and only dude who can rock that name.

KINGSTON

Hold up. Are we all missing something big here? Rico Dane Junior happens to be Ruby's brother, correct?

Your point?

KINGSTON

I'm just saying, it's weird that you've never helped anyone other than one of us and Cassie, and that was because her mom helped Grammie, and now you're helping a dude you can't stand. I wonder why? 🐿️

NASH

He does make a good point.

HAYES

Rico is a complete fuck-up. Are you asking us to help him, or are you asking us to help Ruby?

ROMEO

My question exactly.

I groaned. If I said it was for Rico, they wouldn't do it. Everyone in town knew the dude couldn't hold down a job. No one was going to agree to help him. But I also didn't want to get bombarded with a shit ton of questions.

Does it really matter?

HAYES

Yes.

NASH

100%.

ROMEO

Absolutely.

KINGSTON

I just want to hear you say it so I can drop this mirror off at your house later, and you can check to see if you've still got your balls. 😍

KINGSTON

Waiting.

It's for Ruby.

ROMEO

Done. I can find some handiwork at the gym or at the house.

NASH

I need some yard work done this weekend.

HAYES

My fence is falling apart, and it could use some paint.

KINGSTON

My heart is full, brother. I'll find something for your lover's brother to do.

Thanks.

I set my phone down and leaned back in my chair. I knew I shouldn't be helping this asshole out.

But I knew that Ruby needed someone to step up and help her.

And for whatever reason, I wanted to be that guy.

16

Ruby

"Do you guys need anything else?" I asked, as Kingston, Romeo, and Hayes sat at their usual table, though River wasn't there. I knew Nash was home with Cutler, but I was fairly certain River was avoiding me. I had to make a real effort to hide my disappointment. He hadn't come into the bar since the day I'd berated him for helping Rico.

Four days ago.

And I hadn't seen him when I'd gone to the hospital to see my dad. I'd even gone at the times that I knew he usually went, but my father would say that River had come early that day.

Every. Single. Time.

The bastard knew how to get under my skin.

"Nah, we're good. I've got this one." Kingston handed me his card to close out the tab.

I swiped it through the little handheld machine. "Where's Demi tonight?"

"She's with her mom over at the house, showing her the layout and talking about some decorating ideas. If this house ever gets finished." Romeo shrugged. "Hey, your brother came over yesterday, and he actually did a good job raking the area where the barn is going to go."

"Rico? He was at your place?" I asked, as I handed King his credit card back and tore off the receipt to give him. I hadn't heard from my brother since I'd turned him down when he'd asked for a job, and I hadn't reached out either. I was setting some boundaries, and they would all have to adapt to them.

"Oh. You look surprised," Kingston said, and I saw the excitement on his face.

I put one hand on my hip. "Why does he look like he's got some big secret he can't wait to tell me?"

Hayes chuckled. "He always looks like that. He's a gossipy little fucker."

Romeo nodded with a wicked grin on his face. "He definitely couldn't keep a secret if his life depended on it."

"Hey now. I knew about you and Demi before you told us, and I kept that to myself." He raised a brow at Romeo. "You're welcome."

I snapped my fingers. "What is happening here? Were you going to tell me something?"

Kingston smirked. "Ah, yes. We've all come up with a few things for *Rico Junior* to do for us. My big brother was eager to find him work. And you know, River isn't big on helping people he doesn't like. And he definitely isn't doing it for *Rico Junior*."

I raised a brow. "Is there a reason you keep calling him *Rico Junior*?"

"Well, we certainly didn't hire Rico Senior. My point was that it's very out of character for my brother to want to help someone the way he's helping Rico Junior."

Now it was my turn to laugh because Kingston Pierce was ridiculous most of the time and impossible not to find charming. "So why is he helping my brother, then?"

"You tell me, Ruby Rose," he said, waggling his brows.

"How would I know? He hasn't been in here in several days. I think I pissed him off," I said, and I hated that I cared.

"Don't take it too personally. The wind can piss off River. But it's rare for a woman to get under his skin," Hayes said, and I was fairly certain that was the most he'd ever spoken to me.

Romeo nodded and rubbed his hands together. "You definitely get under his skin."

"So, he is mad at me, then? Has he said anything?" I pressed, and I wanted to kick myself for how desperate I sounded.

"Oh, sweet, sweet Ruby. It's what he hasn't said that says it all." Kingston slipped his credit card back into his wallet and tucked it into his back pocket.

"That makes no fucking sense." Hayes pushed to his feet. "He hasn't said anything. But he did ask us to help Rico, and he said it was for you."

My heart squeezed, and I freaking hated it.

I wasn't a tenderhearted girl, nor did I want to be.

But River had asked them to help my brother . . . for me.

Had anyone ever done that for me before?

"You're awfully chatty tonight," Romeo said, elbowing Hayes in the arm and smiling. "Trust me. He doesn't ask us for favors, and he asked for one. Obviously, it wasn't for Rico."

"Senior or Junior," Kingston piped in.

"It was for you." Romeo clapped me on the shoulder. "We'll see you later. I need to go pick up my girl."

"Have a good night," I said. "Tell Demi I'll stop by Magnolia Beans tomorrow."

"Will do." Romeo led his friends toward the door, and Hayes gave me a quick nod with a forced smile.

"See you later, Ruby Rose." Kingston leaned down and kissed my cheek like the sappy bastard he was.

I spent the next forty-five minutes cleaning up and closing out the register. I walked the short distance home, and I passed

River's house, where I saw his car parked out front in the driveway.

Before I could stop myself, I marched up the walkway leading to his front door. There was a light on inside, and I took that as a good sign that he was still awake.

But it was late.

I had no real reason to be here, but I couldn't seem to walk away.

I knocked on the door and instantly panicked at the thoughts racing through my mind.

He could have a woman here.

Hell, he could have multiple women here. I didn't know what he did in his private life.

Why was I even here?

I owed him an apology, but it could definitely wait until it wasn't after midnight.

I should wait.

This is crazy.

What am I thinking?

I turned on my heels just as the door pulled open. "Hey, Queenie."

I whipped around, and my mouth fell open at the sight of him. Dark, unruly, wavy hair, a pair of dark jeans that were slung low on his hips. His chest was bare and muscled, and my eyes moved down to the deep V that had my mouth going dry. He leaned against the door frame with his arms crossed over that perfectly sculpted chest.

I suddenly couldn't remember why I was there.

"Oh, hey. I was just walking by and thought I would see if you were up."

His eyes narrowed. "Why the fuck are you walking alone at this hour?"

"Well, don't go all caveman on me. I'm very capable of taking care of myself. I believe I've told you that many times." And

142

now I remembered why I was here. "That's the reason we got into it the other day. And you've been avoiding me ever since."

"I wouldn't say I'm avoiding you. I'd say I'm putting some distance there."

"That's the same damn thing. Why are you putting distance there? Are you that sensitive that you can't handle a little disagreement?" I rolled my eyes.

"Nah. It's not like that."

"What's it like?"

"Well, there are two reasons. The first one is that you were clearly pissed off at me for trying to help and do something fucking nice for you, and I figured you didn't want to see me because I've gotten Rico a few side jobs."

"Yeah. I heard that. I actually wanted to come and apologize for the way I acted."

His lips turned up in the corners. "Wow. An apology. Is that why you're knocking on my door after midnight? You had this need to apologize to me right now?"

"I overreacted. I'm not used to people helping me. And I guess it makes me nervous that you're helping Rico."

His gaze softened. "Tell me why."

"Because he will most likely not follow through. And that reflects poorly on me. I've worked hard to prove—" I looked away. I didn't know what I was trying to say, and this was going deeper than I'd meant it to.

"Hard to prove what? That you're worth it? That you're not your mother or your brothers?"

I looked back at him. "Something like that."

"You've got nothing to prove to me, Queenie. I know who you are. I know who your brother is."

"Yet you're getting your friends to help him?"

"Correct. Because you deserve a break," he said, as he glanced up at the tree when a gust of wind moved around us, and the leaves rustled beneath the moonlight.

His tongue swiped out and slid along his bottom lip, and I felt this pull toward him.

This feral need to reach for him.

I took a step closer, and he just watched me with that dark gaze of his.

"You said there were two reasons that you'd been staying away. What was the second?" I asked.

His hand found the side of my neck. "The second reason is because I can't stop thinking about you. About the way you came apart for me. The way your eyes were almost gold when you cried out my name. The way your hands fisted in my hair as you rocked that sweet pussy against my lips. The way you taste. The way you laugh. The way you try to act like you don't need anybody. That's why I stayed away."

Good. Freaking. Answer.

"What if I don't want you to stay away?"

"Then you'll need to say that. And if you want me as badly as I want you, you're going to need to say that, too."

What was I doing?

I shouldn't be here.

But I couldn't seem to leave.

"One time," I whispered.

His gaze searched mine. "I'm not setting a fucking timer, Ruby. If you come into this house and you tell me you want this, it's going to take a lot longer than sixty fucking seconds. I'm going to enjoy every inch of your body and make you come so many times you'll be thinking about me long after you leave town."

I sucked in a breath. "Promises, promises."

He smiled. A genuine, full-bodied smile that had my stomach flipping around like a schoolgirl with a crush.

This was dangerous.

Risky.

One time would never be enough.

144

"Say it. Tell me what you want."

My hands found his chest, and I tipped my head back. "I want one night with you. No timers. No rules. One night to do what we want."

"One night," he said, as his hand stroked my hair, tucking it behind my ear. "You better plan on not sleeping much, then."

My heart was pounding in my ears, and I was certain he could hear it. "Tomorrow, we go back to normal."

"All right. You'll have to tell me in the morning how the fuck I'm supposed to act. Right now, I don't want to think about that." His hands moved behind me, cupping my ass and lifting me off the ground with ease. My legs wrapped around his waist as he walked backward and sealed his lips to mine.

I heard the door close.

There was music playing in the distance in his house.

And his tongue slipped inside my mouth, and I groaned.

The way I needed this man wasn't natural.

Not to me, at least.

I'd never needed anyone aside from my father, and even then, I stopped needing him at a very young age.

Depending on people had not been a good plan for me.

Depending on people had always been painful.

A reminder that the only person I could truly count on was myself.

But I was lost in a River Pierce haze. A mix of passion and desire and want.

He carried me through the house and set me down, unlocking his lips with mine.

I missed him the minute he pulled away.

I knew I was playing with fire, but I stayed right there.

In the middle of the flames. So willing to get burned.

He smiled, his large hands on each side of my face. "Did you eat?"

"Did I eat?" I asked, stunned by the question.

"Did I stutter? I asked if you ate."

"No. But I'm not hungry." I leaned forward and nipped at his bottom lip. "At least not for food."

He growled. "You sure? I don't want you hungry when I'm having my way with you."

"Do you feed all the women you bring home, Wild River?" I teased, but his gaze hardened.

"No. But I think we both know that you're different."

I shook my head. I didn't want this to go deep. Why did it feel like this man could read every thought in my head? Like he could see into my soul.

Like if I let myself go, he would catch me.

"I'm not hungry right now."

"Fine. I'll feed you after. But I plan to eat very well right now," he said, his hand moving between my legs and beneath my skirt. He slid my panties to the side, and my head fell back.

"Shit," I hissed as his finger dipped inside me.

And then he pulled it back and raised his finger to his mouth, his eyes darker than I'd ever seen them. He sucked his finger between his lips, moaning as he did it.

This man was so sexy it should be illegal.

I knew in this moment that I'd never be the same after one night with River.

But when he lifted me off the counter, my legs came around his waist, and my hands moved around his neck.

And I couldn't wait to see where he was taking me.

17

River

I carried her down the hall. The taste of her was fresh on my tongue.

I couldn't wait to bury myself deep inside her.

But I was determined to take my time.

When Ruby said she was giving me one night, I should have been fine with that.

It was all I'd ever offered anyone else.

But I knew it would never be enough. So I'd enjoy every fucking minute until it was over. And that meant going slow. Staying in control.

This wasn't just a fuck for me.

I didn't know what it was, because that was all sex had ever been before now.

But this was different.

She was different.

She was *so* fucking different!

I dropped her down on my bed, and she bounced with a fit of laughter. Hearing Ruby laugh felt like I was witnessing something special. Something you earned. Something you cherished.

She pushed up, resting her ass on her heels as she glanced around my room. "It's very you."

"Yeah? How so?" I leaned down, my knees moving between her thighs as I tipped her back and took her in. Dark waves of hair tumbled around her as her chest rose and fell rapidly.

"It's sort of dark and mysterious. The black bedding. Moody lighting." She smiled, and she was so sexy I didn't know what the fuck I'd done to deserve to have her in my bed.

"There are no lights on. That's the moon coming through the curtains."

"And there he is. Moody, just like the lighting."

"I'm not really very mysterious," I said, leaning down and kissing along her jaw.

"Trust me, you're mysterious."

My lips moved down her neck. "What you see is what you get with me."

She arched up as my tongue traced a path down her neck and chest, moving between her perfect tits as her tee dipped low between her breasts.

"I see a guarded man who keeps to himself most of the time," she whispered.

I wasn't used to talking to a woman when we were in my bed, but for whatever reason, I liked the sound of Ruby's voice.

I lifted my head, and my gaze locked with hers. "I keep to myself because I like it that way. I'm not guarded for any particular reason, other than I don't feel the need for more."

She smiled. "We're two peas in a pod. I feel the exact same way."

"Then we have nothing to worry about." My fingers found the hem of her tee, and she raised her arms so I could pull it over her head before tossing it onto the floor.

And fuck me.

Red lace covered her perky tits, and I nearly came in my pants at the sight of her.

A woman's breasts covered by lacy fabric had never gotten me off before.

But here we were.

"Jesus. Look at you," I said, my fingers tracing over her hard peaks. I couldn't fucking handle how beautiful she was.

Her eyes watered the slightest bit; her lips were swollen from where I'd kissed her, and her teeth sank into her juicy bottom lip, as if she needed to stop herself from saying something.

I tugged the fabric down, exposing her tits, and I tweaked her nipples with my fingers before leaning forward and flicking them with my tongue. Twirling around the outside and teasing each one over and over as she started rocking her hips beneath me. My hand moved behind her back to unsnap her bra because I didn't want anything between us. I pulled the straps down her arms and let it fall to the floor with her shirt as I covered one of her perfect tits with my mouth.

I'd thought about this for weeks, and now that I had her here, I wanted all of her.

I moved my lips to the other side, tasting her again, as her hips bucked faster beneath me.

Her breaths came hard and fast, just from my mouth on her tits.

Damn, I was going to enjoy this.

"River." She panted. "It's too much."

I pulled back to look at her. "Buckle up. I'm just getting started, Queenie."

I sat back on my feet and pulled her skirt down her legs as my fingers traced the skimpy lace covering her beautiful pussy. I teased the edge with my fingers before pulling her panties down her legs and taking her in. My hand moved between her thighs, finding her soaked, and my mouth covered her breast again. My tongue swirled around her hard peak as I dipped one finger inside, feeling her walls tighten around me. My thumb found her clit, and she bucked against me as I slid my finger in and out of her before adding a second. My mouth devoured her tits as I felt her start convulsing.

"Oh my god," she whispered. She writhed frantically, her fingers finding my hair and tugging hard as she gasped over and over.

I continued moving, letting her ride out every last bit of pleasure.

Loving the little noises that escaped her sweet mouth.

I lifted my head, needing to see her. Her eyes were half-mast, and her lips were open as she tried to catch her breath. Her dark hair was a wild mess, and her skin was covered in a layer of sweat.

I'd never seen anything more beautiful.

Ruby Rose coming apart for me was fucking better than anything I'd ever experienced.

I pulled my hand back when her breathing settled, and I stroked her hair away from her gorgeous face. "You have perfect tits."

"You have perfect fingers. And perfect lips."

I chuckled as I pushed forward and moved to lie beside her. Her head settled against my chest, and I wrapped my arms around her. Breathing her in.

"Wait till you see what my dick can do."

Her shoulders shook against me, and she chuckled. "I'm sure he's just as impressive as the rest of you."

"I think he might be my best feature."

She pushed up on her elbow to look at me. "Thank you for helping my brother. I'm sorry I was such a bitch about it. I'm not used to anyone helping me. And I'm used to that, you know? So, I didn't know how to handle it."

"Is this how I get you to apologize? Just make you come over and over and you'll be putty in my hands?" I teased.

"I mean, it's hard to be angry when my entire body is tingling," she said as her hand moved between us and stroked along my denim-covered dick.

I hissed when she reached for the button of my jeans and pulled down the zipper, slipping her hand into my briefs like she couldn't wait one more second.

I shoved my jeans and briefs down, letting my cock spring free, as she continued running her hand up and down my shaft. My mouth found hers, our tongues tangling, desperate for more.

"Ruby," I said, pulling back. "I need to be inside you right fucking now."

She nodded, her breathing frantic once again. I pushed to my feet, shoving my pants and briefs down my legs and kicking them aside.

Ruby pushed up on her elbows and watched me. Her tongue slid along her lower lip, making me harder than I'd ever been. I yanked open the nightstand drawer, grabbed a condom, and tore the top off the wrapper, covering myself as quickly as I could without tearing the condom.

"You're even more impressive than I remembered. Seeing you completely naked, with all that ink covering your arms— damn, you're the whole package."

I climbed back over her, my eyes locking with hers. "And you're fucking beautiful. I want you to ride me. Set the pace. Do what feels good."

"What feels good for you?" she asked, and I loved seeing this side of her. She had such a tough exterior, but she was all sweetness beneath that façade.

Vulnerable and real.

"Your pussy wrapped around me is all I care about. I want you to take control."

"I'm happy to oblige." Her voice was all tease as I rolled over, taking her with me. I was flat on my back, and she settled above me, one leg on each side of me.

Fucking perfect.

Round tits, with her long hair falling all around her. My

fingers traced down between her breasts and along her flat stomach before gripping her hips as she ground up against me.

Teasing and taunting me as I groaned.

She gripped my dick and moved it along her entrance before slowly sliding down. Her gaze was on mine. The moonlight allowed just enough light to see everything in her gorgeous gaze.

Dark sapphire, emerald green, and pops of gold.

She took me in—inch by glorious inch.

I was fucking mesmerized by her.

She paused, a sigh escaping her perfect mouth. She was adjusting to my size, and it was sexy as hell.

"Breathe," I said, and her eyes locked with mine. "You can take it, Queenie. All of it."

My hands moved up to cup her breasts, and I teased her nipples, knowing just what she needed. Her head fell back, and she slid further down my shaft until she took all of me in.

A feral groan escaped my lips at the feel of her around me.

This woman was fucking made for me.

She started moving, finding her rhythm.

I pushed up to sit forward, my back against the headboard, my hands wrapped around her waist, running up and down her back, as my mouth covered her breast.

I couldn't get enough.

And she rode me, slow at first.

We found our rhythm, and nothing had ever felt better.

She met me thrust for thrust, and we moved faster.

Harder.

Needier.

I reached up, tangling my fingers in her hair and pulling her mouth down to mine. I wanted to feel her cry out my name on my tongue when she came.

She continued riding me into oblivion.

I felt her tighten around me, and our kiss was a mix of moans and pants and desperation. But I kept her right there.

Needing all of her.

And she moaned my name against my lips before her head fell back, and she shattered in the most glorious fucking way I'd ever witnessed.

Her tits bounced, and her hair grazed the tops of my thighs, and I gripped her hips and drove into her three more times before going right over the edge with her.

"Fuck," I hissed, as we continued riding out every last bit of pleasure.

It was fucking euphoric.

I'd even venture to say it felt life-changing in the moment.

And I wasn't a man who got emotional over sex, but this was next level.

This was fucking powerful and beautiful and not like anything I'd ever experienced.

I didn't know what to make of it.

She fell forward and collapsed on top of me, and our breaths were the only audible sound in the room.

I rolled her to the side and pushed all that silky, long, dark hair away from her face. Her lips parted, eyes blazing gold as she looked up at me, and we just lay there, staring at one another for a few seconds.

"That was . . . impressive," she said, her voice silky and sexy.

I shifted her and pulled out slowly, trying to process the fact that I missed the feel of her the minute I wasn't inside her.

That was some crazy shit right there, because I normally started working on my exit strategy the minute sex was over.

But I wanted to keep her right here.

To bury myself inside her again and again.

"I don't think that word does what just happened any justice," I said, keeping my voice light because this was the deal.

One-and-done.

I pushed to my feet and made my way to the bathroom, pulling off the condom and tying a knot at the end before dropping it into the trash can. I turned to look in the mirror and splashed some water on my face.

It was just really good sex. Don't overthink it.

I made my way back to the bedroom, and she was sitting up in bed, reaching for her clothes.

"You're not fucking leaving. You said one night, and I told you I was going to take my time."

"Oh. You don't strike me as a cuddler." Her voice was all tease.

"I'm not." I ran a hand through my hair and dove back onto the bed, pulling her down beside me. What the fuck was I doing?

"Are you holding me hostage?" she said, over a fit of laughter.

"We had a deal. I'm holding up my end of the bargain. Plus, you might want to go a few more rounds," I said.

She rolled to her side, and I did the same so we were facing one another. "Fine. I'm yours until the sun comes up."

"And then what? You're a vampire, and you disappear in the daylight?"

Her teeth sank into her bottom lip. "Something like that."

I stroked her hair, and my fingers trailed down her neck and across her breasts. "I've never seen more perfect tits. Seriously, they're works of art."

Her head tipped back in laughter. I loved seeing this side of her, all light and relaxed. "That's awfully poetic. I've never been very impressed with them. They aren't big, but they aren't too small either. They're just . . . average."

"Nothing average about them," I said, my fingers trailing from one to the next, and her nipples were hard enough to cut glass now. "They're the perfect handful, with pretty pink nipples, full enough, yet I can still get my mouth around them."

"Oh my God," she groaned. "Stop talking about my boobs."

"Fine. I'll stop talking about them if I can keep touching them."

"They're yours till the sun comes up, remember?"

"I remember, Queenie."

We were quiet for a few minutes, and now she was running her fingers up and down my arm.

"Tell me about the ink you've got. I love all the colors, and I've tried to make out the writing, but you never stand still long enough for me to do that," she whispered.

"My parents' names are in script here," I said, placing a hand over hers and moving it to my right shoulder.

"They passed away when you were young, right?" she whispered.

It was quiet again. This was not something I talked about with anyone. Hell, I didn't even talk about it with Kingston very often.

"They were killed in a car accident when I was five years old. That's when Kingston and I moved to Magnolia Falls to live with my grandparents."

She stilled for a moment before her fingers trailed along my arm again. "I'm so sorry, River. Were they the only ones in the car?"

"No. I was in the back seat. They were taking me to my first hockey game for my birthday. Apparently, I wanted to be a hockey player when I was young," I said, trying hard to keep my tone light, when the back of my throat was already burning. I didn't like to talk about this shit.

"Were you hurt?"

"I spent six months in the hospital, recovering. My grandmother stayed with me the whole time."

"King wasn't in the car with you?"

"He was home with the babysitter because he was too young to go. The dude had the attention span of a Labrador puppy back then. Hell, he's the same way now. He doesn't really remember much about them or about that time, which I guess is both a blessing and a curse."

She pushed up on an elbow, one hand resting on my chest as she looked down at me. "But you remember them? You remember the accident?"

"I remember things about them. The way they loved us, I guess. I remember my mom's smile and my dad's laugh. I remember being in the hospital and feeling really fucking sad. But that's as deep as it goes."

She ran a finger over my eyebrows, down the bridge of my nose, and along my bottom lip. "That's pretty deep. Those memories can't be easy."

"Shit happens, right?"

I nodded. "Yeah. I guess shit does happen. But that doesn't mean you can't grieve or be sad or struggle with it."

"Okay, Dr. Rose. That's enough psychoanalyzing for the day." I pulled her down and wrapped my arms around her.

I'd never slept with a woman in my arms.

Never wanted to.

But I really wanted to keep her right here.

At least for now.

18

Ruby

The sun came through the curtains, and I used my hand to shield my eyes. Something shifted beneath me, and I turned quickly, realizing I was sprawled over River's body.

Flashes of the night were coming back to me.

We'd dozed off and woken up in the middle of the night for round two. Then he'd taken me to the kitchen and fed me cheese and crackers and fruit, which I'd teased him about.

I'd expected a refrigerator full of beer and leftover pizza. But River had a lot of food in there. His house was immaculate. He didn't live like the wild child I'd imagined.

And then we'd gone for round three, and I'd fallen asleep a few hours ago.

"Hey," he said, his voice gruff. "How do you feel?"

I shifted slightly and groaned because I was sore, which had never happened after sex.

I'd also never had sex three times in one night.

It had never lasted for hours either.

And I'd never been with anyone that was as large as River.

"I'm definitely a little sore this morning," I admitted,

because there'd be no hiding it when I tried to walk out of here.

He sprung forward like I'd just told him the house was on fire. "I hurt you?"

I chuckled. "No. Your dick is unusually large, and we did it multiple times. That's not something I'm used to." Nor was I used to orgasming during sex.

All. Three. Times.

And that wasn't even counting the time with his fingers and tongue.

I was this weird mix of sore and sated this morning.

His gaze narrowed, and he looked so freaking sexy first thing in the morning. I was in this weird, hellish place of want and discomfort. I wanted nothing more than to pull him close again, but the thought of having sex right now had me squirming and wincing at the same time.

He was out of bed and striding toward the bathroom. The sound of the water turning on had me sitting forward. I pulled the sheet up to cover myself when I remembered I was still naked. He came striding back toward me, not a stitch of clothing; he was hard once again, and my eyes widened as I took him in.

Wild, unruly dark hair, strong muscles, colorful ink, and all the confidence in the world.

He didn't so much as hesitate as he reached for my hand and tossed me over his shoulder.

Naked.

I was freaking naked, and the bastard had tossed me over his shoulder like a rag doll.

I slapped his ass and tried to act angry over my laughter. "What the hell are you doing?"

He carried me straight into the large walk-in shower and set me down on my feet beneath the hot spray of water, and he stepped in and stood in front of me. I shook my head with disbelief, although I'd be lying if I didn't admit that it felt damn good.

He just smiled as the water splashed off his handsome face, and he reached for the body wash and poured it into his hands. I put my hand out, but he ignored me.

"Turn around," he commanded, and I raised a brow in challenge, but I did what he said because I'd pretty much do anything he asked right now, seeing as I was still in some sort of sex haze from last night.

"You better not do anything weird back there," I grumped over my shoulder.

He chuckled against my ear as his soapy hands found my shoulders, and he massaged them. His thumbs pressed into my lower neck and up toward my scalp, and I was done for.

Putty in his hands.

Well, naked putty in his hands.

He reached for another bottle and proceeded to wash my hair, taking his time and massaging my scalp. This was like a head orgasm, and I moaned as my eyes closed when he rinsed my hair with a separate hose that he held in his hand. The rain shower continued pouring down on me from above. He rinsed my hair and then proceeded to condition it.

"Are you a hairdresser on the side?" I asked, my voice playful. My eyes were closed, and my back rested against his chest.

"Well, you've pointed out that I'm not very lawyerly, right?"

I chuckled, and he rinsed the conditioner out of my hair. "So, you moonlight at a salon?"

"I've been washing my own hair for a long time, so it's not that difficult to wash yours." He turned me around to face him.

"Do you wash all your lovers' hair after you spend the night with them?"

"I've never showered with a woman, so it would be weird to wash their hair when it was dry." His gaze narrowed. "Spread your legs."

I was still processing the *never showered with a woman before* comment, before I realized what he'd asked me to do. "Why? What are you doing?"

"Just stop fucking arguing and spread your goddamn legs," he hissed, dropping down on his knees and tipping his head up to look at me. Water droplets ran down his cheeks, and his lips turned up in the corners.

God, he was a beautiful man.

I moved my feet apart and sucked in a breath, unsure what he was up to.

He reached for the body wash and poured it into his hands before massaging his way up my legs and then, ever so gently, washing between them.

Holy shit.

I'd normally find this kind of care appalling, but for whatever reason, it was sexy and romantic and sweet.

Completely unexpected after the way he'd ravished me a few hours ago.

He had a filthy mouth, and he didn't hold back.

And I'd loved every second of it.

But this?

This was the kind of shit someone put in a romance book. He continued gently stroking me as he kissed my lower stomach.

And then he pushed to his feet, reached for the handheld nozzle, and rinsed my soapy body.

"Thank you," I said, as a lump formed in my throat.

Had anyone ever cared for me like this?

He didn't say anything, just turned off the water, opened the door, and reached out for a towel, which he wrapped around my body. Then he grabbed another one and wrapped it around his waist before we stepped out of the shower. He opened the cabinet beneath the vanity, pulled out a smaller hand towel, and proceeded to pat dry my hair before he started brushing it. I watched him in the mirror as he stood behind me.

I didn't make any jokes about it because it meant something to me.

I'd told him that I was sore, and he'd done everything he could to make me feel better.

There was nothing funny about that.

"Better?" he asked.

"Yeah. Thanks."

"I mean, you gave me one whole night. I couldn't send you out of here in shambles, right?" He chuckled as I followed him into his bedroom.

"I was supposed to be gone before the sun came up," I teased, since we were back to our playful banter again.

"Well, seeing as I kept you up awfully late, I think it's fine that we extended it a few hours."

"I guess bending the rules and spending a little more time with you isn't the worst thing that could happen."

"That might be the nicest thing you've ever said to me, Queenie."

My head fell back in laughter. I couldn't remember a time that I'd laughed this much.

He opened a drawer and pulled out a pair of black boxer briefs as I reached for my panties and bra and started getting dressed, as well. He pulled a tee over his head and slipped on a fresh pair of jeans just as his phone vibrated on the nightstand. He glanced down to read it as I shimmied my skirt up my legs and tugged my T-shirt over my head.

"Hey, Demi's mom is out of town, and Romeo said they're going to have a barbecue over there. Eat, swim in the lake, relax a little. Do you want to go?" he asked, not even the slightest bit hesitant.

I cleared my throat as my phone vibrated in my purse. I reached for it and read the message from Demi, inviting me over.

"She just texted me. I just—I don't know. I've got things I should do."

"It's Saturday. The bar isn't even open until later, and Doreen always works the early shift on the weekends, right?"

I huffed and sat down to pull on my black boots and lace them up. I wasn't used to being asked to go places. I normally just always worked. Or I hung out on my own. When I was dating Dereck, we'd go to dinner and occasionally a movie. But we both worked a lot, and I didn't like attachments, so I appreciated that he never pushed for more.

"Look at me," he said, making it clear that he was losing his patience.

I turned around to face him. "Yes, Your Highness."

"I did just get down on my knees and wash your pussy, so how about you lose the attitude?" He smirked.

My mouth fell open. The nerve of this guy. "I didn't ask you to do it."

"You didn't have to. That's not what I'm saying." He groaned as he ran a hand through his hair. "Listen, I was happy to do it. You've got the best pussy I've ever been acquainted with."

Now I was laughing again. "Who knew? An award-winning vagina and gold-medal breasts."

He nodded, a wicked grin spreading across his face. "Anyway, stop overthinking it. It's a fucking barbecue. No one's proposing marriage here. We both know what this is. A one-and-done. I got it. You've got it. But we're still going to see each other at the bar and the hospital every day, so no reason we can't have a fucking burger with friends together."

"Ahhh . . . there's the poet again. Fine. I could eat. Turns out, being felt up in the shower really works up a girl's appetite."

162

I texted Demi back to let her know I'd be coming over and then followed him toward the front door and outside as he pulled open the passenger door to his car.

I gaped at him. "I'm walking home. I have to change my clothes."

"You're walking like you just got bucked off a badass bull. I'm giving you a ride home. Get in the fucking car."

"Such a gentleman," I hissed, because it was just our schtick, I guess. Maybe we'd been too nice this morning, and we needed to get things back to normal. I climbed into the passenger seat, and he slammed the door dramatically.

The heathen.

He drove me home in silence, and that bothered me.

"So now you're not talking to me?"

"You know, there are a lot of women in this town that wouldn't mind spending a night with me and getting a ride home. You act like I'm going to fucking murder you." His hands were gripping the steering wheel so hard I could see the whites of his knuckles, and I couldn't help but laugh.

He looked over and glared at me, and I just kept laughing because now that I'd started, I couldn't stop. He pulled up in front of my house and turned to face me.

"Are you done?"

I pulled myself together. "Sorry. I don't think you're going to murder me."

"You're just laughing because . . . ?" He raised a brow.

"Because you're just kind of cute when you get your feelings hurt." I shrugged.

"I hardly have hurt feelings. It's not really my style. I'm offended that you're so ridiculous. We fucked. It's not that big of a deal." Wow. He was really worked up. I had a feeling there was more going on here than my moodiness because that certainly wasn't new.

"First of all, the reason I didn't want a ride home was

because I thought you'd want me to ride with you to the barbecue after I changed clothes, and then everyone would think something was going on between us."

He rolled his eyes and then glanced out the window like I was boring him. "I hate to break it to you, Queenie. Everyone already thinks something is going on between us. Kingston is convinced we're fucking. What's the second thing?"

"How do you know there's a second thing?"

"Because you said, '*first of all*,' which usually implies there's something else."

"Fine. Secondly," I said, clearing my throat because I was sure I'd offend him with this one. "You seem so defensive about us having sex and saying it wasn't that big of a deal, but I think you liked it. And I think that's freaking you out."

"You think I'm freaking out?" He smirked.

The cocky bastard.

"Shall I say it again, slower?" I moved closer to him, my mouth a breath away from his as I spoke annoyingly slowly. "I . . . think . . . you're . . . freaking . . . out."

He glared at me, and before I could stop myself, I lunged forward and kissed him.

I freaking kissed him.

After insisting this was a one-and-done deal.

Insisting I wouldn't ride with him to the barbecue.

Here I was, mauling this man in the front seat of his car in broad daylight.

He tugged me over the center console and onto his lap as we made out like savages.

I pulled back to look at him, and he looked quite pleased with himself.

"Am I still the one who's freaking out?" He smiled.

I climbed off his lap and back into the passenger seat. "That was just a goodbye kiss to thank you for, you know, washing my hair and my lady business."

His head fell back, and laughter echoed around the car. "Your lady business? So proper, Queenie."

I groaned. "Goodbye, River. I'll see you at the barbecue."

"I'd offer you a ride, but I wouldn't want anyone to think anything was going on." He oozed sarcasm. "Unless one of the nosy neighbors saw you climbing me like a tree just now. Word travels fast here in Magnolia Falls."

I flipped him the bird and pushed out of the car. "Don't flatter yourself. This is over."

"Pending you can keep your hands to yourself this afternoon." He winked.

I slammed the door and stormed up the walkway to my front door.

I was definitely irritated, but I couldn't wipe the smile off my face.

19

River

"You seem a little off today," Kingston said, because God forbid my brother didn't say every single thing he thought aloud.

"I'm sitting here, listening to you guys talk like I always do. How am I off?"

"I don't know. Does he seem different to you guys?" he asked Romeo, Hayes, and Nash, who were sitting in the chairs around the fire pit.

Demi, Peyton, Saylor, and Ruby were swimming in the lake with Cutler, but we didn't feel like going in just yet.

"He seems like his usual grumpy self," Hayes said, holding up his water bottle to clink with mine.

"Takes one to know one."

"Touché," he said.

"Well, of course, you don't notice, Hayes. You're as moody as he is." Kingston laughed, taking a long pull from his beer. "Come on, Romeo, you notice it."

Romeo turned to look at me, his lips twitching a little, so I knew he was going to give me shit. "He's a little more smug than usual."

"For fuck's sake. You're making this shit up."

"Nash, what do you think?" Kingston asked.

"I think he got laid last night. He's got that relaxed air about him."

"Spoken like a man who hasn't gotten laid in a long time. You're so horny that you've convinced yourself that everyone else is getting some." I raised a brow, hoping I'd shut this shit down.

Nash barked out a laugh. "That could be true. Cutler is definitely the world's biggest cock block."

"What do you mean?" Kingston gasped. "That kid gets you more attention from women than I've ever seen."

"Correct. They love Beefcake." He laughed some more. "But I'm a fucking dad. I have you guys watch him when I'm working. But it's not so easy to get laid when you've got a six-year-old at home."

"Hey, nooners aren't a bad idea," Kingston said as he waggled his brows.

"As hard as this is for you to believe, there aren't a ton of women who are available for an afternoon quickie."

"You know we'll watch him at night if you want to go out," Romeo said. "Hell, Demi is working with Brinkley's sister-in-law, Reese, that designer we hired, to come up with a room design just for Cutler at the new house."

Brinkley was Romeo's sister-in-law from Cottonwood Cove, and he'd told us about her brother's wife, who was an interior designer and was helping them with their house.

"He doesn't need his own room. And he sure as fuck doesn't need it professionally decorated." Nash shook his head as he stared out at the water as all the women took turns swimming with him. "That little dude gets way too much attention from everyone."

My eyes moved to Ruby. I swear she was fucking with me when she showed up in that little red string bikini and cut-off denim shorts. She knew I thought she had the best tits I'd ever seen, and this suit was just driving that fact home. And then she'd peeled off those goddamn shorts and bent over, reminding me about that award-winning pussy.

She was an evil queen sometimes.

"You going to tell us what's going on with you and Ruby?" Romeo asked as he turned to me.

"Nothing." I wasn't a guy who would disrespect a woman by talking about that shit, but I also never lied to these guys. They were my brothers in every sense of the word.

"Your eyes bugged out of your head when she showed up in that bikini." Kingston was laughing now because he was an asshole, and he enjoyed seeing me struggle.

I flipped him the bird. "She's a cool girl. There, I said it. Can we stop talking about it now?"

Romeo smiled. "Yeah, brother. We can stop talking about it."

"I heard John Cook is thinking of retiring next year," I said, anxious for a subject change. John was the captain at the Magnolia Falls firehouse where Hayes worked.

"Yeah. He's ready. He said he's got a few more months in him." Hayes shrugged like he hadn't been waiting for this day for the last few years.

"You putting your name in the hat?" Nash asked, as he stared out at the water where Cutler was jumping off the dock and the girls were catching him.

"He knows I want it, but fucking Lenny Davis is pushing for it, too. And apparently, they like a well-balanced dude, and Lenny being married to Kimber now makes him appealing. The dude will stab you in the back and throw you in the flames, but he's got a social-climbing wife, so that makes him appealing? It's such bullshit."

"Play the fucking game," I hissed. "The system isn't always fair, so you've got to play by their rules."

I fucking hated injustice, and there was a lot of it out there. It was the reason I got into law.

"I'm not going to get married just to get a job. I'm fucking good at what I do, and they know it. Who gives a shit if I have a wife?"

"Well, obviously, the people in charge care." Kingston chuckled.

"Why would they give a shit if you were married?" Nash asked as he sipped his beer.

"It's not necessarily about me being married. They like the firehouse to be an extension of family. John's wife, Elise, is always throwing family picnics for everyone in the park, and it builds community or some shit." He shook his head. "Kimber is nothing like Elise Cook, and I don't see her doing any of that shit, but now, she's suddenly bringing cookies to the firehouse every week. Fucking Lenny knows how to play the game."

"So, play the game, too," Romeo said. "You don't have to be married. You could start dating again. I think a stable relationship might do the trick."

"Been there. Done that. We all know how that turned out," Hayes hissed.

"Not everyone is like Kate Campbell," Kingston said.

"I almost walked down the aisle with the devil. I'm reminded of it every fucking day I have to see Lenny. Every fucking time I have to run into Kate in town. Not everyone needs to have that shit, and it definitely should not be a reason why I get promoted. It pisses me the fuck off." Hayes crossed his arms over his chest.

"Really? It's hard to tell that you're pissed off with that vein about to burst in the side of your neck." I chuckled. "You dodged a bullet, brother. And the day you give us the thumbs-up to kick Lenny's ass, I promise you we will sic Romeo on him in a dark alley."

More laughter.

Hayes was engaged to Kate, whom he'd dated for several years. I'd never been a fan of her. The way she flirted with all of us had never seemed playful. She was desperate for attention, and she'd get it any way that she could. Hayes had always been guarded, but for whatever reason, he'd let his guard down with her. And she'd fucked him over in the worst way.

"Trust me . . . I'd love to unleash Golden Boy on his arrogant ass. There'd been a rumor that he was thinking about transferring a few months ago, but with Cook letting word get out that he might be retiring, Lenny is suddenly determined to stay here," Hayes said, letting out a frustrated breath. "My disdain for the guy just gets worse every time I'm around him."

"Yeah. He's a real piece of shit," I said, and Nash, Romeo, and Kingston all nodded in agreement.

"Well, you've got time. He's not leaving for a while. Maybe the right woman will knock you on your ass." Nash stretched his legs and crossed them at the ankles.

"I think meeting the wrong woman first, sort of ruins it for all future women." Hayes barked out a laugh. "And then I look at the men my mom has picked, and the truth is, some people are better off alone."

"I get that. I mean, my reasons are different. I just personally can't imagine only being with one woman. It's like being told you can only have vanilla ice cream for the rest of your life. I like mint chocolate chip. Sometimes I feel like cookies and cream." Kingston smirked.

"Baby, did King just basically compare me to vanilla ice cream?" Demi said with a laugh from where she stood behind Kingston's chair.

"Ah, not you, Beans. If I met a girl that was all the flavors mixed together, I'd for sure change my ways."

"Nice save." Demi sauntered over and sat down on Romeo's lap. "What are we talking about?"

"Hayes is telling us why he's never going to date anyone

again after the shit Kate pulled on him," Romeo said before he kissed her cheek. She looked over at Hayes, and her gaze softened.

"Yes, there are bad people in the world, Hayes. But not everyone is bad." She smiled at him.

"I've just met too many of them to ever go all in again." He shrugged.

"Don't you worry that you'll get lonely?" she asked.

"I do just fine, Beans. Don't you worry about me." Hayes winked at her.

"Yeah, the women in Magnolia Falls love a broody, damaged firefighter," Nash said.

Hayes chucked his napkin at him. "Hey, I'll own the broody firefighter, but I take offense to the damaged part."

Now we were all laughing.

Demi shook her head and pushed to her feet. "I'm going to go get the cookies and bring them out. Cutler is ready for something sweet."

"So am I," Romeo teased, and she waggled her brows.

When she'd walked far enough away, he leaned forward, elbows on his knees, as he looked at each of us. "I was going to wait to tell you guys this week when we met at the gym, but since we're here shooting the shit, I may as well tell you now."

"Is something up?" I asked.

"I'm going to propose to Demi soon. We're working on this house together, and we spend every damn day together, and I don't know. It feels right."

"She's all the flavors, brother," Kingston said, pushing to his feet and pulling Romeo in for a hug.

"I'd lock that shit down, too." Nash stood and gave him a bro hug, and we all stood and did the same.

"Happy for you, Romeo. She's one of the good ones." Hayes clapped him on the shoulder.

I studied him for a long minute. I'd known Romeo since

we were just kids. He'd always been the toughest guy I knew, but he had a heart of gold and would walk through fire for the people he loved. I'd seen something there right away with them, and I couldn't be happier for him. He and I had been through a lot of shit, and we'd come out the other side still standing.

"I knew there was a tender heart beneath all that tough-guy shit." I pulled him in for a hug. "You deserve this, brother."

"Thanks. I may need you guys to come with me to pick out a ring. Demi's got nice taste, and I don't know shit about diamonds."

"Beans deserves the biggest one out there," Kingston said.

"Nah, she doesn't give a shit about the size of the diamond; she only cares about the man behind it," Hayes said, and we all turned and gaped at him.

"Dude. That was deep. Where the fuck did that come from?" Nash said over his laughter.

"Just saying. I went all in on Kate's ring, and she went and fucked my coworker. It's not about the diamond; it's about the girl you're giving it to." Hayes raised a brow.

"You got that ring back, right?" Romeo asked.

Hayes glanced over at me, and the corners of his lips turned up. "Yeah. River managed to get it back for me."

"I paid a visit to good ole Kate while she was crying on Lenny's shoulder about getting caught in bed with him, and I may have used some intimidation to get the job done. But let's just say, she handed over that ring real fast, and Lenny looked like he was going to piss himself when I showed up."

"That's right. I remember now," Kingston said. "We were all so busy trying to keep Hayes from losing his shit on Lenny that I forgot you went and got that ring back."

"Where's the ring now?" Nash asked.

"It's just been collecting dust for the last few years. I just want it gone. If any of you want it, it's yours."

We all turned to Romeo, who held his hands up. "Fuck that. I'm not giving Demi a cursed ring. You need to sell it and get your money back."

"So, I guess we're all going ring shopping," Kingston said as he looked at each of us with a big grin on his face.

"Those are words I never thought I'd hear for us," I said.

"Lincoln thinks we should road-trip to Cottonwood Cove so no one can tip her off here in town." Romeo's brother turned out to be a great guy.

"Who are we shopping for a ring for?" Ruby popped her head in between Romeo and Kingston.

"Shit. This is why I can't tell you guys anything," Romeo groaned.

"She won't say anything, will you, Queenie?"

"Please. I'm a vault. You'd have to kill me to get a secret out of me." She waggled her brows at me. "Although River would probably enjoy seeing bodily harm come to me, wouldn't you?"

There was a lot I wanted to do to this woman at the moment.

But killing her wasn't one of them.

Unless it was a silent death by orgasm.

That, I could get on board with.

20

Ruby

The day had been so much better than I'd anticipated. Perhaps it was the company. I really liked everyone in this group, which was saying a lot because most people annoyed me after a while.

It could also be that I was just in a good mood from all the fabulous sex I'd had last night.

The postcoital daze.

The orgasmic bliss.

Either way, it had been a great day. Cutler was by far the cutest kid I'd ever met. Cool and quirky and uniquely himself.

I'd changed clothes and was just finishing eating a cookie that Demi insisted I try because she'd made them, and she wouldn't tell any of us what was in them.

"Should Cutler be eating these *special* cookies?" Nash teased, because they'd all asked if they were cannabis cookies.

"Hey, Pops. It's Beefcake. And I like the cookies," he said, leaning his head against my arm as he sat next to me on the bench by the fire pit.

"Fine. I'll tell you. These cookies you all love so much are made with applesauce and gluten-free flour." Demi beamed.

The guys all groaned, and Peyton, Saylor, and I all told her how fabulous they were.

"I'm going to hit it. How about you pack me up a few to drop off with Lionel? I'm heading over to the hospital now," River said.

I turned, and my gaze locked with his. "I'm going there, as well."

"Well, what do you know . . . you're both going to the same place," Kingston teased.

River flashed him the bird before turning his attention to me. "Did you walk here?"

"Yes." I raised a brow.

"You want a ride to the hospital? We're both going to the same place."

My heart raced, per usual, and I was considering talking to a doctor about a medication to get this madness to stop.

But how do you medicate yourself for something that only happens around one particular man?

I'd caught him staring at me several times today, and that was only because I couldn't seem to stop looking at him.

River Pierce was not the guy you fell for.

He was heartache just waiting to happen.

The professor was the kind of guy you went all in on. There was no room for heartache there. And that was how I liked it.

"No, thanks. I prefer to walk."

His lips turned up in the corners just the slightest bit. "Suit yourself. See you there."

Demi handed him a baggie of cookies for my father, and we both said our goodbyes to everyone and walked out toward his car in silence. He paused when he reached for the door handle and dangled the keys around on his finger.

"Last chance. It's awfully warm out here today," he said.

"I like the sun," I lied. My shoulders were sunburned, and I was overheated from all my time in the water today.

"Said no vampire ever."

"Can you not come up with anything else than calling me a bloodsucker?"

"Sure. I think you're an amazing cocksucker."

A laugh escaped my lips, and I quickly corrected myself and started walking before shouting my lame response over my shoulder. "Takes one to know one."

When I turned down the street leading to the hospital, he drove past me slowly. "You're looking a little red, Queenie. Sure you don't want to get into this air-conditioned car? You might get sun poisoning."

"Well, I'm heading to the hospital, so I'll seek medical attention there if needed."

"All right. See you later."

He drove off, and I tried to talk some sense into myself. Why was I so drawn to him? Was it the sex? Obviously, it had been mind-blowing, but I'd been drawn to him even before the sex.

It was classic behavior. I'd had an unstable childhood. An unfit mother figure.

I'd had to grow up far too young.

Of course, I'd be drawn to a walking tornado.

A sexy, tempting, witty wrecking ball.

But I knew better than to let this go any further. I'd dipped my toes into the sexually explosive waters, and now it was time to tap out.

Or tap that.

Damn. There I go again.

No more River Pierce.

I needed distance and space and all the willpower that I could muster.

My phone rang, and I pulled it from my back pocket and saw Dereck's name on the screen. It had been a while since I'd spoken to him, so I answered the call.

"Hey. How are you?" I asked.

"I'm well. How about you? How's your father?" His voice was deep and void of emotion. He was the calmest person I'd ever met. There were no highs, no lows, no ups and downs with him. He was always steady.

Which also translated to extremely boring.

But at least there was no drama.

"He's doing all right. He's in a rehab facility, and he's got a long road ahead of him, but he's making good progress."

"That's good news, Ruby. I, er, I wanted to reach out for a few reasons."

"Okay, what's up?"

"Well, Dean Langston came to speak to me yesterday about the letter of recommendation that I wrote for you. He's really hoping you take the position in the fall. Have you considered it any further?"

I sighed. "I just don't know that teaching is what I want to do. I was honest with Dean Langston that I have applied for several jobs, and I just want to weigh out my options. He said that he wanted to hold the position for me for a couple of weeks to give me time to decide."

"I understand that. But you could always take it and see if you like it. You were the strongest TA I've ever had. You're very relatable, and the students like you."

I saw the hospital a few feet ahead, and I was ready to get out of this heat. "When do you think I'd need to let them know?"

"I would make a decision pretty soon. These aren't positions that come up often, and there are a lot of people who would jump at the opportunity to teach at one of the most prestigious universities in the country." There was always a bit of arrogance in his tone when he spoke, but he was a humble guy when you got to know him. We were from two completely different worlds, but aside from our work ethics, we didn't have much in common. Our twelve-year age gap was probably the most exciting thing about our short-lived, passionless relationship.

"All right. I'll think about it."

"I'll try to buy you some more time," he said. "I do miss you, Ruby."

I winced because I hadn't expected that. There really was nothing to miss. We didn't know one another well enough to miss each other. We had a very professional relationship until we crossed the line two months before I graduated.

"That's kind of you to say," I said, making an effort to keep my voice light. I didn't want to lie and say that I missed him, because I hadn't really thought about him since I'd left. But I also didn't believe he'd missed me. I think he missed the idea of me. The excitement of sneaking around with someone he wasn't supposed to be dating. Having sex with a younger woman, maybe. But we hadn't gone deep. I didn't know anything about him other than his educational journey and the fact that he'd traveled a ton over the years.

"I think you underestimate your allure."

"Thank you." I approached the hospital, and I was desperate for a water now.

"You're welcome. Let me know when you decide what you're going to do. I'm guessing it's your best option; you'd be foolish to pass it up."

He was probably right, but his comment annoyed me at the same time.

"I'll keep you posted. I'm at the hospital, so I need to go."

"All right. We'll talk soon. Goodbye."

I ended the call and tugged the door open, on a mission to head straight to the drinking fountain, when I looked up to see River leaning against the wall near the gift shop. He wore a black fitted tee and dark jeans. His face was tan from all the sun he'd gotten today, and his hair was a wild mess of dark waves. He held a bottle of water between two fingers and dangled it back and forth, taunting me. "I thought you might be needing this."

I didn't say a word. I just hustled over to him and attempted to snatch the water from his hand, but he pulled it back.

"Are you seriously not giving it to me?" I huffed.

He leaned forward. His face was so close to mine that I sucked in a breath. "Just say it."

"Say what?"

"Just say that you were being stubborn, and you should have just gotten in the car with me." He smirked.

"Fine. I should have gotten in the car. Can you please stop torturing me and give me the bottle of water?"

"Was that so difficult?" He held it out to me, and I grabbed it and untwisted the lid before tipping my head back and guzzling the whole damn thing in one long sip.

"Thank you," I said, wiping my mouth with the back of my hand and tossing the bottle into the recycling section of the garbage can beside the elevators.

"You're welcome." He held the door open to the elevator and motioned for me to step on, and he walked in behind me.

We were silent, and I glanced up to see him watching me, but he turned away the minute my gaze caught his. We stepped off the elevator and walked side by side toward my father's room.

"Did you have fun today?" he asked.

"Surprisingly, yes."

"See, this town isn't all bad."

His comment struck me. He was right. I'd been avoiding my mother's calls, and Rico seemed to be keeping busy with odd jobs that River had found for him. Zane had stopped by the bar twice this week and hadn't asked for money or needed me to solve any major problems for him.

And I'd actually been enjoying being home.

"Don't get cocky. It was one good day," I said, as I paused at my father's door.

"And one really good night," he whispered in my ear and then winked before pushing ahead of me and walking in first.

The bastard.

"My two favorite people are here," Dad said as he looked up from the chair he was sitting at, working on a puzzle.

A memory of doing puzzles with him as a young girl flashed through my mind. We'd spend hours working on them. He'd even had a few framed, and they hung in the hallway at the house.

I pulled up a chair, sitting beside him as I glanced at the box with a picture of mountains and a large lake. "This is pretty."

"Yeah, it reminded me of the area we used to kayak to in that little cove."

River pulled up another chair and placed it on the other side of him. "So, I'm one of your favorite people, huh?"

"Of course, that's what you focused on. And by the way, you're definitely his second favorite."

"Well, you are his child. I would hope I didn't knock you out of the top spot."

"In your dreams," I grouched and reached for a few puzzle pieces and got to work.

My father just laughed as we continued to banter back and forth before Dad jumped in and started chatting with me.

"How's it going with Wendy?" my father asked, as we continued working on the puzzle.

River was ridiculously competitive and pointed out every time he found a match and started keeping score.

"Better, actually. I haven't been taking her calls lately. Her rent is paid. The boys are fine. And I've been busy at the bar."

"That's good to hear, Rubes. And the boys are men, keep that in mind. I hope you're having some fun. I asked River to keep an eye on you for me."

"I'm definitely keeping an eye on her. *Showering* her with lots of attention." He looked up at me with this wickedly sexy grin on his face, and I wanted to lunge over the table and throat-punch him.

And also crash my mouth into his because I liked kissing him.

Damn it. This happened every time I was around him.

My dad didn't even notice the comment he'd made. "Good. She's always worked too much, and she's young. She needs to have a little fun, too."

"I couldn't agree more," River said.

We spent the next hour working on the puzzle and chatting, and every time I looked up, I caught River looking at me. We couldn't seem to keep our eyes off one another.

"All right, I'm going to head home and change and get over to the bar." I stood and kissed my father's cheek.

"You work too hard, Rubes," Dad said, smiling up at me. "I'll try to get out of here as quickly as I can so you can get back to your real life."

"It's fine. I've got a few weeks to decide if I want to take that job at the university." I didn't necessarily want that job, but it wasn't like I had a ton of other offers coming in, and the salary they were offering was impressive. I wouldn't mind making enough money to live comfortably for once. To not stress over bills.

"You need a ride?" River asked, leaning back in his chair as his eyes scanned me from my head down to my feet.

Slowly perusing, as his tongue swiped out to wet his bottom lip.

I squeezed my thighs together and glared at him. "Nope. I prefer to walk."

I heard him chuckle as I made my way out of the room.

I'd rather blister in the hot sun on my walk home than be alone with River Pierce in his car.

Because I already knew where that would lead.

21

River

It had been a week since I'd seen Ruby, and I was going out of my fucking mind. She'd made it clear that she wanted space, and damn if the woman didn't stick to it. I thought she'd break.

Expected a booty call text after the night we'd shared.

But she'd gone radio silent.

And I sure as hell wasn't going to beg her to talk to me. The ball was in her court.

If only her brother wasn't such a clingy motherfucker. I couldn't shake this guy. He'd texted me every day, and I was running out of odd jobs for the bastard. He'd been the laziest guy on the planet before I'd agreed to help him out, and now he was suddenly the most reliable dude on the planet.

So, I'd made up a bullshit job and asked him to stain my dock today while I was at the office. It was a large dock, and it was a shitty job, so I figured he'd be a no-show for this one. I'd left the stain and the brushes on the back porch and texted him that it was there if he wanted to get started. A part of me hoped he'd flake because I didn't have much more for him to do.

I pulled up at my house, and his car wasn't there.

Finally. I'd given him more than he could handle.

I walked around to the backyard and saw Rico lying in the middle of the grass with the hose beside him, and I'd be damned if the dock wasn't rocking a new coat of stain and completely finished.

"Wow. You did the whole thing?" I asked.

He sprung forward and held up a hand. "Yep. All done."

"What's with the hose?"

"It's hot out here, and I didn't have any water. So, I'm drinking Magnolia Falls' finest."

"You didn't bring water? Where's your car?"

"My battery is dead, and I need to get it fixed." They lived out a ways, so that had to be about a two-mile walk.

Rico was full of surprises.

"Come inside and get a Gatorade and something to eat. Have you been out here all day?"

"Yep. Got here around 8 a.m."

I led him inside and handed him a bottle of blue sugar water and a banana. I didn't know when I became a babysitter, but Rico had definitely attached himself to me.

"The dock looks really good. Thank you. I didn't expect you to do it all today." I pulled out my wallet and handed him the cash. I paid him a lot more than usual because he'd done a hell of a job.

"Well, Romeo needs me at the gym the next few days, so I didn't want to leave you hanging with a half-finished dock."

Damn. Romeo was doing that all on his own now. This wasn't a favor anymore; Rico had actually proven he could be reliable.

I glanced down at my watch. I'd promised my grandmother I'd be by to see her in an hour.

"Give me five minutes to change clothes, and I'll give you a ride home on my way to my appointment."

"You got it, River. I'll be here, staring at my good-looking stain job."

I made my way down the hall and changed clothes quickly before we got in the car.

"How's your sister doing?" I couldn't help but ask. I'd missed her at the hospital, and I hadn't been by the bar because I'd wanted her to come to me, but I couldn't get her out of my fucking head.

"You know Ruby, she's always good. It's just who she is." He shrugged, and I took a minute to process his words.

"No one is always good. I think she just hides it well."

"Yeah, you're probably right. I'm trying to get my shit together because, I don't know, I think she's tired of me being a pain in the ass. She deals with everyone else's crap, you know? The least I could do is not add to it."

It was about fucking time someone got on board and had her back.

"It's a good thing to get your shit together. You're not a kid anymore. Time to grow up." I pulled in front of the trailer just as Ruby came walking outside.

"Speak of the devil," Rico said with a laugh as he pushed out of the car. "What's up, sis?"

I didn't miss the way her eyes widened and her lips turned up the slightest bit as I stepped out of the car.

I had a feeling she'd missed me as much as I'd missed her.

"Hey. Where are you two coming from?"

"Your brother just stained my entire dock, so I figured the least I could do was give him a ride home."

A genuine smile spread across her face. "Really? That's amazing, Rico."

"Thanks. What are you doing here?"

"Mom needed some groceries, and I cleaned up a little. She's wallowing again." Ruby shrugged, but her eyes never left mine.

"I'll take it from here." Rico kissed her cheek. "You working tonight?"

"No. I'm actually taking the night off. I'm going to take the kayak out and relax a little."

"Not to be a total pain in the ass, but my car isn't working. Any chance I could use yours to take Panda to dinner? I'll bring it by in the morning, and I promise to fill it with gas."

She reached into her pocket and tossed him her keys. "Sure. I'm not going anywhere."

"Thanks. I'll text you later in the week, River, and see if you have anything for me. I'll be busy at the gym for the next few days."

"Yeah. No problem. Thanks for doing the dock." I held up a hand, and he walked into the trailer.

Ruby strode toward me. "Hey."

"Hey, Queenie. Long time no see."

"Yeah. You haven't been by the bar in a while," she said.

"Ah, is this your way of telling me you missed me?"

She rolled her eyes. "No. Just an observation."

"You want a ride home?"

"I can walk," she said, clearing her throat.

I moved closer, my hand grazing hers. "I didn't ask if you were capable of walking. I know how capable you are. I asked if you *wanted* a ride."

"Is this your way of telling me you missed me?" she mimicked my words back to me. And for whatever reason, I didn't hold back.

"Yeah. I fucking missed you."

Her eyes widened with surprise. "Well, if you missed me, I guess the least I can do is take the ride and grace you with my presence."

I chuckled and walked around to the passenger door and opened it as she slipped inside. Why the fuck was I so happy? She'd agreed to a goddamn ride home, nothing more.

Once I settled into the driver's seat, I turned to look at her. "You want to go somewhere with me?"

"Can you be more specific? Are you taking me to a cult meeting? A gunfight? Swimming with sharks? How can I agree with no information?"

I barked out a laugh because she was funny as hell, and we just sort of got one another. "I'm going to see my grandmother, and she'd probably like to see a pretty face."

She smiled. A genuine, real smile. That was the second one I'd seen today. "Flattery will get you everywhere, Wild River. Sure. I'll go with you to see your grandmother. She was always my favorite."

"Yeah? You said you knew her from the library?" I pulled out of the trailer park and made my way toward Magnolia Haven.

"Yep."

"You used to spend a lot of time there?" I asked, glancing over at her when I stopped at the light.

"Yeah. The lake was always my favorite place, but the library was a close second."

"I always hated the library."

She laughed as I took the final turn and pulled into a parking spot. I turned the car off and shifted so I was facing her. "I wasn't lying when I said I'd missed you."

"Yet you've avoided the bar for a week?"

"I was trying to give you your space. I thought you'd realize that you missed me." The words left my mouth before I could stop them.

Her hand was beside mine on the center console, and her pinky finger wrapped around mine. "Didn't take you for such a sap, Wild River."

"Never been sappy before." I started to pull my hand away to get out of the car, but she wrapped her hand around mine and stopped me.

"I missed you. I was disappointed you didn't come by the bar the first day, but after a week, well, I've been—*unhappy*."

"The evil queen has feelings?" I teased, leaning closer to her and nipping at her bottom lip.

"If you tell anyone, I'll torture you slowly."

"I'm down for being tortured slowly by you any time." I pulled back to look at her.

"I don't think this is a good idea."

"What isn't a good idea?"

"You and me." Her voice was just above a whisper, and I fucking loved the vulnerable side of this woman.

"Listen. I'm not going to lie to you. I don't know what this is. But I've missed you. So, make of it what you want. Your time here in Magnolia Falls is temporary, so how about we just take it one day at a time and hang out when we feel like hanging out?"

"I'm not sleeping with you again," she said, her teeth sinking into that juicy bottom lip.

"Because it was so good, you're terrified to do it again and actually enjoy yourself?" I teased.

"Something like that. Let's go."

I'd never brought a woman with me to see my grandmother. But I didn't think twice about bringing Ruby.

Because everything about this girl was different.

22

Ruby

We'd spent the last hour with Pearl Pierce, and the comfort with her was unexplainable. I remember feeling it when I was young. At a time in my life when I didn't trust easily, and not that it had changed a whole lot, but I was wiser now, at least I hoped I was.

But back then, I was even more cautious of people.

Maybe it was just fear or some form of self-preservation. My mom had broken marriages and burned a lot of bridges in this town, and I'd always been aware of that. Felt some of the judgment fall onto me, being the daughter of Wendy.

But Pearl had always been different.

Warm and kind and genuine.

I'd had no hesitation when I'd spend time talking about books with her.

And today had been no different.

From the second I'd walked through the door, her face had lit up.

"I'm so proud of all that you've accomplished. Not surprised at all. I always saw big things for you, Ruby," she said as she squeezed my hand.

"Thank you. You were always so encouraging to me." I cleared my throat and glanced over to see River watching us before I turned my attention back to the lovely woman sitting in front of me. "It meant a lot."

"I know good people when I see them." She smiled. "Do you ever get to read for pleasure now? I know you've been in school for so long, but now that you're done, maybe you can get lost in some fiction?"

I chuckled. "Funny you should say that. Demi, Peyton, and Saylor just had me add several romance books to my Kindle library. I guess I'm going to dabble in a little fiction."

"Oh, I love romance. It's my favorite genre," she said, as she clapped her hands together once.

"Really? Well, it sounds like I've been missing out," I said. "I think I'll start one tonight."

"You will be addicted. And let me tell you, my husband appreciated me reading all those sexy books." She waggled her brows, and River groaned.

"Hey, what's wrong with reading romance?" I said, narrowing my gaze at him.

"Nothing. I just don't want to hear my grandmother talking about sexy books and my grandfather's appreciation of them."

My head fell back in laughter, and I added a few of her recommendations to the growing library on my Kindle app.

"Don't be a baby. Gramps gave you the birds and the bees talk a long time ago." Pearl smiled at her grandson as he walked over, wrapped an arm around her shoulder, and sat beside her on the bed.

"He did. I love you. We're going to head out." He kissed her cheek.

I pushed to my feet and hugged her goodbye, promising to come back and visit her soon.

When we were back in the car, he told me he was taking me to his house because he had a larger kayak, so apparently, we were now kayaking together.

The thought made me happy, so I wasn't going to overthink it.

"I love your grandmother."

"Yeah, she's one of the good ones."

"When you were in the bathroom, she mentioned something about you going to speak at the juvenile detention center later this week. Is that something you do often?"

He pulled into his driveway and put the car in park. "Nope. It's my first time. There's a new program director, and he seems like a cool dude. He asked Romeo and me if we'd come to speak to the kids and tell them about our experience and how we made changes for the better after being there."

He glanced out the window, shoulders stiff and jaw flexing with tension.

"Are you going with Romeo?"

"No. He went last week. He said it wasn't bad at all. I just don't like dredging up shit." He ran a hand through his hair and turned back to look at me. "It wasn't a good experience for either of us. And sure, we're okay now, but it wasn't because that place shaped us in any way. Hell, we shouldn't have even been there."

"Why were you sent there? It was for an incident at the Daily Market, right? I remember my dad telling me about it. That you and Romeo hadn't done anything, and you were set up for a crime that someone else committed?"

"Yeah. It was actually Slade Crawford and his scumbag friend who stole some booze, vandalized the place, and then knocked Walt Salden down. He sustained a pretty bad head injury."

"Demi's brother was the one who did it?" I asked with surprise.

191

"Yep. He was fucked-up on drugs at the time, and her father covered it up. He let us take the fall. We were in the wrong place at the wrong time."

"And you tried telling everyone what happened? That you didn't do anything wrong?"

He nodded, and there was a deep sadness in his gaze when it locked with mine. "Slade's father had a lot of money. Romeo's dad had just gone to prison, and his mom wasn't equipped to go to bat for us. My grandparents were old, and they didn't know what to do. Grammie just cried all the time, and Gramps was devastated when they took me away. But shit happens, right? You move forward."

I climbed over the console and onto his lap before I could stop myself. I wrapped my arms around him and hugged him as tight as I could. My heart was aching for these two boys who'd been sent away for something they didn't do. They must have been terrified.

"Yes. Shit happens. But that doesn't make it any easier. I'm sorry that you went through that," I whispered in his ear.

His hands came around me, and he held me there. "It's fine, Queenie."

I pulled back to look at him, and a tear broke free and moved down my cheek. "It's not fine. I'm sure it was scary. I know what it's like to feel judged for things you didn't do."

He reached up, his thumb swiping away the single tear trailing down my face. "Don't you shed even one tear for me, Ruby Rose." His lips turned up in the corners. "I'm not your dog or your dad. I don't deserve that tear."

My hands moved to each side of his face. "You deserve more than you think you do."

"You're making a habit of climbing onto my lap in the car, aren't you?"

I chuckled. "What can I say? It's pretty cozy over here."

"I'm fine. I don't think about it often. I just don't know that

192

I want to go visit a place that I don't have fond memories of, you know?"

I nodded, my hands stroking the sides of his face. "Yeah, but maybe you could make it better for those kids that are there now. Maybe you could make it less awful for them."

"Never thought about it that way. That wouldn't be a bad thing."

"You want me to go with you?"

"You're going to go with me to the juvenile detention center and watch me speak to a bunch of troubled kids?"

"Yes. Troubled kids are my favorite."

And River Pierce is my favorite, too, but I won't say that out loud.

"You're something else. You're willing to do that, but you won't have sex with me again?" His voice was all tease as his hands settled on my hips. I could feel his bulge beneath my ass, and I tried to hide my smile.

"Come on, lover boy. Let's go take the kayak out and maybe I'll read you some romance from the book I'm planning to start tonight. You can learn a thing or two about women."

"I'm an expert on women." He was up and out of the car with me in his arms in no time. My legs wrapped around his waist, and my head fell back in laughter.

"Pretty smooth, right?"

"You can put me down now," I said, as he pushed into the house.

"Nah. I like carrying you around when you're feeling sorry for me. Otherwise, you're glaring at me and fighting with me. So let me enjoy this moment."

"I don't feel sorry for you," I said, over more laughter as I tried to push down and get to my feet.

"I don't know, Queenie. I was just a kid back then, and there were some scary fuckers in that place. It was pretty terrifying." His voice was all tease.

I wrapped my arms around his neck and hugged him. "You play dirty, River Pierce."

"You have no idea," he said, as he walked through the house and set me down on the kitchen island.

He grabbed a couple of bottles of water, a box of crackers, and some grapes and dropped them all into a bag. I left my purse on the counter and jumped down, tucking my phone into the back pocket of my jean shorts and following him out to the backyard.

"Your brother did a good job. He's actually surprised me. I didn't think he'd last more than a day, and the guys have not gone easy on him."

He dropped the bag into the kayak, and we both climbed in.

"I'm surprised, too. Maybe there's hope for him."

He reached for the paddles, and we started gliding through the water.

"I think when you stop saving him, he'll be forced to figure his own shit out."

I nodded, leaning back as the sun shined down and warmed my skin. I loved it out here. He made his way around the bend, and we moved toward the cove. I couldn't stop thinking about what he'd shared in the car.

"That must have been complicated for Romeo and Demi, with what her brother and father did to you guys."

"Yeah. They didn't have an easy path, but they got through it. Hell, I held shit against her that had nothing to do with her for years. And now Slade will be coming back to town and working for Romeo at the gym. I guess sometimes you need to let shit go. Forgive people for their mistakes, right?"

I thought about it. "Agreed. It's not good to hold on to anger."

We came to a stop under the large tree that was creating some shade beneath its lush canopy.

He set the paddles in the kayak and leaned back on his elbows. Even with his gold aviators, I could see he was watching me.

"Thanks for coming with me to see my grandmother and for not being a stubborn ass and getting in the car."

I pulled off my sunglasses and rolled my eyes dramatically. "I'm not a stubborn ass."

"Yeah, you are. But I like it."

I slid my sunglasses back onto my face and leaned back. "Well, you're pretty stubborn yourself."

"I won't argue that. But I'm glad you agreed to hang out. I wasn't lying when I said I'd missed you."

My stomach did that twisty thing that made me want to throw myself overboard for being so sappy.

"I think we need to have some rules," I said, thinking about how this would all play out.

He groaned. "Why the fuck do we need rules? We're consenting adults. We can do whatever the fuck we feel like doing."

"I like to know what I'm getting into. You're a lawyer, for God's sake. You should love this. It's like a contract. An agreement. You know, so things don't get messy."

He sat forward and sighed. "Okay. Let's hear your terms."

"The first and most important rule is that we both remember this is temporary. We need to agree to an NCF clause."

"I can't wait to hear what that means."

"No catching feelings," I said. "That's where things get messy."

He chuckled. "You don't have to worry about that with me. I give you my word. I will not catch feelings. You aggravate me, and you turn me on. You annoy me, and you make me laugh. That's all this is."

"Right. I feel the same about you. I hate you as much as I

like you. So, obviously, that can't go anywhere, or we'd end up killing one another."

"Agreed. So, we have nothing to worry about," he said, as his tongue swiped out to wet his lips. "What, exactly, do your rules allow under these strict guidelines?"

"Well, we're friends who are attracted to one another and also irritate one another. But we like to eat, so I think meals are allowed."

"Good. Are we talking about eating food or your pussy?" His voice was all tease, but my body was most definitely not laughing at the comment. I squeezed my thighs together and made a serious effort to remain in control.

"Both are approved."

"Fucking fabulous. So, meals, both at a restaurant and between your sexy thighs. What about sex?"

"I think sex is a yes, but we touch base after each time we cross the line. If either of us starts to feel like we're catching feelings—we take sex off the table. Trust me, I've had this problem with men in the past. Take the professor, for example. He didn't think it would happen, and then it happened."

"That's because it wasn't an equal relationship. He reaped all the pleasure and did nothing for you. Of course, he caught feelings. But this is a mutual pleasure deal. We both give, and we both receive. Therefore, we're in a safe zone. The balance is there."

"That makes no sense," I said.

"Neither does your ridiculous contract, but here we are." He yawned, pretending to be bored. "Anyway. Food. Sex. All the orgasms. Check in and make sure we're still annoyed by one another. What else?"

"Do you have any requests?" I asked.

"Hmmm . . . Are we telling anyone?"

"No. This stays between us. Why? Do you want to tell someone?"

"Not really. I don't give a shit who knows what's going on, but the guys already suspect, and I won't lie about it."

"Agreed. If anyone asks, we just say that it's casual, and we're having fun. I like getting this all squared away. This is very adult of us."

"Very. We know where we stand. I'm good with it. I've never had an agreement with anyone I've been fucking, but I'm here for it."

"Ahhh, glad you brought that up. Let's add an addendum. No dipping your wiener schnitzel in any other ladies when you're sleeping with me."

Loud laughter escaped his lips, and it echoed around the cove. "Deal. But that means you stay the fuck away from all other wiener schnitzels while you're enjoying mine."

"I can do that."

"Well, we have an agreement, and I wouldn't be a very good non-boyfriend if I didn't stick to the terms."

"How about I read us some romance and see if it gets you in the mood?" I said, waggling my brows.

"Fine. But just so you know, I'm always in the mood when you're around."

I leaned back, opened my Kindle app, and offered him a few options. "We've got a small-town romance, a mafia romance, and a billionaire romance. Do you have a preference?"

"Will one of those lead to you getting naked on this kayak?"

"Maybe." I laughed and leaned back, swiping to chapter one. "Let's do the small-town romance. I'll read one chapter, and you read the next."

"No fucking way. That wasn't in the contract. You read, and I listen."

"That's not fair. Why am I doing all the reading?"

"Because I don't want to read this book. How about you read, and I bury my face between your thighs while I listen? Then we'll both be doing some work."

My teeth sank into my bottom lip, and I shifted my legs apart. "Deal."

I was fairly certain that this non-relationship was going to be the best one I'd ever had.

He moved so fast the boat shook, and he was suddenly between my legs and did exactly what he said he would.

And I enjoyed every second of it.

23

River

"Wipe the frown off your face. They're already stuck somewhere they don't want to be. The least you can do is try to look friendly," she said.

"You know, for a non-girlfriend, you're awfully bossy."

She smiled. "Deal with it. You look like a grump."

"You didn't seem to mind when I was on top of you this morning, making you cry out my name," I teased.

Yeah, this arrangement was working out fantastically. We had sex whenever we wanted to, which was all the time. I'd buried my face between her legs that day we were out on the kayak, and that would go down as one of my favorite memories to date. Watching her try to control herself and not tip the boat while I brought her right to the edge over and over again, torturing her slowly, until I finally let her go over. She was ridiculously sexy when she came, and I'd never get enough.

And now we ended our days with her reading her book to me about some dude who was damaged and broken and in love with the girl next door. Literally, I shit you not. She lived next door. They were high school sweethearts, and he'd fucked it all up, because, well, he's a dude, and he doesn't have a fucking clue how to deal with all his feelings.

I couldn't say I minded the book as much as I pretended to be uninterested.

Maybe it was just the sound of her voice that I liked so much. She read a chapter to me every night before we went to sleep and every morning when we first woke up.

Yeah, we'd spent every night together since we'd come up with our little agreement. Normally, this would feel like a death sentence to me, but with Ruby, it was the opposite.

I only wanted more.

"Just because I enjoy having sex with you does not mean that I won't tell you when you're being an asshole. Go in there and give these kids some hope. The guy that asked you here did it because he thinks you'll be an inspiration to these kids. You're a freaking attorney, and a damn good one. You took something shitty and turned it into something positive," she said, her hands flailing around.

I smiled. Couldn't help myself. "I thought I wasn't very good at being lawyerly?"

She covered her mouth with her hand in an attempt to hold back her laughter. "I just say that to get under your skin. You're sort of a rock star, River Pierce. You're an amazing friend, a fabulous uncle, a wonderful grandson, and a damn good attorney and human being. And you're not too shabby in the sack. There. Are you happy?"

"I want to fuck you right now. Right here in this car."

"And now you're fucking crazy," she said, as I leaned over and tickled her senseless. "We're parked outside a juvenile hall, you lunatic. Stop being a perv and pull your shit together."

I kissed her hard before jumping out of the car and going around to open her door. "Let's get this done."

"It's not the death chamber," she mumbled beside me, before glancing up to find me smiling down at her. "Stop acting like you hate this. I think you're actually excited to talk to them, aren't you?"

"No. I'm excited that you just made it clear how amazing I am."

She pinched my arm hard, and I laughed before wrapping an arm around her shoulder as we approached the building.

Once we were inside, we were greeted by Terrence Juniper, the director of operations at Fresh Start Juvenile Detention Center. He'd taken the position six months ago and had reached out to both me and Romeo. He led us to his office first, and we took the two seats across from his desk as he sat and faced us.

"Romeo was very open about your situation. I assume I'm free to speak in front of your friend here?" Terrence said.

"Absolutely. Ruby just graduated with her Ph.D. in psychology; I think she can handle whatever you want to share."

She feigned being annoyed that I'd thrown her fancy degree out there, but I saw the way her cheeks pinked the slightest bit. She'd accomplished something impressive, and I wanted Terrence to know it. I did that a lot lately when we spent time together.

Ruby Rose was impressive as fuck, and the world needed to know it.

She liked to act all tough and hard around the edges, but I saw through it.

Saw the vulnerable side of her.

"That's quite a feat. Congratulations, Ruby. I'd love to speak to you about some programs we've set up for the kids here. We're hoping to provide them more support to deal with the reason they are here and the challenges of being away from their families during their stay."

"I'd like that. And I'm happy to help in any way I can. I'll leave you my phone number and you can give me a call.

Today, I'd like to focus on why River is here, what he went through, and all that he has overcome since."

I turned, my gaze locking with hers, before shifting my attention back to the man in front of me.

"I know things were different back when you were here, and I want to apologize for that."

I cleared my throat, curious how he'd have a fucking clue about the shit we lived through back then. "How do you know what went down when Romeo and I were here?"

"Because I was here a few months before you. It was abusive and scary as hell, and I know that you found your way into the legal world after, and I'm guessing it was to make a difference in the world. Romeo obviously became a professional fighter, and I went the route of studying psychology like Ruby. I guess we're all just trying to make things better, right?" He smiled, and his gaze moved between us.

There was no doubt that Terrence was a straight shooter. No bullshit. I was fairly good at reading people, and there was nothing manipulative or calculating here.

"None of that was your fault. I'm glad things are different for the sake of the kids here now," I said. "So, what exactly would you like me to talk about today?"

"I thought you could share your story from the perspective of how it affected your life after you left. How you pursued a career in the legal world. How one set of circumstances changed the trajectory of your life."

I nodded. It surprised me that I felt relaxed and fairly at ease, considering I'd hated this place with a passion. "I can do that."

"I was hoping you could speak to the group first and then after, maybe spend some time talking to them individually or in small groups?"

"I'm fine with that."

He nodded and glanced over at Ruby. "Maybe you'll be willing to stick around after and talk with the kids?"

"Yeah, I'm here for as long as River's here," she said, and for whatever reason, my chest puffed up like I was some fucking caveman who'd just impressed his girl.

I pushed to my feet, and we made our way out to the hallway and down to a room with maybe thirty chairs facing the front, filled with young men who looked to be around fourteen to maybe seventeen years old.

"You ready for this?" Ruby asked as we followed Terrence toward the front of the room.

"As ready as I'm going to be. Not big on talking about this stuff, but Romeo said it wasn't too bad, and we're here."

She nodded. Terrence came to a stop and held his hand out for Ruby to take the seat in the front row. She looked up at me. "Break a leg, Wild River."

I smirked before making my way to the stage, and Terrence took the microphone and introduced me.

"River was here for eight months when he was seventeen years old, and he is an attorney now. I thought he could offer some insight about his journey that you might find helpful," Terrence said, before stepping aside.

"Hey, I'm River Pierce, and as Terrence said, I spent some time here when I was seventeen years old. I think you recently met one of my best friends, Romeo Knight, and we were here together," I said, as a few people cheered for my boy. They'd obviously remembered him. It didn't hurt that Romeo's name was all over the news after winning his fight recently, so he was not only a badass but also somewhat of a celebrity at the moment. I gathered my thoughts. "So, here's what I'm going to tell you. At the end of the day, you're going to make mistakes that are big and small. But it's what you do with them that matters. My reason for being sent here all those years ago wasn't for something that I actually did. It was for something that someone else had done. And for a long time, that shit ate me up. But the truth is, I wasn't a perfect kid, and spending time here gave me a lot of time to think about what I wanted out of life. I spent eight months here, and it wasn't pleasant. I missed most of my senior year of high school." I paused and reached for the water bottle that Terrence had set there for me. You could hear a pin drop in the room, as everyone was completely silent, waiting for me to screw the lid back on my water bottle. "So, I decided to make some serious changes when I left this place. I knew that what happened to me wasn't fair, and I was going to do something about it. I didn't retaliate against the dude who let me take the fall for his crime, though I didn't care for the asshole." I paused as laughter erupted around the room. "I thought about what I could do to make a difference moving forward, and that took me to college. It wasn't an easy path. I had to make up for the time I'd missed and repeat my senior year in high school. And guess what, I got straight A's that year. I'd never done that before."

A few people clapped and cheered, and I glanced over at Ruby, who was listening like I was giving a presidential acceptance speech.

"How'd you pull that off?" someone yelled from the back.

"I put my head down and worked my ass off. Because when I left here, I made a decision that no one was going to tell me who I was moving forward. I was going to decide who I was. I was going to decide who I wanted to be. And that's exactly what I did. I went to community college first and then transferred to a larger university, and then I went on to earn a full-ride scholarship to law school. If you want it bad enough, if you stay determined, you can make your dreams a reality. I wanted to make a difference in this world. There were a lot of people who were betting against me, but do you know what matters most at the end of the day?" I paused and glanced around the room, my gaze landing on Ruby's briefly before turning my attention back to the center of the room. "*You.*

Who you believe you are. Who you want to be. No one gets to decide that for you. Now, you've got to follow the rules while you're here, stay the course, toe the line, and all that shit. And it's the same thing when you leave here. You've got to be smart and do your time, in and out of here, to pursue what you want. But in the end, you get to decide your path. I work for myself now. I represent people who can't represent themselves. I get to be the voice for those who aren't equipped to speak on their behalf. And I get to fight for things that I believe in. That's what you need to figure out." I paused and took another sip from my water bottle. "What do you believe in? Who do you want to be? Because only you have the power to make that happen."

Everyone clapped and whistled, and I chuckled and held my hands up. "I'll hang out for a while and come around and chat with you. And if you want to know anything important, I've got my friend, Ruby, here," I said, motioning to where she sat in the front row. "She's actually a doctor, so she's a hell of a lot smarter than I am, and I'm sure she'd be better at talking to you than I would."

More whistling and clapping.

I stepped off the stage, and Terrence told everyone to head to the lunchroom, letting them know that we'd be in to chat soon.

"Nice job, River. They like you. They relate to you. You can make a difference here just by sharing your story," Terrence said, leading us down to the cafeteria.

The next hour was spent with both me and Ruby moving around and talking to the kids. They were fascinated by her, and I understood it, because I was too.

"You're a real doctor, Ruby?" Jonah asked. He was fifteen years old, and he'd been sent here because he'd broken into his neighbor's house and taken food, which he'd said was for his younger siblings who were hungry. The neighbors had called the police, and they'd found a pocketknife in his jacket, which made it a much more serious crime, and here he was.

"I'm not a medical doctor. I have my Ph.D. in psychology."

"So, you're a doctor of the mind. Do you work in a hospital with sick people?" Patrick asked with a big smile on his face. He was sixteen years old and hadn't disclosed why he was there. But at the end of the day, these were kids. Just young men who'd made some mistakes and were paying the price.

"I'm just someone who knows a bit about psychology," she said. "And I just graduated, so now I have to figure out what to do with that."

"What would you like to do?" Jonah asked.

"I think I'd like to work with kids to some extent."

"You're a real lady boss," Patrick said, and the other kids started laughing.

"She is a lady boss," I said with a smirk.

"Is she your girlfriend?" Duncan asked. He was the youngest kid here at fourteen. He looked even younger, and I saw the sadness in his eyes. Recognized that the minute I looked at him.

"Nope. She's calling the shots, and she doesn't want a boyfriend," I teased, and all the kids erupted in laughter, taking turns slapping me on the shoulder.

"Don't give up, dawg," Patrick said as he fist-bumped me like we were old friends.

"Did you ever get in trouble for anything, Ruby?" Duncan asked, and the rest of the kids turned their attention back to her.

"I got into a few fights when I was young, and I wasn't the best with authority because I always thought I knew better."

Shocker. She still did.

"And now you're a real doctor? How'd you do that?"

"I didn't have a perfect life. But I knew that education was important at a young age, and I was determined to take that as far as I could. I didn't have money or people pushing me to go to college in my family, outside of my dad, who supported my decision to go. But it wasn't important to him. He just respected that I wanted something more for myself."

"Your mom wasn't around?" Duncan asked, his voice making him sound even younger than he was.

Shit. He was Romeo's age when he'd been sent here. The one thing I'd always been grateful for was that I'd been here with him. That we'd been together when we were here. We'd had one another's backs, and we'd been forced to defend ourselves more times than I wanted to think about. But we'd made it because we'd had one another.

I didn't know if Duncan had anyone in his corner.

"Not a whole lot. And it wasn't necessarily a bad thing. My dad is a really great guy, and that was enough, you know? But what River said is true, only you can decide your future."

"I like that."

"How about you? Does your family come to visit?" she asked.

"He's got a family here, don't you, Duncan?" Patrick said. I saw the bond there, and it was going to help get them through this.

"I do. These are my boys. And my dad's never been in my life. My mom tries, but she has her hands full with my two younger siblings. My stepdad doesn't like me much," he admitted, and I could see the hurt written all over his face.

The loneliness.

The wounded young kid who was trying to put on a brave face.

I've been there.

"Lots of people didn't like me when I was young. That doesn't mean anything. People are tough on kids. Do you like who you are?" Ruby asked.

His eyes widened. "Well, I can be a jerk to my mom sometimes. I get pissed off and act like an asshole."

"How about you stop doing that? Because you know who that hurts in the end, right?" she said.

"Me."

"Yep. Does your mom love you? Does she deserve to be treated like that?"

"She loves me a lot. I know she's sad that I'm here."

"Well, then maybe you can make the best of the time you've got here, like River said. Think about who you want to be when you leave."

Damn. This kid was looking at Ruby like she set the sun. Hell, I glanced around, and they all looked at her that way.

"I'd like to be a fireman someday," Duncan said unexpectedly. "But my stepdad said it won't happen because I'm not big enough."

"Pfft," Ruby huffed as she shook her head. "You're fourteen years old. You don't know how big you'll be when you're older. But do you know what the best revenge is when someone tells you that you can't do something you're determined to do?"

"What?" he asked.

"You go out there and you do it. You leave here, and you work hard in school, because you need to be a good student to become a firefighter. It's competitive, and they won't hire someone who causes trouble. So, you put your head down and start making good decisions. It doesn't mean that you won't make mistakes, but when you make them, you learn from them. And you keep that goal of becoming a firefighter in your mind the whole way. Let that drive you toward becoming everything that you want to be."

"Is that what you did?" he asked.

"Yeah, something like that." She smiled just as Terrence came over and told us it was time for the kids to go outside and get some fresh air.

He walked Ruby and me back to the front lobby and asked for her number to see about her coming back to speak to the kids again sometime.

We thanked him, and when we were both in the car, she turned to look at me.

"You were great in there."

"You were fucking amazing. You had those kids eating out of the palm of your hand," I said.

"Whatever. They idolized you." She shrugged. "You were very inspiring, River Pierce."

"Remember that when we're naked later."

I could feel myself getting pulled in deeper with this woman.

It should terrify me, but it didn't.

I only wanted more.

24

Ruby

I had a call with Dean Langston, and my palms were already sweating. Over the last two weeks, I'd had a few interviews for positions I'd applied to for different programs working with children in varying capacities. So far, I'd been told that I was overqualified for almost every single position.

And the truth was, I needed to have a job lined up when my father came home, which was not as far away as it once was. It was the Fourth of July weekend, and time was flying.

I couldn't put the dean off much longer, as the fall semester was right around the corner.

I clicked on the Zoom link on my laptop, adjusting the collar on the button-up I was wearing, and smiled as Dean Langston came into view.

"Dr. Rose, hello. It's lovely to see you," he said. There was nothing informal about this man, and there would be no sense wasting energy asking him to call me Ruby. He'd called me Ms. Rose when I was a teaching assistant at the university for the last two years.

"Hello, Dean Langston. Thank you for taking the time to meet with me."

"Of course. Obviously, we've already interviewed you, and I'm sure you've had interviews at several other universities over the last few weeks. I would expect nothing less. However, time is ticking, and we're going to need an answer now, as we have several applicants for the position. We offer what I would guess is one of the most competitive packages, so I'm hoping you have a decision made."

I cleared my throat. I hadn't officially made a decision, although I didn't have any other viable options at this point. This was a grown-up position. I'd be a professor. It meant a generous salary, fabulous benefits, summers off, and any future children—which I had no idea if I'd ever have—would get a very impressive discount on tuition. Apparently, that was a big selling point for most professors.

"I'm so grateful you've given me the time to explore my options. I was actually looking into different ways I could work with students that are a bit younger—you know, kids that maybe need that support."

A pretentious laugh escaped his mouth, and he shook his head. "You didn't go through all this schooling to be underpaid, did you? You've earned the right to teach at the collegiate level. The hours are great; it's a nice career. Why would you want to mess with younger, troubled kids?"

Spoken like a wealthy asshole.

"Probably because I once was one." I met his gaze via the computer screen. "I think psychology offers many avenues where I can put my education to use."

"And let me guess—they've all said you were overqualified."

"I've heard that a few times," I admitted.

"If you wanted to be a school counselor and break up schoolyard arguments, you could have taken a different path in your education. You have a Ph.D."

Yeah, no shit, Sherlock.

"I was just looking into a few different things. But I agree,

211

teaching at the collegiate level is probably my best option for a number of reasons."

"Spoken like a true doctor of psychology," he said, his lips pursed and his unibrow impossible for me to look away from.

My stomach twisted at the thought of what I was agreeing to. It didn't feel right. Maybe that was just part of growing up. That I'd just decided what I was going to do for the next thirty years. I was agreeing to be the next Dereck Hamilton. I'd buy a house, drink wine, and go to happy hour with all the professors once a month. I'd stand in front of the classroom, pretend to be an expert in my craft, and go through the motions until I retired.

It was boring and mundane.

But consistent and responsible.

"My only concern is that my father will not be home until the first or second week of August, and I know you'd need me there by the first of the month when classes start. Perhaps I could start my contract mid-year and start in January for the second semester?"

The thought of spending six months here made me feel better. I wasn't ready to leave. I'd fallen into a routine that I was enjoying. And I wanted to spend some time with my father once he came home.

"Don't worry about it. We'll hire a substitute professor to cover for you until you arrive. I'll have your contract sent over in the next week or two for you to sign. Welcome to the family, Ruby."

I nodded, but an enormous lump formed in my throat.

"Thank you for being so understanding. I appreciate it."

"I'll be in touch. Take care." He ended the call, and I sat back in my chair, processing the conversation. I should be excited. This was what I'd wanted, right? No more driving myself crazy about what I wanted to do with my life. No more struggling to make rent. No more living month to month.

I would even be able to help my father financially so that he didn't have to work so much if he didn't want to.

There was a knock on the door. I moved to my feet, and when I pulled it open, both of my brothers came barreling through.

"Hey, sis, we came to take you to dinner," Zane said, as he scooped me up and spun me around like the barbarian he was.

"What? You've never taken me to dinner."

"Well, I got hired at Knockout Gym full-time. Romeo was impressed with the job I did painting the locker room, and his maintenance guy is moving, so he offered me the job," Rico said. "We thought we'd take you out to celebrate."

"Hey. I also got promoted at the auto shop. I came to pay you back the money I owe you from when you paid off Sam for me. So, Rico will be buying dinner," Zane said over his laughter as Rico flipped him the bird.

I was stunned. Zane had never made an effort to pay me back, and Rico holding down a job had surprised me as well.

All of it surprised me.

I'd barely heard from my mother over the last few weeks, which meant she was doing better.

No news was good news in the life of Wendy Rose-Dane-Holt-Smith-Slaughter.

"Well, don't look so stunned that we want to do something nice for you," Rico said, looking sheepish. "We like having you home. It's been nice."

"Don't get too attached. I just accepted a teaching position at the university. I'll be leaving as soon as my dad comes home."

"Then I guess we better savor this time together," Zane said, wrapping an arm around my shoulder.

"Savor? Look at you, talking all fancy," Rico said over his laughter.

"Hey, my older sister is a professor at the University of Western California. People will expect that from me now."

I grabbed my purse and followed them out the door.

When we arrived at the Golden Goose, Midge reached for the menus and walked us to our table.

"I heard that Oscar got Boone back," I said, as my brothers stopped to talk to everyone that we passed on our way to the table.

Midge turned around. "I know you think I'm a terrible person, but I love animals, and Boone just showed up at my doorstep one day, just like your pup had done."

For the first time since I'd known her, Midge Longhorn didn't look guilty—she looked downright pathetic.

Sad and heartbroken.

The dog wasn't even hers. What was her deal?

"You do know that you can go and rescue a dog of your own from the pound, right?"

Her shoulders stiffened, and she glanced around before her eyes met mine, and she kept her voice low. "Doug Callan has run the pound for the last twenty-five years."

"I know that. Do you not like him?"

"I was married to him right out of high school. We were young. It didn't work out. He's rejected every application I've filled out over the years, so I stopped trying. And I'm not buying a boutique dog from a fancy breeder."

She has a problem with breeders but not with stealing dogs?

I sighed. "Did you break the guy's heart? Why would he do that?"

"I married his brother." She held up her hands in defense. "I was young. I divorced him a few years later."

This shouldn't thrill me, but it does.

Midge was a rebel, and I kind of loved it.

"Well, that doesn't give him the right to block you from having a dog."

"I agree, but that hasn't stopped him." She shrugged just

214

as my brothers waltzed over and slid into the booth, grabbing their menus.

"Let me look into this," I said, and she nodded before walking away.

I moved into the booth beside Rico as Zane proceeded to read every item on the menu aloud. We'd been coming here since we were practically babies. The menu hadn't changed.

I reached for my phone to send a quick text to River.

> Hey. I need a favor.

ARROGANT PRICK

> Sixty seconds of my time?

I'd put him in my phone under the name *Arrogant Prick* when he'd first texted me, and I'd kept it there because it drove him crazy.

> So cocky. That's not the favor, though.

We spent an unusual amount of time together. Every night. Every minute we weren't working, we found a way to hang out. I wasn't overthinking it anymore; I was just going with it.

ARROGANT PRICK

> Name it.

> Midge wants a dog.

ARROGANT PRICK

> You want me to steal one for her? 😈

No. Of course not. I want you to help her rescue one.

ARROGANT PRICK

Why can't she do that herself? Why do you need me?

It's a long story. I need you to scare Doug Callan with some legal jargon.

ARROGANT PRICK

I thought I wasn't good at being lawyerly?

Stop pouting about that. I told you that you're brilliant.

ARROGANT PRICK

You better not still have me in your phone as Arrogant Prick. I will do no favors for you if you don't change it.

Of course, I changed it. 😉

ARROGANT PRICK

I want a screenshot. Not doing any favors until I see proof.

Damn you. Changing it now.

HOT LAWYER

Nice. I'll take it. Why the fuck do I need to scare Doug Callan? Anyone can adopt a dog from the pound.

He keeps rejecting her because they used to be married.

HOT LAWYER

No shit?

Yes, shit. And . . . Are you ready for it?

HOT LAWYER

Waiting with bated breath.

She broke his heart and married his brother.

HOT LAWYER

Dennis Callan? He's a preacher, isn't he?

Bless you. Midge is full of surprises. 🙏

HOT LAWYER

Fine. We'll go down there tomorrow before my first client. How did your call go with the dean?

I chewed on my fingernail. We both knew this would be ending soon. Why was I nervous to say it?

> Good. I took the job.

HOT LAWYER

> I thought you didn't want the job.

> It's my best option.

Three little dots moved around the screen, but no message came through.

> Are you at a loss for words because you're going to miss me?

HOT LAWYER

> I guess I better get in as much time with you as I can then, huh? Where are you?

> Dinner with my brothers. Rico is treating.

HOT LAWYER

> I heard Romeo offered him a full-time job. Good for him. And he should treat you.

> Don't get sentimental. Our clock is ticking. Our arrangement is coming to an end.

HOT LAWYER

You better take what you want from me now, Queenie. You're going to miss this. 👆

Don't flatter yourself.

HOT LAWYER

Get your hot little ass over here when you're done with dinner. I'll show you what you're going to be missing when you leave.

See you soon.

We placed our orders, and both of my brothers started talking a mile a minute. They'd been by the bar a few times over the last few weeks, but things had been fairly uneventful. Now that Rico was working all the time, he wasn't going out as much.

Maybe they were both actually growing up a bit.

"So, Zane and I are thinking of getting our own place. Panda will move in with us, as well. We've started looking."

My eyes widened, and I quickly fixed my features so as not to be an asshole and act completely shocked.

But I was completely shocked.

"You want to move out? Does Mom know?"

Zane rubbed a hand along the back of his neck. "We can't live with her forever, and honestly, it's a shitshow over there. She and Jimbo are always breaking up or making up, and Mom's moods are a lot to take."

I figured that out at a very young age. Dealing with someone who was an emotional roller coaster all the time was not pleasant. You never knew which Wendy you were going to get.

I was happy they were recognizing that.

"I cleaned the trailer yesterday, and then Jimbo showed up with a bunch of friends, and he and Mom partied their asses off. The place was a mess this morning. I spent the night at Panda's because they were so fucking loud."

"I'm proud of you guys. I think that's a step in the right direction." I smiled as our food was set down in front of us.

A weight lifted off my shoulders.

My brothers were going to figure things out.

My mother probably never would, and that was okay.

It wasn't my job to fix her.

25

River

"It's stupid to go to the Fourth of July party separately. You're here. Who gives a shit?" I wrapped my arms around her and pulled her close.

She'd spent the night at my place.

Again.

Hell, we'd managed to spend the night together every single night over the last few days. We used different excuses to appease ourselves.

We opened a bottle of wine, and we shouldn't drive.

Even though we live within walking distance from one another.

One night, we'd both said it was too cold to get out of bed, so we might as well stay there. It was fucking July. It was hot as hell outside.

We were both full of shit, and neither of us cared.

We had a deal. We'd agreed to do this until we didn't want to do it anymore. But the thing was, I liked being with her.

In and out of the bedroom.

It didn't matter. She was leaving in a few weeks, so I wasn't going to overthink it.

She burrowed into me, jasmine and orange flooding my senses.

"We don't need everyone thinking there's something going on between us." She tipped her head back to look up at me.

This morning, her eyes were emerald green with sapphire blue rings surrounding them. I loved the way the color of her eyes changed depending on her mood.

Right now, she was relaxed.

"You do realize that everyone already thinks something's going on, right?"

"No. They think we hate each other. Because we do—most of the time."

I chuckled. "Your dad asked me if something was going on."

She reared back. "What? What did you tell him?"

"I said we were hanging out. You were leaving soon. That was all there was to it."

"Why did you tell him that?"

"Weren't you the one who was pissed that your dad lied to you about what was going on with his health?"

Her brows furrowed as she thought it over. "That's true. But there is nothing going on. We're just hanging out while I'm here. It's nothing."

I'd always been the guy who'd made it clear I didn't want anything. But I was getting fucking tired of her telling me the same shit over and over.

We were nothing.

I got it.

Yet, here we were, in bed together, day after day.

I didn't know what exactly qualified something to be an actual relationship, because I'd never had anything serious with a woman before.

But this sure as shit isn't nothing.

I placed a hand on her cheek, waiting for her gaze to meet

mine. "I've seen you every day over the last couple of weeks. We text when we aren't together. I've woken up with you every day this week. I know you aren't staying. I know this isn't going anywhere. But stop fucking saying that it's nothing. It's more than I've ever had with anyone else, and it's starting to piss me the fuck off that you keep saying that."

She pushed up, placing her hand on my chest as her gaze searched mine. "You've said it, too."

"No. I haven't said it in a while. You're the one who reminds me daily that this is nothing. I got it. I know there is an end to this, but right now, we're in it. And I want to go to the fucking Fourth of July party with you."

A slow, easy smile spread across her pretty face. "You like me, don't you?"

"Don't get cocky. I just don't like you belittling this."

She sighed. "Fine. I like you, too. I'll go with you to the Fourth of July party."

"Thank you. Was that so fucking difficult?" I asked as she settled her cheek against my chest.

"No. None of it has been difficult, if I'm being honest."

"What do you mean?" I stroked her long, silky hair away from her face, and her fingers traced along my shoulder and down my arm.

"When I was with the professor, and even the two guys I dated before him, I had rules. I didn't like spending the night more than once a week. It wasn't like this."

"I get that. I've never had a woman stay the night repeatedly. I usually need my space, and I get irritated pretty easily."

She chuckled and tipped her head back to look at me. "Really? You? Say it isn't so."

"It is so, you smart-ass. But I like having you in my bed."

"Maybe it's because we both know it's ending soon, so we don't have to worry about it becoming anything."

"Yeah, that's probably it," I lied. Our connection was

something I'd never shared with anyone before. And I knew it terrified her because it terrified me, too. And not for the reasons that it should.

I wasn't afraid of falling for Ruby Rose.

Hell, I'd already fallen.

I was afraid of what would happen when she left. So I was doing my best to keep things under control, but somewhere along the way, I'd lost control with this woman.

I didn't want her to leave, and that thought alone was fucking with my head.

"You should come with me to Fresh Start to see the boys this week. Duncan is going back home on Friday," she said.

Terrence had reached out to Ruby after our visit, and she was going out there to work with the kids whenever she could. She had her afternoons free before she went to the bar, and she was volunteering there.

"I'll see if Cassie can clear my schedule in the afternoon. You've been going out there a lot, huh? You like it?"

"Yeah. I hadn't planned on going daily, but I made a schedule, and you wouldn't believe how many of them signed up to talk to me next week. I think they're just wanting someone to tell them that they're going to be okay."

"And they all have big, fat crushes on the hot doctor."

"You're ridiculous. I like talking to these kids. I feel like it's making a difference, you know? Terrence said they're talking more about their futures now, as well. So it feels good."

"Look at you, Queenie. Out there, making a difference in the big, bad world." I kissed the top of her head. "Did you send the contract back to the university with the changes I made?"

I'd looked over the contract that the dean had sent over, and the wording was vague, so I'd made a few suggestions for her before signing it.

"Yeah. They didn't seem thrilled that I'd requested the

wording to be changed, but they said they'd get to it after the holiday weekend," she said. "I don't think they expected me to have an attorney on hand."

"Not a bad thing to have, eh? And contracts can be complicated. You always want to have an exit strategy because you don't know where life is taking you most of the time."

"Is that what you do? Have an exit strategy at all times?" she asked.

"I always know how to leave a situation I don't want to be in."

"Do you think it's because of losing your parents so young? You don't like to get too comfortable?"

"Are you analyzing me again, Dr. Rose?"

"I mean, I am in your bed. You gave me free legal counsel. The least I can do is tell you what I see."

"And what is it you see?" I asked, thrusting against her as my morning wood was aching with her hot little body pressed against mine.

Her hand slipped between us, as we were both naked, which was how I preferred it when I was with Ruby. She stroked me a few times, and I groaned.

"I see a man who fiercely loves the few people he lets in. But he doesn't trust easily. He doesn't like most people, but the ones he likes, he'll walk through fire for them. And he has the sexiest eyes and a very impressive dick."

A gruff laugh escaped my lips, and I ran my hand up the side of her hip before cupping her breast. I flicked her nipple with the tip of my thumb, then rolled her onto her back and settled between her thighs.

She sucked in a breath, both hands on each side of my face now. Her eyes searched mine for something, but I didn't know what.

"Tell me what you want," I said. Because I'd fucking give this girl the moon if she asked me for it. I'd do whatever it took to put a smile on her face every goddamn day if I had the chance.

"I want to feel you. All of you." Her lips parted, and her gaze was wet with emotion. "I've never been with anyone without protection. And I'm on the pill. I've just always doubled up."

"I've never been with a woman without a condom either. Never actually wanted to before now." I'd always feared being trapped by someone. Never trusted anyone enough to go there. But I trusted Ruby. I wanted Ruby in a way I'd never wanted anyone. "But I want to feel all of you, too, Queenie. Every goddamn inch of you."

"No catching feelings, Wild River," she whispered.

"I can turn them off when it's time. But right now, I want to feel all of it," I admitted, and a single tear ran down her cheek. I swiped it with the pad of my thumb. "No one's stealing your puppy. No one's hurting your father. This is just two people who want to have sex without a condom. Don't go freaking out on me."

She smiled. "I won't."

"You ready to take all of this with nothing between us?" I asked, thrusting the tip of my dick against her core.

"Yes," she hissed, as her head fell back, and she squeezed her eyes closed. "Please. I want you right now."

I flipped her over in one fast movement so I was lying on my back and she was straddling me. Her hair tumbled around her shoulders, falling across her luscious breasts. I gripped her hips and lifted her, and she slowly slid down my erection, inch by motherfucking inch.

And I felt everything.

All of her sweetness.

All of her warmth.

It was the most erotic thing I'd ever experienced. There was nothing between us.

Just me and her.

She bit down on her bottom lip as her gaze locked with mine, and she took me all the way in on a moan.

She was wet and tight and so fucking perfect.

"Don't move yet. I want to savor every second of this. You're fucking perfect."

She stayed completely still, and I wrapped a hand around the back of her head and tugged her down before kissing her hard. My tongue explored her mouth just as she started to move.

She rode me slowly at first before we found our rhythm.

She pulled back, and her fingers interlocked with mine as she slid up and down my cock, meeting me thrust for thrust.

That was the thing about Ruby.

She always met me thrust for thrust. If we were sparring verbally, fucking our brains out, or laughing our asses off.

She was right there.

Almost like she was made for me.

She moved faster, her breaths more labored now.

Cheeks flushed, lips parted, and eyes deep and soulful.

"River," she groaned, and I felt her start to tighten around me. I pulled one hand away, moving it between us.

Knowing just what she wanted. What she needed.

I circled her clit with the pad of my thumb and watched as she gasped and bucked against me, desperate and needy.

So fucking sexy.

And when she cried out my name, I realized it was my favorite sound in the world.

The sound of her coming apart.

Wild and free.

Like the fucking queen she was.

She went over the edge right before my eyes, tits bouncing and body trembling as I thrust into her two more times.

Hard.

Fast.

Lights exploded behind my eyes, and a guttural sound left my lips.

I followed her into oblivion.

And I didn't ever want to return.

26

Ruby

"Is it possible that you're nicer than you pretend to be?" River asked, as he pulled into the parking lot at the pound.

"No. It's not possible," I said dryly.

He turned off the car and shifted to face me. "You've volunteered at Fresh Start every day for weeks, you visit my grandmother at the nursing home all the time, and now you've dragged me to the pound to get a dog for your childhood nemesis."

I rolled my eyes dramatically. "First off, I smoked all the ladies at gin rummy, so it was hardly a hardship. Fresh Start is like my mother ship. I've always fit in with troubled souls, so I feel comfortable there. And lastly, calling Midge Longhorn my childhood nemesis is a bit dramatic, no?"

His lips turned up in the corners. There were moments with River when I tried hard to memorize every detail of his handsome face. I'd never felt so much joy at seeing someone smile as I did him. Like I'd earned something the rest of the world didn't get to experience. He smiled a lot with me. And I liked it.

"It was the one time in over two decades that you'd cried.

Are you claiming you like her now?" He smirked. "You going soft on me, Queenie?"

"Don't misread empathy for being soft. I know what it's like to want something so badly it hurts." The words were out of my mouth before I realized what I was saying.

"Yeah?" he asked, reaching for my hand and intertwining our fingers. This was our thing now. We were sappy bastards ever since the Fourth of July three weeks ago. He'd kissed me in front of our friends and then announced that I was leaving soon, and it was temporary, so they should get used to it for a few weeks. And no one seemed slightly surprised by the act. "What do you want so badly that it hurts?"

The first thing that popped into my mind was River.

Wild River.

The man who made me feel comfortable in my own skin. The man who made me laugh and even made me cry during sex multiple times. He was perfectly unattainable. The worst kind of torture, yet I just kept falling deeper.

I was no longer harnessed to any sort of safe space. I was just falling a little more every day, knowing how much it was going to hurt when it ended.

I'd never let myself do that before.

I'd never let myself feel this much.

I knew better, yet here I was.

You.

"Bullet, remember?" I smirked.

"But you're here getting the woman who stole Bullet a dog. And why the fuck isn't Midge here? Why is this our problem?"

"Hey, lose the attitude, dude. I agreed to let you kiss me in public. You owe me."

He laughed, and it echoed around the cab. "I owe you, huh? How about I pay you right now?"

"How do you plan to do that?"

"I can pull you into the back seat, lift that little skirt you've got on, and let you ride me until you come so hard you forget where we are."

Did it just get hot in here?

"You've got a filthy mouth, River Pierce, but that's a hard no right now. Midge is meeting us here, and I am not about to risk her catching me having sex in the back seat with my non-boyfriend. Let's get in there and have you intimidate the shit out of Doug Callan. If Midge leaves with a dog, you just might get lucky tonight."

He got lucky every night. I was kind of a sure thing when it came to River. But it was still fun to tease him.

"You know, when I went to law school, I never imagined I'd be intimidating some old dude just to get the woman I'm not dating a dog for her nemesis."

"What can I say? Life is full of surprises." I waggled my brows, and he jumped out of the car and came around to get my door.

He was a walking contradiction. A dirty-talking gentleman. He had no problem whispering filthy things in my ear or pissing me off by challenging me at the most ridiculous things—yet he always opened my door and pulled out my chair for me.

"Speaking of surprises, did the dean like the latest tweaks I made to the contract?"

Yes, we were still negotiating the contract. River found yet another loophole that he insisted could screw me over if I signed it, so we'd returned it for the third time.

"He didn't make any snide comments this time. He said he'd get it back to me this week, and he was looking forward to me having a long career teaching there."

Three weeks. That was what we were down to. My father was coming home in two weeks, as he'd made amazing progress. But I'd have one week with him at home to help him adjust, and I'd worked out a schedule at the bar with the staff, which meant he didn't need to work long hours anymore.

Everything had come together.

"Good. Now, don't try to get involved in what's about to go down in here. You got me? I've got this handled. What time is Midge getting here?" he asked, and I looked down to see a message from her that had just come in.

"The yellow canary has landed." I chuckled before typing back a message for her to wait for my text before coming inside. I needed to make sure we had Doug on board before he did anything to upset her. Turns out, Midge Longhorn was just lonely. She desperately wanted a dog, and I wasn't leaving Magnolia Falls until she had one.

One that wasn't stolen and belonged to her.

"Who the hell is the yellow canary?" River whisper-hissed as he pulled the door open and motioned for me to step inside.

"Do you not watch spy movies? The yellow canary is Midge in this scenario."

"I don't think she'd be a canary. She's more like a vulture."

I snapped my fingers in front of his face. "Stay focused. It's game time."

He shook his head and walked toward the front desk. "Is Doug Callan in?"

"Yes. May I ask who's asking?" the teenage girl working behind the counter asked.

"Sure. Tell Doug it's his worst freaking nightmare that's asking, how about that?" I spewed, and the girl's eyes went wide before she ran off.

"What was the one thing that I asked you to do?" River asked, voice totally even and in control as he looked at me.

"Sorry. My adrenaline is pumping."

He leaned down so his lips were grazing the side of my ear. "If you plan on getting *pumped* later . . . you best close that mouth of yours and let me handle this."

I smiled when he pulled back. "I like how you tied that together."

232

"You're talking again." He raised a brow, his eyes darker than usual. "I know a way to shut that pretty mouth of yours up."

Damn. Normally I would throat-punch a guy for saying that to me, but the way River was saying it was hot as hell.

I pressed forward, wanting his mouth on mine because now he'd completely ruined my adrenaline rush, and I was horny as hell.

He nipped at my bottom lip. "Not yet, Queenie."

"Can I help you?" the older man walking our way said. He had an edge for a man in his sixties with a beer belly. He sported a few tattoos on his forearms, and his T-shirt read: *I'm just here for the pussy*. Not at all what I was expecting, but I was ready to see River work his magic.

"Yes, you can," River said, turning to face the man who was two or three inches shorter than him. "I have a friend who's been trying to adopt a dog for, what is it, honey?" He turned to me, using that smart-ass tone of his. "Twenty-five years now, she's been trying to get a dog?"

"Yes. You're spot on, darling." I raised a brow before glaring at Doug, the douchebag.

"Let me guess, Midge Longhorn sent you here." He chuckled this maniacal laugh that you'd hear in a movie from the lead mean girl. He was a little old for this role, but I wouldn't have expected Midge to have an ex-boyfriend who wasn't a little unusual.

"You'd be correct. I'm River Pierce, Midge's lawyer."

"Oh, for fuck's sake," Doug groaned. "It's not a crime to deny someone's application for a pet. She's unfit, and she isn't getting a dog."

I started to huff, and River's hand found mine, squeezing just enough to remind me to keep quiet.

"Let me tell you why you're wrong, Doug," he said, his voice sexy and gruff as he squared his shoulders. "It is unlawful to deny a woman's application for a pet just because she broke your heart."

"How about she married my brother? Does that seem lawful to you?"

"Listen, I understand why you're angry with her. I really do. But the woman wants to adopt a dog, and she'll provide a good home, so she should be allowed to do so." River paused, and his shoulders relaxed. "Come on, dude. You've punished her for twenty-five years. Let's call a truce."

"What the fuck is in it for you?" Doug crossed his arms over his chest.

"I'll tell you, man-to-man, what's in it for me. You see this gorgeous woman beside me?"

Doug peered around River's shoulder and looked at me. "Yes."

"Well, she hates me most of the time, and I've only got her here for three more weeks, and she's agreed to go home with me tonight if you give Midge the dog. So, basically, Doug, I'm not leaving here without that fucking dog. I can make things very uncomfortable for you. You've got plenty of violations going on outside this building, with extension cords running across the sidewalk and duct tape on the windows. I'd hate to bring the city down here to check that out."

"Damn. You've clearly got it bad, and you're willing to fuck me over if I don't do what you want. All for a woman?" Doug said, shaking his head with disgust.

"We seem to understand one another," was all River said.

"So, if I give Midge the dog, you leave, and we don't have a problem?"

"That's the deal." River glanced over his shoulder and winked at me.

Too smooth for his own good.

"Fine. Let's make it quick."

"She's actually here. I'll text her to come inside and take a look at the dogs," I said, typing out a message to Midge.

"I'm assuming you don't want to see her?" River said.

"Oh, I'm definitely going to see her. I go to The Golden Goose once a week just to glare at her."

River barked out a laugh. "This ought to be interesting."

Midge came walking through the door with a wicked grin on her face, like she'd just won some big feat. She looked between the three of us, and her gaze landed on Doug's. "Hello, asshole."

"Hello, home-wrecker," Doug said.

"You sure like to bring up my faults, but you fail to mention that you slept with my best friend before things started with your brother," she hissed.

I wished I had a bucket of popcorn because this was like watching reality TV at its finest.

"I've told you many times that I never slept with Rhonda!" He was shouting now.

"Oh, I just caught you in her bed for a sleepover?" She moved closer to him and pointed her finger in his face. "Payback is a bitch, Dougy boy. Now, take me to see the dogs."

"Family is off-limits, and you know that," he grumped.

"You don't even like him!" she shouted.

"Yeah, because he married my goddamn wife," Doug hissed.

"Listen," River said, pinching the bridge of his nose. "As riveting as this conversation is, I've got things to do. Can you continue this after she gets the dog, please?"

"That's fine with me." Midge shrugged. "We could discuss it further over coffee if you'd like."

Doug's eyes widened. "I wouldn't mind that. I could use the caffeine."

"Great. You can help me get my new pup settled, and I'll

put on a pot of coffee. I keep your favorite hazelnut creamer at the house." She shrugged.

My mouth gaped open, and I looked up to see River watching me with a smile on his face.

We'd recently discovered that we had a gift for communicating without words. Basically, I could tell him he was annoying me without saying it aloud, and he could do the same.

So, I gave him a look. *Midge still has feelings for Doug, and I think he has feelings for her, too.*

He raised a brow, and one side of his mouth quirked up like the cocky bastard he was. *No shit, Sherlock.*

Doug led us into the back, and we walked past two rows of kennels with adorable dogs just waiting to be adopted.

I wouldn't mind adopting one myself. Hell, I'd been out riding horses with Demi and Cutler every weekend, and a part of me wondered what it would be like to have a ranch house with animals here.

A totally different life than the one I'd just agreed to start living in a few weeks.

27

River

"I can't believe everyone is going to help paint the new place for my brothers," she said, as we pulled in front of the rental house that Zane, Rico, and Panda were moving into.

"I offered them free pizza and beer, and they were all in." I put the car in park. Rico had attached himself to me, and I can't say I minded it. Maybe it was that he was her brother. Hell, I didn't know, but I was all right with the dude needing to lean on me. At least for now. "Hey, I emailed you the contract back. That pretentious prick of a dean you are going to work for actually agreed to everything we'd asked for. He upped your salary, increased your vacation time, and took out some of that fucked-up wording he'd had in there."

She was leaving in ten days. Her dad would be home in three days. Everything was about to change.

I'd known it was coming.

Hell, this was my MO. Short and sweet. No feelings. We were just having a good time.

Nothing more.

She'd been ready to get out of this place since the day she'd arrived. She talked about it often. How this wasn't her home.

Maybe there were too many memories here that she wanted to forget.

But like it or not, her time here had been better than she'd expected. She'd made friends. She was out riding horses every weekend, which was something she couldn't do in the city. She was spending a lot of time with her father, helping out the kids at the Fresh Start, and whether either of us wanted to admit it or not, we'd grown attached to one another. It hadn't been the plan, but I couldn't have stopped it if I'd wanted to.

The good thing about me—I was a pro at turning off my feelings. I'd had losses that were devastating, and I'd learned how to bounce back.

Losing my parents at a young age taught me that attachments were not permanent. You had to set your life up in a way that meant you could survive if any of it were taken away.

Maybe it was a good thing that Ruby was leaving. Because if she stayed much longer, I knew in my gut that I wouldn't survive if she left me, and that scared the shit out of me.

It was for the better.

This was a fling. Nothing more.

Hell, I'd found the only woman that was as guarded as I was. We were a safe bet. We'd known that there was an expiration date for us from the beginning.

I just had to remember that it was coming soon.

"Thanks for doing that for me." She turned to face me. "Do you think you'll miss me when I leave?"

Do bears shit in the woods? Fuck yeah, I'll miss you.

"It'll be fine. This was the plan." I studied her, saying something I knew I shouldn't. "You want to take the job there, right?"

"Sure. And all the women in Magnolia Falls will be all over you once I'm gone. Evie was seething when she saw me sitting on your lap when we watched the fireworks."

"Does that make you jealous, Queenie? Knowing Evie

wants to be in my bed the minute you aren't?" It was a shitty thing to say. I had no intention of having Evie in my bed. I didn't want anyone else in my bed. But I wanted to see if it bothered her.

"Never. I know what this is. That's why it works. We both want the same thing." She shrugged, and I saw something in her gaze. Sadness, maybe.

I think we both knew nothing had gone according to plan. I should just cut the cord now and make this easier on both of us. But I couldn't seem to do it. I'd thought about it several times over the last week, but here we were.

"And what is this?" I asked.

"Two people who don't want anything serious, getting what they need from the other."

I nodded. "Sounds about right. Let's go paint this house."

She helped me carry in several boxes of pizza, a few six-packs of beer, and some sodas.

Rico and Panda were both wearing matching baggy jumpsuits that I assumed were for painting, and they looked absolutely ridiculous. Zane was in an old T-shirt and a pair of faded jeans. When I walked around the corner, Demi and Romeo were checking out the kitchen. Saylor was talking with Kingston at the small table in the corner, Nash and Hayes were out in the backyard, looking around, and Cutler came running toward Ruby.

"Rubes, I missed you. We're going to ride tomorrow, right?"

I took what she had in her hands and set it on the counter, and she bent down to his level so she could hug him. She was so tough on the outside, but there was nothing but heart beneath that exterior.

"Yep. I wouldn't miss riding with you and Demi for anything."

"I wish you weren't moving. My dad said it's coming up pretty soon." He pouted.

You and me both, little dude.

"I'm going to miss you, but I'll come back to visit."

He turned to look at me and lunged. "Hi, Uncle River. Did you bring my favorite pizza?"

"Of course I did. That's why I'm your favorite uncle," I said, as I fist-bumped him.

He looked up at me and winked. This fucking kid was too smooth for his own good.

"Hey, we don't have favorites," Kingston said, shooting me a glare. "Unless, of course, your favorite is Uncle King. And who could blame you?"

Everyone laughed, and Ruby started passing out plates so they could eat before her brothers offered to show her around the house. Obviously, this wasn't my first time here. She didn't know that.

She didn't need to know that.

"I'm going to start in the bedrooms. Let's bust this out," Nash said, spoken like a true contractor. He and Kingston had already been here with me to check out the place. Romeo nodded and followed Nash down the hall.

Kingston grabbed Hayes and Saylor and said they'd get started on the family room, and Ruby and Zane headed for the guest bedroom, while Rico and Panda were taking on the laundry room.

"Looks like you and me are doing the kitchen," Demi said.

I grabbed a slice of pizza and took a few bites. "Let's do this, Beans."

She stood on the step stool and started taping off the ceiling, and I got the paint brushes and rollers out before filling the bin with paint. Kingston had recommended we paint the whole place in a light gray color. Just getting some fresh paint on the walls was going to make a big difference.

The house didn't need much. I normally invested in dumps that we could flip, but these were Ruby's brothers, and they'd been eager to get their own place, so I'd bought this one in pretty decent shape as is.

I knew it would be better for her not to be worrying so much about them after she left.

Her mother wasn't changing, but her brothers were proving to be capable of more than they'd shown up until now. Maybe having their sister back here had made a difference or motivated them in some way.

"Okay, what's the plan?" Demi asked, as she held up a paintbrush and smiled at me.

"How about I do the large space and roll the paint on most of the wall, and you do all the edging?"

"Sounds good to me." She dipped her brush into the fresh paint and got to work.

I could hear voices in the distance, laughter coming from one end, music coming from another. Everyone was pitching in because that was just what we did for one another.

"You going to be okay when she leaves?" Demi asked, looking up at me with her hair tied in a knot on top of her head.

"Of course, I will. I'm always okay, Beans."

"I know you are. But it's also okay if you're not."

"I'll be fine. It'll be good to get back to normal," I said.

"Have you thought about asking her to stay?"

"No. She doesn't want to stay. Hell, she hasn't even applied for jobs here. She only applied out of state. This isn't where she wants to be." I rolled the paint across the length of the wall and moved to my right as Demi filled in the spots along the trim that I couldn't get to.

"Maybe she doesn't know you may want her to stay." She paused. "If it were up to you, would you want her to stay?"

Fuck. It isn't up to me. So, I'm not going to go there.

"You know I'm not big on fairy tales. I'm fine, Demi. I like being alone."

I always had—up until recently. I'd preferred it for the longest time. That was why my relationship with Ruby was catching me off guard.

"That isn't what I asked you, River."

I dipped my roller into the fresh paint, and my gaze locked with hers. "It's not up to me. End of story. Tell me about the progress on the house."

She groaned and started painting along the bottom of the wall again. "Reese is driving out this week to go over some ideas for furniture and décor. I'm excited. Things are really coming along."

"Yeah, every time I stop by, there's more progress. You guys will be moving in before you know it."

"Hey, River," she said, her voice low and steady.

"Yep." I knew she wasn't done with our earlier conversation.

"Just because you don't believe in fairy tales doesn't mean they can't happen. You deserve your happily ever after, just like everyone else."

I watched as the fresh new paint covered the old, faded color with ease. Maybe that was how life worked. You could just keep putting on new coats of paint and starting over.

That was what I'd done most of my life.

"Sure. But everyone's happily ever after might look different."

"Yeah, I know. But it's hard when you see it before your eyes, not to hope that someone grasps it, you know?"

"What do you mean?"

"I see it. This sort of magic that lives between you two. I love watching you guys together. All that banter and laughter—it's pretty special."

I rolled my eyes. "You think watching us argue and fight is special? I think you might be romanticizing things."

"Even Romeo sees it. Hell, we all do. I just don't want

you to miss it, River. To let something good get away because you're too stubborn to admit how you feel."

I let her words sink in. Normally I would shut this shit down immediately, but this was Demi, and there was some truth to what she was saying.

What I had with Ruby was different from anything I'd ever had with a woman. But I also knew when someone had one foot out the door because it was normally me. And Ruby Rose had one foot out the door. She wanted bigger things than I had to offer, and she deserved them.

"How about this?" I paused and looked down at her. "I hear you. I'll think about it, okay?"

Her lips turned up in the corners, and she nodded. "Fair enough."

But what I didn't have the heart to tell her was that life wasn't always fair.

And I knew that better than most.

28

Ruby

We'd been painting for hours, and everyone was getting exhausted. I was thrilled that my brothers were moving out of my mom's trailer. It was a change for the better, for both of them. My mother had called me, whining that she wouldn't be able to cover her bills if they left, and I'd agreed to help her out until she got on her feet.

I'd be making more money soon, and I didn't want her guilting them when they were finally branching out on their own.

Rico had been working at the gym for a few weeks now, and he actually seemed like he'd found his niche. He was training on the side with Romeo, and I was happy to see him feeling passionate about something.

He idolized River, that much was obvious. Rico called him every freaking day, and I told River that I'd tell him to back off, but he said he didn't mind. I think my brother looked up to him, and seeing as it was the first time Rico had ever been motivated, I wasn't going to do anything to interfere.

And I appreciated it.

I'd have to do something to thank him.

I stepped out into the garage with two bags of trash as we were just getting the place cleaned up.

"It's a nice house, right? It's got to make you feel better knowing they are going to be living in their own home now," Kingston said, as he came up behind me.

King and I had become very friendly. He was hilarious, and he loved razzing his brother as much as I did, so we'd bonded over that. "Yeah. I'll worry a whole lot less. And honestly, I want to thank all of you for what you did for Rico. Helping him find work and giving him a purpose that he's never had before."

"He's a good guy, actually. And he works hard." He shrugged. "He's a big fan of my brother, too."

I chuckled. "He is. I hope it doesn't drive River too crazy."

"I don't think River would have bought this house if he wasn't equally invested," he said.

"What? Bought what house? This house?"

"Fuck," he said under his breath. "I didn't realize he hadn't told you yet. Don't throw me under the bus because the dude is so on edge lately. I don't want him all over my ass for something that shouldn't be a secret anyway."

"I won't say anything. Why would he buy this house, and why is it a secret?"

"I don't know, Ruby. What's the deal with you two? From where I'm sitting, you're always together. My brother has never seemed happier. Even when you're fighting with one another, he's—I don't know, he's lighter. More content than I've ever seen him."

"You probably just didn't pay much attention when he was with other women in the past. You know he likes to keep to himself." I cleared my throat because that lump was there again.

"He's never dated anyone," he said, holding his hands up

to stop me from interrupting that thought. "I know, I know, you two aren't dating. You're just hanging out—or whatever the hell you're calling it. But he's never hung out with one woman like this. For this long. This consistently. Buying houses for her family members and finding them jobs. He's fucking invested, no matter what you two want to call this. And yeah, he's bought homes before. He invests in things that he thinks will make him money. The dude is smart as hell. But this house is different. He didn't buy it for the investment. Hell, it's not as much of a fixer-upper as he usually gets. He bought this home to help out your brothers. And sure, he likes Rico, but he sure as shit wouldn't be buying him a house if he wasn't your brother."

My heart raced so fast and loud, I was certain Kingston could hear it. "This is temporary. Neither of us is any good at this type of thing. He doesn't want anything long-term either. I was a safe bet because I'm leaving. He's just riding out his time."

"If that's what you think, then you don't know River as well as I thought you did."

"What does that mean?"

"It means my brother wouldn't give a shit if you were staying or going if he didn't like you. If he wasn't crazy about you. He may not be admitting it to us, or even to himself, for all I know, but we all see it. If River wasn't all in, he'd have bailed a long time ago. It's different with you. It has been from the day you rolled into town."

"We've talked about it. He's fine with me leaving."

"Yeah? How about you? Are you fine with walking away? Because if you really are, then I'm glad you're leaving soon, as much as I hate to see you go, Ruby. Because I love having you here. Love seeing you with my brother and the two of you giving one another shit and laughing your asses off most of the time. But my brother has been through a lot in his life. A lot of

246

loss and trauma at a young age. And I know he doesn't open up easily, but something is different here. We've all noticed it. And if you don't feel it, then it's best you walk away sooner rather than later. He doesn't deserve any more pain in his lifetime, you know?"

I couldn't breathe. His words were sitting heavily on my chest, stealing the air from my lungs.

I do feel it, don't I?

"I don't know how to trust someone like that," I whispered.

"Come on now, girl. You already have. He's involved with your dad and your brothers. He's helping you with the contract for your job. You're volunteering at Fresh Start with the kids, which used to be a dark cloud for him, and you're bringing all your light there. If you think this is the real deal the way that I do, you're going to have to take that step. Because he won't do it. He'll think he's holding you back or some shit. You're the psychology genius; you probably know what the hell it all means. Maybe he makes up excuses to protect himself? I don't fucking know. But I do know this." Kingston paused and shoved his hands into his pockets. "River can be a difficult bastard when he wants to be, but that man is the best guy I know. And he's worth the risk. And he deserves to be happy, just like you do."

The garage door pulled open, and River stood there, looking between us. "What's going on out here?"

I didn't miss the way King's shoulders stiffened, so I spoke before he could throw himself under the bus.

"He's trying to convince me that my brothers should have a pool table out here," I said with a laugh.

"Oh, yeah?" River scratched the back of his neck. "That's not a horrible idea."

"Well, we might be in need of a new one at the bar soon, so I'll let them know if my dad decides to sell the current one."

"That's a good plan. You ready to go? Everyone is heading out," he said, and it hit me in that moment that everything Kingston was saying made sense. River was always checking on me. Making sure I was okay. Even if most of the time he did it in a broody, overbearing way. It was his way of showing that he cared.

"Yeah. I'm pretty tired." I moved toward him, and he pushed the door open, and Kingston followed me inside.

The conversation was over, but his words were still moving through my mind.

Getting into something with someone with no expectations was very different than planning a future together.

We'd never talked about anything beyond right now. It wasn't his style, and in many ways, it wasn't mine. I'd become a pro at guarding my heart.

And loving River was dangerous.

The chances that we would implode together were high.

We were just having fun right now.

What was I going to do? Give up a job that was a once-in-a-lifetime position for one that I didn't have here? For a man who would possibly never be able to tell me how he felt about me, because he was too guarded? The closest we'd ever come to saying anything, as far as our feelings go, was the rare occasion when we admitted that we didn't hate one another all the time.

Or the moment when he said that we weren't *nothing*.

So, we didn't hate one another, and we were more than nothing. That wasn't a strong foundation.

"Ruby, I was telling everyone how pissed you were that I stole your blue sweater before you left for college," Panda said when we stepped inside, and everyone laughed.

"I never did get that back, did I?" I raised a brow.

"I just wanted to look cool like you. Ruby was always this badass, confident girl from the first time I met her, and the rest

248

of us were just trying to keep up," she said. Her words startled me, because I'd never seen myself that way before.

I'd always felt like I had something to prove.

To myself.

To everyone around me.

Maybe I'd been the one who'd had so much armor surrounding me that I couldn't see the good that was there.

Maybe I was still doing it.

"Thanks. I hardly think I was a badass, but if the navy sweater made you feel empowered, have at it." I chuckled as we all walked toward the door.

"Thanks for doing this," Rico said to everyone, clearing his throat. "We appreciate it a lot."

"Happy to help." Demi beamed, and Romeo wrapped an arm around her shoulder.

"But I don't care how sore your arms are tomorrow. I'll see you at the gym in the morning."

More laughter and we all said our goodbyes.

My brothers hugged me tighter than usual, and I quickly pulled away.

Thinking about leaving was weighing on me lately.

River and I made the short drive to his house. We were quiet.

"The house looks good, doesn't it?" I asked.

"Yeah. It's amazing what a fresh coat of paint can do for a place."

We parked in the garage and walked inside. He hadn't asked if I was coming over. It was just assumed at this point. Because it was what we did now.

How had I let things get this deep?

Go this far?

I was in a full-blown relationship without even realizing it.

I followed him into the kitchen, and he flipped on the lights

LAURA PAVLOV

as I jumped up on the counter, and he poured us each a glass of water.

"I'm happy Rico and Zane are moving out."

He handed me a glass and moved to stand between my legs. "Yeah. I think it will be good for them."

"Something you want to tell me about the house?" I peered over the edge of the glass as I took a sip.

"That fucking loose-lipped brother of mine can't keep his damn mouth shut, can he?"

I chuckled. "Why should he? Why is it a secret?"

"Because I knew it would be turned into a big deal. I didn't want you to freak out. The house came up for sale, and I've been looking for a new property. Your brothers were looking to rent one. It was a win for both of us."

I nodded. "I wouldn't freak out about it. It's very nice of you to do that for them. Hell, you've done so much for Rico, and I'm just—I'm grateful."

"What is that? *The Ruby Rose* isn't pissed off that someone did something nice for her?" His voice was all tease as his large hand moved to the side of my neck. His thumb tipped my chin up so my gaze would meet his.

"Calling me *The Ruby Rose* is just creepy." I smiled.

"Ah, I'm creepy now, huh?"

My gaze searched his for the longest time, feeling that overwhelming feeling take over again. The lump in my throat was there. My eyes were blinking rapidly as I pushed away the tears that threatened to fall.

"Thank you, Wild River."

"You're welcome, Queenie."

Say something. Ask him how he feels. Tear off the bandage.

"Are you upset that I'm leaving?" I whispered.

He studied me, his thumb stroking along my jawline. "I'm never upset to see you living your dreams. We knew the score when we started this. I'm fine, so don't you worry about me."

250

"You're probably relieved."

He nodded the slightest bit. "Are you relieved? You ready to go and chase your dreams and all that shit?"

"Sure." My heart was beating so loud in my ears that I couldn't think straight.

"That's all I need to hear." He scooped me up off the counter and carried me down the hall to his bedroom.

River was always carrying me around, and normally, if a man wanted to carry me through his home, I would want to kick him in the balls for treating me like a helpless woman.

But when River took care of me, it never felt like that.

It never felt like he didn't think that I could take care of myself.

It felt like he wanted to worship me, care for me—not because I couldn't do it for myself, but because he just wanted the opportunity to do it, too.

"You sore from all that painting?" he asked after he dropped me onto the bed.

"Not sore at all." I waggled my brows.

"How about you let me taste you first? And then I'll let you ride me into oblivion."

"How can I say no to that?" My voice was all tease, but the anticipation already had me squirming.

He reached for the top of my jean shorts and unbuttoned the button before pulling down the zipper. He tugged them down my legs, then ran his fingers over the lace of my pink panties.

"I love your fucking body. I love your pink lace panties and your military boots. You're such a walking contradiction, and I fucking love it," he said, finding my hands and pinning them above my head. "Keep these right here."

His words had my head spinning once again.

I love you.

I wanted to say it. For the first time in my life, I wanted to tell a man that I loved him. Because I loved River in a way I never knew was possible.

But saying it would change everything.

Walk away now and no one will get hurt beyond repair.

I closed my eyes as he pulled my panties down my legs. I kept my arms above my head where he'd left them.

His head settled between my thighs as his tongue swiped across my clit, and I gasped. My hand came down to tangle in his hair, and he stopped and looked up at me.

"Hands above your head or you don't get to come. I want you to feel everything that I'm giving you. I don't want you guiding me where you want me. I know what you want, Queenie. I want you to trust that."

I raised my arm back above my head, intertwining my fingers to keep them there, and I gave him the slightest nod.

And River delivered exactly as he promised.

His tongue, his lips, his fingers—it was pure ecstasy.

He knew my body.

He knew my mind.

He knew what I needed and how to please me.

My entire body started to shake. I squeezed my hands together, desperate to reach for him, yet not allowing myself to.

Because I did trust him.

More than I'd ever trusted anyone.

His tongue was pure torture. Moving and teasing me over and over. He slipped a finger in, and his lips covered my clit, and he sucked hard, causing me to arch and buck in response.

He slipped in another finger, and lights sparked behind my eyes.

My lips parted on a cry, and I shattered.

I went over the edge with the most powerful orgasm of my life.

And he held me right there, riding out every last bit of pleasure.

I knew in that moment that I was ruined for all future men.

Because this man owned me.

He owned my body, and he owned my heart.

Two things I'd never planned to give away.

29

River

"Why are you in an unusually bad mood today? And that's saying a lot for you, because bad moods are sort of your thing," Kingston said as we stood huddled around a glass display case filled with fancy rings.

We were at a jewelry store in Cottonwood Cove, where Romeo's brother, Lincoln, had purchased a ring for his wife, Brinkley. Romeo was convinced that buying Demi a ring in Magnolia Falls would never stay a secret, and he was probably right. He wanted to surprise her. So, Lincoln had flown us here in a private plane this morning, and we'd be home by tonight.

"You know, if you spent half the time figuring out your own shit than you did analyzing my moods, we'd all be happier," I hissed.

"How about we focus on finding the ring and talk about River's notable bad mood over lunch?" Hayes glanced between my brother and me.

How about we shut the fuck up about my bad mood and talk about something else?

I didn't say it aloud because then that would be a whole other conversation.

I nodded as Romeo held up one ring and studied it. "This is it. This is the one."

"Ah, beautiful choice, sir. That's a gorgeous princess-cut diamond. Classy and elegant," the older man who owned the place said.

"Beans is classy and elegant," Kingston said, and I slapped him upside the head just because it made me feel better.

Everyone chuckled, and Lincoln glanced at Romeo and nodded. "I agree. It's perfect."

"I'll take it." Romeo looked at each of us. "Thanks for being here. Biggest decision of my life, and I wanted to get it right."

"Ride or die, brother," Nash said, clapping him on the shoulder.

"Honored to be here with you," Lincoln said. "And I'm glad my brother has good friends around him all the time."

We were all getting sappy at the thought of Romeo tying the knot with Demi. We all loved her, and I knew they'd have a long, happy life together.

Something I'd never wanted myself, but lately, I was all over the fucking place with my thoughts.

Maybe it was because I saw how happy Romeo was.

Maybe it was because I was getting older.

Maybe it was because Ruby Rose had come into my life and turned it upside down. Making me want things that I shouldn't.

Queenie.

Romeo paid the bill and tucked the ring box into his coat pocket, and we all walked the short distance to Reynolds' Bar & Grill.

Lincoln's brother and sister-in-law, Hugh and Lila Reynolds, owned the place, and they supposedly had the best food in town.

When we arrived at the restaurant, we were led to the back,

where a table was set up for us. A big dude with long hair made his rounds, introducing himself as the owner, Hugh. He was a nice guy, that much I could tell right away, and Lincoln made introductions as the next few guys walked in. There was Maddox Lancaster and his brother, Wyle, whom Romeo had talked about before. Maddox was married to Brinkley's sister, Georgia. They shook our hands and congratulated Romeo on coming to town to pick out an engagement ring. Next came Finn Reynolds, who I recognized right away, as he starred in a show called *Big Sky Ranch* that Ruby had insisted we binge last weekend. He was pretty famous, but you wouldn't know it; he just acted like a regular dude. The broody guy beside him, his older brother, Cage Reynolds, settled in the chair beside me. We seemed to be putting off equally grumpy energy, so I was good with that. Hugh asked if we were all okay with the ribs, which we were, and he ordered a shit ton of appetizers for the table, as well.

"So, first, you win the fight of the century, and now, you're proposing to your girl. It's a good year to be Romeo Knight," Finn said.

Romeo nodded in thanks, and the conversation started flowing. Cage and Nash were deep in conversation about their kids, who were the same age, and they were both complaining about all the homework kids had these days.

Lincoln sat on the other side of me, and we both reached for the onion rings that were set in the center of the table.

"I'm telling you, it's the best food you'll ever have. I can't get enough," he said, and I laughed as I shoved an entire onion ring into my mouth and nodded.

"Damn right. Whiskey Falls needs to step up their game."

"I've eaten there a few times, and it's a damn close second place to this food." He reached for his water. "Thanks for coming here to help him pick out his ring. You guys are family to Romeo, which means you're family to me."

"Same, brother." I tipped my chin up, because I was not only a fan of the number one quarterback in the league, but I liked the dude a lot. He was down to earth, and he'd shown up for Romeo and his sister, Tia, from the moment he found out he had siblings he hadn't known about.

"So, what's this moodier-than-usual shit you've got going on about? You want to talk about it?" he asked.

"Oh, for fuck's sake. Why is everyone always analyzing the grumpy dudes? Maybe we just like being quiet," Cage grumped from the other side of me.

"Trust me, he's not being quiet. He's being a moody little bitch because he's in love and too chickenshit to admit it," Kingston said.

And now the whole table turned their attention my way, and they were all going to get involved.

"Did you not get enough *me time* this morning? Did you not work your feelings out in your Zen garden and write in your diary before we left to come here?" I hissed.

Kingston's head fell back in laughter, and Finn did the same.

"Damn. I like this guy." Cage nudged me, and the table erupted in laughter again.

"Two fucking peas in a pod right here," Lincoln said, looking between me and Cage. "So, give us the breakdown. There's a girl involved?"

"Oh, yeah," Romeo said. "It's always about a girl."

"Well, that is, until your girl fucks your coworker," Hayes said, and now everyone was laughing.

"There are good ones and bad ones. Lucky for me, I found myself the best girl around," Maddox said, and his brother smirked.

"I could say the same," Wyle said proudly, as the server set our food down in front of us.

"So, is there a girl, River?" Finn asked. "Does she have you all messed up?"

The table was quiet as I ate a rib and dropped the bone onto the plate and wiped my mouth. "There's a girl."

These fuckers all started cheering and hollering like I'd just said something out of left field.

"There always is," Cage said. "It's always that one fucking girl that gets you wrapped around the axel. Hell, it took me years to finally get my shit together. So I'm kind of an expert now."

"Oh, for fuck's sake," Finn said. "Now you're a therapist?"

"He has been more sensitive than he used to be since he and Presley got married." Hugh reached for a rib and started eating again.

"I've been there, buddy," Maddox said, as he set his drink down on the table and looked at me. "There's no running from it. Once you meet the right one, it's pretty much over. So just surrender to it."

"It's not a death sentence," Lincoln said over his laughter. "It's a good thing."

"Unless she fucks your coworker," Kingston said, winking at Hayes.

"True that," Hayes said.

"Nah, Ruby's a good one. That's not the problem." Nash wiped his face with his napkin and tossed it onto the table beside his plate.

"So, what's the problem?" Cage asked.

I just sat back, arms folded over my chest, as I let them all figure out my shit.

"Well, Ruby and River are both stubborn asses. That's the biggest problem I see," Kingston said, tossing me a wink across the table.

"So poetic, brother." I flipped him the bird.

"What King means to say," Romeo interjected over his laughter, "is that Ruby and River are both strong people, and they've both been single for a long time. Demi says they're both guarded."

"What the hell is this? Some kind of psychotherapy where you insult me the whole time?" I hissed.

"Don't fight it, my man. They do it to me all the time, but it usually leads somewhere." Cage shrugged, and Finn chucked a dinner roll across the table at him, but Cage caught it with one hand, taking a bite without missing a beat.

"The issue is that we weren't looking for anything. This was temporary, and we both agreed to that. And she doesn't live in Magnolia Falls. She was home, helping her father while he recovered from a stroke, and now she's going back for a new job in a week. I knew the score, and I'll deal with it. I just don't need to be analyzed about it every second of the fucking day."

The table was quiet as they listened to me rant.

"Do you spend a lot of time together?" Finn asked, breaking the silence.

"Every fucking day," Kingston said. "They spend every night together. They hang out whenever they aren't working. He just bought a house so her brothers could rent it."

Hugh and Finn both whistled, and Lincoln clapped me on the shoulder as if he were consoling me.

"Says my brother, who hasn't had a fucking relationship in his life. The perpetual playboy. Now you're a relationship expert?" I growled.

"Hey. I know who I am. I'm not guarded; I'm just attentionally challenged. My heart beats for the ladies. I just can't seem to find one that makes it want to beat for them and no one else." Kingston took a bite of his roll and raised a brow at me.

"He does make a valid point," Nash said. "He is in one relationship after the next. There's nothing guarded about King."

"Yeah. He's like a twenty-four-hour open house. Everyone is welcome," Hayes said, and the table erupted in laughter.

"Hey, I don't think there's anything wrong with being

guarded," Romeo said, turning to look at me. "But there's also nothing wrong with changing the plan. You never saw this coming, but that doesn't mean it's a bad thing. I felt that, and I was terrified of messing it up, but being with Demi is the best thing that's ever happened to me."

I nodded. "And I'm happy for you, brother. I'm not being guarded; I'm being real. First off, I can't ask her to stay for something I'm not sure I can even do. We got into this knowing it had an expiration date. I've never been with one woman for a long period of time. I'm a loner. I like to be on my own. And she does, too."

"Oh, man, do I get that." Cage whistled. "However, just because you thought you liked being alone before doesn't mean you'll want that forever. You hang out with her every day and night? How long has that been going on?"

"For a few weeks." I cleared my throat.

"More like two months, dude," Kingston, the guy who just wasn't capable of not adding in his two cents, said.

"Rest in peace, my brother. You're already in a relationship, you just don't know it." Maddox shrugged, and Wyle nodded at me.

"And if you don't do something about it, you'll just die a lonely, unhappy man," Cage said.

"Way to make him feel like shit." Hugh turned his attention to me. "Just tell her how you feel. You don't have to have it all figured out. But at least let her decide what she wants, and you'll know that you left it all out there."

"That's not really my style. I'm not going to pressure her into something or guilt her to make a decision based on me. People have been doing that her entire life. I won't be that guy." It was the truth. If Ruby wanted to stay, she'd need to do that all on her own. I wasn't going to be another person who needed her to do something for me. "And I can't even be certain how I feel, anyway."

Cage raised a brow. "I'm sorry to tell you, but you've already made it fucking clear how you feel."

"How do you figure that, when I just said I don't even know what this is?"

I didn't miss the way their gazes moved around the table, and Finn smiled as he looked at me. "You're putting her needs before your own, buddy. That's what you do when you love someone."

"Thank you!" Kingston shouted, as his hand came down hard on the table. "You're in love with Ruby Rose, you little pussy."

The table roared with laughter, and I shook my head.

It wasn't that I didn't agree with him.

I couldn't argue that I loved her.

But acting on it was a different story.

30

Ruby

"I don't need a babysitter. You don't need to hover so much, Rubes," my dad said, as I cleared his breakfast plate from the table. "I'm ready to head to the bar today and start getting back to normal."

Back to normal.

What did that even mean anymore?

I'd lost sight of normal a long time ago.

My dad had come home from the hospital four days ago, and I'd spent the night here with him every day since.

Alone.

Almost instinctually, I'd started pulling away from River.

We both knew I was leaving.

Things had gone too far.

He hadn't put up a fight, almost like he'd thought it was time to put some distance there, as well.

But I hadn't expected to feel like I'd lost a limb.

Like I couldn't breathe without him.

I hadn't expected the dull ache in my chest to make me feel physically ill.

We hadn't spoken either. We'd just gone radio silent. No texts. No calls.

No sneaking around or booty calls.

"I hired two new people, and you aren't on the schedule until next week. Plus, you are no longer working night shifts. You'll be working day shifts. I need you to take better care of yourself, Dad."

"Rubes," he said, his voice softening. "I'm in my late fifties. I'm not dying. I took a medication that I shouldn't have taken. I understand the danger I put myself in, and I've worked hard to get myself back. But I will be making my own schedule at the bar, and I will work nights again because I like closing the bar down."

I groaned as I crossed my arms over my chest. "Old habits die hard, huh?"

"I'm feeling good, and I don't plan to start drinking again. I'm in the best shape I've been in in years, and I want to continue the physical therapy and exercising every day. And as much as I appreciate all that you did for me at the bar, I need to take my life back. Can you understand that?"

"Yeah, Dad. I can understand that." I glanced down at the contract sitting on the table that I still hadn't signed. Dean Langston had emailed me, letting me know they'd agreed to all my changes, yet here it sat, unsigned.

River had spent so much time making tweaks over the last few weeks, and he'd told me I should never rely on a man who wasn't very lawyerly to be the last set of eyes on the contract. So, I'd promised to read it all the way through before I signed it. I'd made up excuses to Dean Langston that my internet was down, that I'd sent it back, and it must have gotten lost in the universe—but the verbal acceptance seemed to appease him for now.

Tonight, I would sit down and read every damn word of the contract, sign it, and send it back.

I'd planned to do that this morning, but I'd woken up feeling a little off today. I'd felt a little off every day for the last four days.

It was him.

The loss of him.

This had never happened to me before. But here I was.

My chest aching for a man who wasn't mine.

"Tell me what your plans are for today. Doreen is coming to pick me up, and we're going to The Golden Goose for lunch, and then I'm heading over to the bar to check on things."

He didn't want me to baby him; he'd made that clear. "I'm going to stop by to see Pearl Pierce before I head over to Fresh Start. Terrence wants to talk to me before I leave, and I'll get to say goodbye to the kids. I'll be at the bar after. I'm working tonight, so you'll be on your own for dinner."

He smiled. "That'll be just fine. You didn't need to stay an extra week to take care of me. You've done enough. I'm fine on my own, and you need to go start your big job."

"I wanted to make sure you were settled before I left," I said, and that lump formed in my throat again, just like it had been doing more and more the closer I got to leaving.

"It's still what you want, right? The professor job? You've worked so hard and accomplished so much." And that sent my thoughts spiraling all over again.

"Yeah, Dad. I—" What did I want? Why was I struggling so much? "I just worry about you."

"We're not doing that, Rubes. I'm fine," Dad gruffed, then hit me again with another worry of mine. "You sure spend a lot of time out there at Fresh Start with the kids, huh? You like it, don't you?"

"Yeah. It's been really great. I feel like I'm making a difference by helping them see an attainable future and hopefully realizing that they aren't stuck just because of one bad choice. I've really enjoyed my time there." And I did. I'd miss it for sure. When I was there, I thought of a young River. I thought about how much I wished someone had been there to protect him during that time.

He smiled, and it reached his eyes. It was one of my favorite things about my dad. "You've always been good at fixing things. Finding broken things and putting them back together."

I rolled my eyes and chuckled at the same time. "These are actual humans, Dad, not things. And they aren't broken; they're just a little damaged."

"I know, but that's your strength. You've done it with your brothers. You've done it with me. Hell, even the guys that you've dated. You find them damaged, and then you fix them before you leave them for good." His voice was all tease, but I startled at his words.

What the actual hell is he talking about?

"I'll agree that I try to do what I can to help my family, but not in my dating life. I don't look for men who need to be fixed. I typically seek out men who want the same thing as me. Nothing too serious." I crossed my arms over my chest defensively.

"Please. I've met three men that you've dated, and they've all had the same issue."

I narrowed my gaze. "What are you talking about?"

"Let's start with your undergrad boyfriend, Dalton. He was a train wreck when you met him."

"He'd found his girlfriend in bed with his roommate. He was slightly broken."

"And you put him back together, made him fall in love again when he thought he never would, and then you hit the road. It's your shtick. You fix them and leave them."

I gasped. "That's not true. He just got too attached, and I didn't feel the same way about him."

He raised a brow and bit down on his apple slice. "Right.

265

You showed him how to love again, and then sent him on his way. And how about Devil? You did the same to him."

"His name is Devlyn, and he'd spent a year in prison in a foreign country right before I met him. He was traumatized. He had no idea that you couldn't travel with marijuana." I shrugged. I hadn't expected this trip down memory lane today. "So he was down on himself, and he didn't feel worthy of love. It was a sad situation."

"Well, by the time you were done with him, he was all in. Didn't he propose to you?"

"You sure are feeling cocky today, aren't you? Yes. He proposed, but we weren't in love. He'd just found himself again and wanted me to be the person who gave him his life back. I was not in love with him. Plus, I had to turn the proposal down. You remember his last name . . . it would have been a big issue for me." I smirked because it still made me laugh every time I thought about it.

"Yes. You would have been Mrs. Ruby Looby." His laughter echoed around the room. "But his name was not the problem."

"Correct. I didn't reciprocate the feelings he had. And we're still good friends. He's married and has a little girl now. So, it all worked out."

"Yep. Your work was done, and you moved on to the professor." He reached for his coffee.

"Don't serial-date-shame me. There was a good year in between each of those relationships. And the professor was fine. He wasn't broken. So, your theory just went down the shitter, Daddy dearest."

He nodded, his gaze locked with mine. "An older man who's never been married. Believes he's incapable of love. And then he falls for his much younger teaching assistant after she fixes him."

"You make it all sound so scandalous. I wasn't looking for

anything long-term, and I've always been open about that. But I enjoyed his company, and I was happy to see him come into his own. He wasn't just an intellect with no personality. He's a good man. He'll make someone very happy someday—that person just isn't me."

"I think we're saying the same thing, sweetheart. You fix them, and you leave them. It's a habit."

"Well, lucky for you, you're all fixed up now, and I will be on my way soon." I kissed his cheek and walked to the sink to rinse my glass.

"What about River? You two seemed to be spending an awful lot of time together these last eight weeks. And now, it's just over, just in time for you to leave?"

"Your theory will for sure die there, Dad. River Pierce does not need fixing. He's a confident man who knows exactly who he is and what he wants. He feels very worthy of being fawned all over." I laughed, but it wasn't genuine, because thinking about him hurt like hell. "There was nothing to fix."

Because he was perfect exactly how he was.

And I wasn't desperate to get away from him because I didn't reciprocate his feelings; I was desperate to get away from him because, for the first time in my life, I was the one with the feelings.

And that scared the hell out of me.

Rule number one: Don't catch feelings.

I'd always been able to live by that motto, until I couldn't.

When it came to River, I'd broken that one pretty quickly.

Maybe things were reversed this time around for me. Because I'd been the broken one when he'd kissed me for the first time all those weeks ago. And in a way, he'd put me back together.

I just didn't know what to do about it.

Everything I thought I knew, thought I wanted, was waiting for me far from here.

All I had to do was sign the contract and head back to my safe little life.

It was what I should do.

I was leaving in three days. Time was ticking.

"He's definitely not broken. You two are actually a lot alike," Dad said.

"How do you figure?" I asked, grabbing my purse and pulling the strap over my shoulder.

"You both like to take care of everyone around you, and you don't need anyone to take care of you. It's brilliant in a lot of ways, but I imagine it could get really lonely, too."

"Okay, you weepy sap. Enough psychoanalyzing me for the day. I'm off to meet Terrence and say goodbye to the boys. I'll call you later."

Our conversation really hit home, and a day I'd thought would be filled with happy goodbyes had actually turned out to be much more difficult than I'd anticipated. I felt like I was leaving my life behind, and that was not how it was supposed to be. I was supposed to be beginning my new life, the one I'd worked so hard for, the one that would make me feel like I'd achieved all that I'd strived for. The one that said I'd made it, and I was now just as good as everyone else. But it didn't feel that way at all.

I'd actually cried when I'd hugged Pearl goodbye, and she'd done the same, catching me completely off guard. I'd then headed to Fresh Start, and again, I'd been caught completely off guard. Meeting with Terrence had been both exciting and confusing. He'd offered me an actual position working with the kids there. He'd spent all these weeks getting a position approved and hadn't wanted to tell me in case it didn't happen. He'd received the paperwork late yesterday and sprung the whole thing on me today.

It was a good offer.

I'd be working with kids all over the state, but I'd have an official office at Fresh Start, which would be my home base.

A place I'd grown to love and feel like I belonged.

A place where I could do the work I'd always wanted to do. Where I could make a difference and be a positive factor in someone's life.

Help kids that needed someone in their corner.

The pay was decent enough.

But it didn't compare to the salary I'd receive as a collegiate professor. Though living in the city would be much more expensive than living here.

The benefits were fewer at Fresh Start, too. And tenure wouldn't be an option, of course, so my future wouldn't be laid out for me the way it would be if I accepted the position at the university.

Then again, when have I ever taken the easy way out?

Am I actually considering this?

I'd sent Demi a text and asked if she could sneak away from work to meet with me for a little bit. We'd grown close, and I trusted her. I was beginning to trust a lot of people these days, more than I'd ever had in my life.

She'd told me to meet her out at the ranch, and we could go for a ride. Talk things out on the horses like we used to do.

She'd been waiting for me when I arrived, and we saddled up and started riding toward the water.

The breeze swirled around us, and the sound of the waves crashing against the shore relaxed me. Demi pulled her horse up beside mine and glanced my way. "Tell me what's going on."

"Well, you know I'm leaving in three days."

"Yep. It actually makes me sick to my stomach. I've gotten used to seeing you almost every day. And now you won't be back but once or twice a year again."

I started almost every day at Magnolia Beans. Demi had become more than a friend to me. She was family in a way now.

They all were.

"Terrence offered me a really good position working with the kids full time." I stared out at the water after bringing my horse to a stop.

She pulled back the reins and turned to face me. "What? I didn't know you'd applied for anything here."

"I didn't. He came up with a job for me all on his own. And I shouldn't be tempted, but I am. It feels right."

"Is the pay as good as the professor position?"

"No. Not even close." I laughed. Because it wasn't just about the money. Obviously, I wanted to be able to live comfortably, but I wasn't going to base my decision on just the financial aspect. I needed to be proud of the work that I did, and sure, teaching college kids also meant that I could make an impact, but it was different. College kids were typically invested in the education process because they were paying a lot of money to be there. But the kids at Fresh Start were facing challenges that would take work to turn around. They may not have the support at home or the resources they'd need to make a change, but that was something I understood. Something I knew I'd be good at.

"You like it here, don't you? The place you were so determined to hate feels like home now, doesn't it?" She smirked.

"Is everyone cocky today? You sound like my dad."

"Maybe we know you better than you think we do. And I know one thing for sure," she said as she locked her gaze with mine. "You would not bring me out here to talk about what job to take. You're the most self-assured person I know. You aren't indecisive. You know what you want. Who you are. There's only one thing you'd come to me for, and we both know it."

My head fell back on a groan. "Is this my karma for trying to read people the minute I meet them? Now everyone knows me better than I know myself? I have no idea what you're talking about. I honestly don't know what to do about the job. I don't want to piss off the dean and burn that bridge, but it just never felt quite right. But I don't know if I should stay either."

She hopped off her horse and motioned for me to do the same, and we tied them to the tree beside us before finding a warm spot by the lake. My fingers settled into the warm sand, and I tipped my head up to the sun, letting it warm my skin.

"Ruby Rose, look at me."

I straightened my face and gave her a look like she had three heads. "Why are you using my full name?"

"Because I don't think this is about the job at all. I think you're in love with River, and that scares the shit out of you. But you've come to the right place. Because I'm here to tell you exactly what to do."

I wanted to argue.

To laugh in her face and tell her she was absolutely ridiculous.

But I didn't do either.

I just stared at her, feeling my eyes well with emotion.

"Tell me what to do," I whispered.

A wide grin spread across her face. "You can work anywhere. But River Pierce is in Magnolia Falls. And you can't leave half of your heart here and expect to be happy. If you want that job at the university, you tell him how you feel and see if he'll go with you."

"I don't think I want the job. It never felt right. And my old life there doesn't feel like mine anymore. This place that I ran from so long ago feels different now. And I think it has a lot to do with River."

She nodded and reached for my hand. "Tell me how it feels here now."

"Like home."

271

31

River

There was a knock on my office door, and I shouted for Cassie to come in. I was having a shit day. Hell, I was having a shit week. It had been four nights that I'd slept alone in my bed, and I didn't fucking like it.

It used to be my favorite place.

Quiet and serene.

And now it felt cold and lonely.

I didn't get lonely. I'd always thrived on being alone. Pitied the fuckers who couldn't handle being by themselves.

And here I was—a sad, fucking pussy-whipped motherfucker.

"Hey, boss," Cassie said, and I pinched the bridge of my nose because I'd asked her no less than eight million fucking times not to call me boss. "Your grandmother is on the line, and I'm going to head out. It's late. You should think about leaving soon, too," Cassie said.

"Have a good night," was all I said.

"Are you okay?" she asked. "You seem a little grumpier than usual."

"I'm fine." I nodded. She turned to leave, and I realized I'd

272

been a real dick lately, and she hadn't let anyone in without an appointment in more than three weeks. "Hey, Cassie."

"Yeah?" She turned around to face me.

"You've done a good job not allowing people to just stop by these last few weeks. I've noticed, and I appreciate it."

She smiled ridiculously big. Had I never complimented her?

"Well, Ruby gave me a tip on how to stop letting people walk all over me, regarding the appointments, when she brought you lunch a few weeks ago."

"What did she say?"

"She said that you'd worked really hard for your practice and that you were the best lawyer she knew. She said that with me being your assistant, I should know that and protect it so you can do your job."

Fuck me. I did not see that coming.

"I told you to send them away dozens of times. All you had to hear was that I was good at my job?" A sarcastic chuckle left my mouth because it was ridiculous, yet my chest puffed up with pride that Ruby had gone to bat for me.

"Well, you're always growling at me, and it makes me nervous, I guess. Ruby just said it plain as day, as if it were common knowledge. And it made sense. So, there you go." She shrugged.

"All right. I better get this call. I'll see you tomorrow."

I picked up the phone. "Hey, Grammie."

"Hello, my boy. Why are you still at work?"

"Because I'm busy," I said.

And I don't want to go home because all I do is think about her.

She was leaving. I'd get over it. But right now, I needed to stay busy.

"Ahhh . . . Ruby came by to see me yesterday. She stopped by on her way to say goodbye to the kids at Fresh Start. Have you said goodbye to her yet?"

"She hasn't left yet, so no. And I haven't seen her in a few days."

"Yes, she mentioned that," Grammie said, and I wanted to know more.

"What did she say?"

"She said that she hadn't seen you and that maybe it was better that way, because she was leaving."

"Typical Ruby. She's always psychoanalyzing everything."

"I think owning it is better than denying how you feel."

"I've got news for you," I said, leaning back in my chair. "You can own it and be in denial at the same time. That girl thinks she knows everything, and she's more in denial than I am."

There. I said it. It was the truth.

"And what exactly is she in denial about?" she pressed, because that was my grandmother's favorite thing to do.

"She's running away. She likes to analyze everyone around her, but she's afraid to look in the goddamn mirror. Afraid to admit how she feels. Not the best quality for a doctor of psychology," I hissed.

"Spoken like a man who knows what he's talking about. Maybe you're in denial, too?"

I groaned. I'd set her up for this conversation, and she was going to enjoy it. "Listen, I'm not in denial. I have always said exactly how I feel. And I was honest with her in the beginning, but then things changed. I haven't said anything because I don't want to pressure her to stay. *I want her to want to stay.* I was giving her time to figure her shit out."

My grandmother was quiet on the other end for a moment before she finally spoke. "Sometimes, people need more. She's not had a lot of people take care of her, River. She might not know how you feel," she said.

"How could she not know? She's a smart woman." And she knows, because I'd written her a note and let her know. And then what did she do? She shut me out. I never heard from her again.

I'm sure I'd freaked her the fuck out.

"And you're a smart man, yet you don't seem to know how she feels. Why don't you stop being a stubborn ass and be the one to take the first step? Just tell her how you feel. What do you have to lose?"

I ran a hand through my hair. "I did. I wrote her a note, and it clearly freaked her out."

"Really? You wrote her a love letter? I'm impressed."

"Well, don't get too excited. It was a sticky note. I put it at the end of the contract so she'd see it before she signed it. Clearly, she saw it. She signed it. And she's avoided me ever since."

"River Pierce. Did I raise you to be a coward? You wrote it on a sticky note?"

"Hey. I put myself out there. I'm a man of few words, but at least I had the balls to say how I feel."

"That's not how a woman wants to hear from a man. Go down and talk to her face-to-face. Stop being a baby. You've never been afraid of anything. Don't start now."

What the hell was happening? Had everyone lost their goddamn minds lately?

"I don't need any more advice on this. I'm good. I need to go. I'll come see you this week."

"I love you," she said.

"Love you, too."

"See, was that so difficult to say? Those three little words." She chuckled, and I shook my head with disbelief.

"Goodbye." I ended the call and looked down to see the group text I'd been ignoring all day going off, per usual.

I quickly caught up on all the mundane shit we talked about. Kingston and Nash went on and on about the renovation at the Silvertons' house, and how Walter Silverton answered the door stark naked. That conversation got a bunch of endless memes and emojis. And not in a good way.

Hayes told us about a bullshit call for a fire last night from Suzie Walters, who simply wanted someone to come over and change the batteries in her smoke detector.

Kingston said how hot she was and that he'd change her batteries anytime.

Normally, I'd find this shit funny, but I wasn't in the mood today. But the next one caught my eye.

NASH

> Cutler has back-to-school night next week, and he wants everyone there to meet his new teacher. I didn't have the heart to tell him that Ruby wouldn't be here next week. Are we going to do a barbecue or something before she leaves so we can all say goodbye? You know how Cutler is. He's going to lose his shit after she's gone.

KINGSTON

> I don't think he's the only one. Are you still being a stubborn prick, brother?

ROMEO

> Everyone deals with things differently. Let him work through it.

HAYES

> This is going to shock the shit out of all of you . . . but I'm with King on this one. Stop being a dumbass and tell the girl how you feel before she leaves.

KINGSTON

Well, looky here. Even a blind
squirrel finds his nuts every once in
a while. Apparently, today is my day.
Even Hayes is on my side. Come on,
Golden Boy and Nash. Jump on the
King train.

ROMEO

You are one crazy fucker. I'm fairly
certain you ruined that saying. The blind
squirrel finds a NUT, not HIS NUTS. 🤯
And I'm on your side, too. I want him
to tell her how he feels, but I think he
should do it in his own way. His own
time.

NASH

Fuck. I don't know who I'm siding with
on this one. You're all making good
points.

That's because they're saying the
same fucking thing. I get it. You want
me to tell her how I feel. Do we not
remember the fucking sticky note?
Wasn't that Kingston's goddamn
idea?

HAYES

I never got on board with professing
your love on a sticky note.

NASH

The problem with writing it in a note, and one that is unusually small, is that you don't know if she got it. And it's not like you have the neatest handwriting.

ROMEO

I liked the note better than King's first idea, which was tattooing it on his chest and tearing his shirt off.

HAYES

That was definitely a little much. Most of King's ideas suck.

KINGSTON

Hey, now. Un-fucking-true, you dick weasels. The tattoo was a stretch, but Ruby's the kind of girl you go big with. The sticky note seems to have flopped, but we don't know for sure if she saw it, right?

Of course, she fucking saw it. She had to have signed the contract by now. She's moving in two days. She said goodbye to Grammie and the kids at Fresh Start yesterday. Obviously, she saw the note. It probably freaked her the fuck out. I should have explained it.

KINGSTON

How do you explain it? I love you kind of says it all, right?

ROMEO

You do realize you're taking advice from a man who's never been in a relationship, right? No offense, King.

HAYES

That's a very good point.

NASH

We should have killed the sticky note idea right away.

KINGSTON

Let's all shoot the fucking messenger. I'm the only one getting shit done. None of you bring anything to the table. 👆

HAYES

Romeo is proposing to his girl, so why don't we let him throw an idea into the hat?

KINGSTON

Let's hear it, Golden Boy.

ROMEO

Well, you could just go down to the bar and tell her how you feel. It would be a lot easier than wondering if she got the note.

NASH

This is a better plan.

KINGSTON

Hindsight and all that, you judgy fuckers.

I'm done with this conversation. I'll check back in later.

My phone continued vibrating, but I shoved it into my pocket and decided to take the goddamn bull by the horns. I'd never been afraid of anything, and I sure as shit was not afraid of Ruby Rose.

What do I have to lose at this point?

I walked the short distance to Whiskey Falls and pulled open the door. Evie shouted my name, her words already slurring from where she sat with a few of her friends. I held up my hand to briefly acknowledge her, as my eyes scanned the bar. No sign of Ruby.

Doreen was behind the bar, and I walked over to her.

"Hey, River, what can I get you?"

"Nothing for now. I thought Ruby was working the night shift tonight?"

"Yeah. She asked me to stay on late because her friend is here, and they've been in the back talking for the last hour. Maybe he's here to help with her move? I don't know, but if you want to tell her to hurry up, that would be great. My feet are killing me, and I'd love to clock out."

My shoulders stiffened.

He's here to help with her move.

"Who is the dude she's with?" I asked, as she stood at the tap, filling a few beer glasses for an order.

"Some guy named Dereck. He's from the city, I think."

The fucking professor.

Well, that didn't take long.

I stormed behind the bar, pushing open the double doors to the kitchen and barreling through like a man on a mission. I nodded at Calvin, who was cooking, and strolled toward the stairs, assuming they were in her office.

The place I'd first been with her.

But I startled when I found them in the corner of the kitchen, her back against the wall, looking like she was trying to convince him of something.

He appeared to be pretty devastated, and she was comforting him like she felt bad about something.

I'll bet she fucking did.

Had they been together this whole time while she'd been fucking around with me?

And now she was going back to her old life.

Back to her routine, with her boring-ass boyfriend who probably had old man balls.

"What the fuck is going on here?" I barked, and they both startled.

Highlight of my day was seeing this motherfucker squirm as he took me in.

"What the hell are you doing?" Ruby narrowed her gaze at me, as I moved toward them like a goddamn stormtrooper on a mission.

"Who do we have here?" I said, my voice smooth and calm, even though I was ready to rip his head from his body. He wore a goddamn polo shirt and khaki pants, and his hair was cut short like he was in the military.

This was the dude she was going back to?

"Hey, I'm Dereck Hamilton," he said, and even his voice was pretentious. He had a slight East Coast Ivy League twang that made him seem like he was better than the rest of us. He extended his hand, and I stared down at it.

"Put your hand away, Professor."

He raised a brow, as if the man had never had anyone deny him anything.

And clearly, the woman I loved wasn't denying him either.

"River, you're being an ass."

"Oh, well, you didn't seem to have a problem with my ass over the last two months, did you?" I smirked.

Her cheeks flamed red, as if she couldn't believe I was saying it aloud.

Yeah, buckle up, Queenie. I'm just getting started.

Rage and anger and something foreign I wasn't used to coursed through my veins.

Maybe disappointment.

Hurt.

I wasn't sure, because the only way I knew how to respond was to hit back.

She'd wounded me, and I wasn't going down without fighting back.

Professor Douchebag looked at her like he wanted to swoop in and save her, and that only infuriated me more.

That wasn't his fucking job.

"Dereck." Ruby's voice cut through the anger buzzing in my ears, and a knife sliced me in the chest at the sound of her calling out to him, even while I stood here, clearly upset. "Can you go out to the bar? I'll be there in a few minutes."

"You sure you're okay?" Dereck asked, and my hands fisted.

"Is she okay? Are you fucking kidding me? Why don't you go pour yourself a nice glass of chardonnay and order a few more polo shirts on your phone, you pretentious prick."

The professor didn't even appear offended. He looked—disappointed, as if he couldn't believe I would speak to him that way.

He had no idea how ugly this could get.

"Oh my god, what is wrong with you?" Ruby grabbed my forearm and turned me to face her, as her boyfriend did what she told him to do and left the kitchen.

"What's wrong with *me*? What the fuck is wrong with *you*? Jesus. I'm an asshole, and even I wouldn't move on this quickly after all the time we've spent together."

She sighed, her eyes showing the hurt she rarely showed. "All right, River. Give me your best. What is it you think I've done wrong?"

Un-fucking-believable.

She was just going to let me give it to her and act as if she was innocent here?

"Oh, you'd like that, wouldn't you?" I leaned in close to her, my face just inches from hers. "Then you could leave Magnolia Falls feeling like the good guy and act like you had a valid reason for hating me."

"I don't hate you," she said as she met my gaze.

"Yeah. We're fine, right? You've got your boyfriend here, and you're moving the fuck on. And that's if anything you've ever told me was the fucking truth."

Her chin tipped up, eyes hardening now, preparing for battle. "What wasn't I truthful about?"

"Have you been with him this whole time? Does your boyfriend think you were here taking care of your father while you've been in my bed? And now you're jumping right back into his, huh? You've played me the whole fucking time." I spewed my anger, wanting to get a reaction out of her.

Needing a fucking reaction out of her.

But she was giving me nothing.

"Are you done?" she asked, as a tear ran down her cheek.

"I'm so fucking done." I stepped back, my finger pointing in her face. "I guess you got the last laugh. But at least you warned me, didn't you?"

"I warned you about what?" She swiped at her cheeks, and she glared at me.

"Rule number one. No catching feelings. I guess the evil queen was the only one still playing the game." I stepped back, my gaze locked with hers. "And don't let that sticky note go to your head. It didn't mean shit. Have a nice life."

"Fuck you, River," she said, anger radiating off her hot little body.

"Well, you've already done that. But I'm sure there are plenty of women out there who would like to take their shot and leave with me right now." I turned and walked out of the kitchen, and people were staring as if they'd heard the fight going on.

Evie was right there, waiting for me.

She reached for my hand and walked beside me toward the exit. I flipped the preppy professor the bird as I passed him, and he just sat there with his wineglass, gaping at me.

When I got to the door, I turned around and found those hazel eyes on me. They were sapphire blue tonight with gold rings around them.

Angry. Hurt. Confused.

Good. I hope she felt a little bit of the pain that I felt.

I needed her to feel something, or it meant that none of this was real.

"You okay?" Evie asked as I pushed through the door, and we made our way outside.

"I will be." I dropped her hand. "But I need to be alone right now. I appreciate you being there, though."

She nodded. "I know you do. I just didn't want you to walk out of there alone."

"Thanks." I held up a hand as I stepped back. "Take care, Evie."

I watched as her friends came walking out of the bar and told her they were heading to The Golden Goose to grab some food, and she fell in line beside them.

I pulled out my phone and opened the group chat and texted my boys.

I need you.

I knew that was all I had to say. When I got to my house, they were already there.

Ride or die.

32

Ruby

"Well, this was an interesting night," Dereck said, as I finished closing the bar. We were the last two people here, and I couldn't wait to get home, because I'd barely been holding it together the last few hours.

"I guess you could say that."

I reached for my keys and walked him through the kitchen to the back door. Thankfully, he had a rental car of his own, and I would finally be alone in my car as soon as I said my goodbyes.

He'd come all the way here to talk to me, and falling apart in front of him wouldn't be fair.

"Listen, Ruby, I know that scene earlier was upsetting." He cleared his throat and reached out to touch my shoulder when we stopped in front of our cars. He was a good guy, and I knew he felt bad for me after he'd witnessed River losing his shit on both me and him.

And unfortunately, River's words were embedded in my head. *And now you're jumping right back into his bed, huh?*

Rule number one. No catching feelings. I guess the evil queen was the only one still playing the game.

I couldn't wrap my head around the way that he'd reacted. I was planning to go talk to him about my decision after work tonight, now that I had spoken to both Dean Langston and Terrence. I saw this day going a whole lot differently than it had.

I also did not expect Dereck to show up in Magnolia Falls. I hadn't returned his calls over the last two days because I didn't know what I was going to do. I'd made the call to Dean Langston this morning and apologized for changing my mind, and Dereck had already been on his way here.

"I'm fine. You don't need to worry about me. It was sweet of you to come here," I said, but all I wanted at the moment was to get into my car and be alone.

"Well, I told you that it was for selfish reasons. I was worried that you hadn't signed the contract because of me. Obviously, I wanted you to come back. You earned that job, and sure, maybe a part of me was still holding out hope," he said, holding his hands up to stop me from interrupting. "That's on me. You made your feelings clear long before you left town. But that didn't stop me from hoping something would change when we spent some time apart. And now I know that it did."

"What do you mean?" I asked, as a slight breeze moved around us.

"That friend of yours, the one who came barreling into the kitchen tonight and made a scene," he said, as he sighed.

"He's hardly my friend at the moment."

"Ruby, you don't have to lie to me to protect my feelings. It actually makes sense why you don't want to leave."

"It has nothing to do with him."

At least it doesn't at the moment.

"Listen, the last thing I want to do is give you advice about another man. But that little scene back there was fueled by a whole lot of feelings. He was jealous and wounded; that much was easy to see."

"He behaved like a jackass, which shouldn't surprise me. He's hotheaded and stubborn and—ridiculous. I can't even believe that he just did that at my place of work." I threw my hands in the air.

Dereck smiled, and I saw the empathy in his eyes. "It's a bar, so it wasn't that out of place. And sometimes your feelings are so strong that you can't control them. I wish I could be that passionate when I needed to be."

"I much prefer a more subdued approach," I said, with a little chuckle, trying to shake off the heaviness of the evening.

"I don't think that's true." His gaze locked with mine. "There's something there, and we both know it. Hell, anyone with eyeballs could see that much. Don't find a reason to run from it just because things got ugly. Find out why he reacted that way. I've never seen you look so wounded either, so obviously, there's something deep here."

"I can't be with someone who flies off the handle at me when he has no idea what's going on. Who does that?"

"Someone who loves a woman more than anything else and thinks he's losing her," he said.

"Well, that's not how you show someone that you love them."

"There's no right or wrong way to show someone how you feel. The question is, do you feel the same way? That's the key." He looked away, and my chest squeezed. Because he'd actually professed his love to me in a mature, normal, caring way, and I'd rejected him.

"Dereck." I shook my head and squeezed his hand. "I'm so sorry if I hurt you. I didn't know that you were feeling that way. You caught me off guard when you told me."

"Don't ever apologize for being honest. I knew it was a long shot." He smirked. "I'm okay, Ruby. I've started dating again, and I've met someone that I've been spending a little time with. She wanted me to come here, too, and get the closure that she thought I needed. I didn't come here to guilt you or try to change your mind. I came here because I was afraid you were turning down the job because you were uncomfortable about working with me. We're friends, and I care about you. But now I know there's a much bigger reason that you didn't take that job. And it actually makes me very happy. I feared you'd never let yourself have it. You deserve happiness, so don't run from that."

I moved forward and wrapped my arms around him. "Thank you. It means a lot that you came here."

He hugged me tight before we both stepped back. "Are you going to be okay?"

"Of course. You know me. I'm always okay."

"I'm always here for you if you need a friend."

"Same. And I want to hear more about this new lady you've met. I'm happy for you. You should give her a chance, Dereck." I jangled my keys and took another step back. "Let's talk soon."

"Looking forward to it."

He waited until I got into my car, and I watched as he did the same, and he pulled out of the lot behind me. I drove a block toward my house and pulled over on the side of the road, put the car in park, and let it all out.

River thought that I'd been with Dereck the whole time. That I was . . . what? Sleeping with both of them? He thought I'd lied the whole time and basically accused me of being a complete asshole.

He is the asshole.

The tears started falling, and they didn't stop, and an unrecognizable sob left my throat. My chest ached. My stomach was twisting.

And I'd never felt so alone.

Like I'd just lost my best friend and the man I loved all in one swoop.

I'd never told a man that I loved him outside of my father, and I'd made a decision to stay here, and that decision had a lot to do with my feelings for River.

Magnolia Falls felt right for me.

But now, I wondered if I'd made a huge mistake.

Love was a bitch, and this was why you didn't give your heart away. Hell, I hadn't even told the man how I felt yet, and he'd already stomped on my heart.

The bastard.

I reached into my purse for some tissue, and my shoulders shook and quaked, and I remembered that time in the elevator when I'd broken down in front of River.

He'd been the one to comfort me.

That day and every day since.

And now I didn't have a clue where we stood.

The more I cried, the angrier I got. I would not allow any man to control my emotions like this.

I pulled the rearview mirror down and cleaned up my face, calmed my breathing, and let out a few deep breaths.

"You're fine. You're in control. You're stronger than this." I repeated those words over and over a few times until I started to believe them.

And then I put the mirror back in place and put the car in drive.

I was moving forward, and for now, River Pierce could kiss my ass.

* * *

It had been three days since my run-in with River at the bar, and my new job started tomorrow, so this was my last official day off. My father had taken over his shifts at the bar, and I was officially done at Whiskey Falls. My dad was absolutely thrilled that I was staying in Magnolia Falls.

I hadn't gone back to the bar, because I had no intention of speaking to River. I didn't know if he knew I was still in town, nor did I care at this point.

Well, that was a lie. I cared a little.

It was all I thought of, if I was being honest.

Dad was at the bar, and I was home alone. Demi, Saylor, and Peyton had all been texting me to see how I was, as they knew I'd decided to stay. I asked them not to share it when they'd all shown up at my house the morning after River had blasted me at the bar. They were equally pissed on my behalf and agreed he didn't deserve to know what my plans were at this point.

He clearly didn't trust me, and he obviously thought very little of me.

They were coming over here today with lunch to celebrate my last day off before I started the new job. It was sweet that they cared. I hadn't told my father anything about what happened with River, as I'd become a pro at hiding my feelings.

The knock on the door startled me from my thoughts, and I opened it to three smiling faces.

"Last day before the new job starts," Demi said, holding up a large bag from The Golden Goose and shaking it in front of me.

I hugged each one of them, and they came inside, setting up our food at the dining table.

"You look like hell. You can't hide from him forever, you know." Peyton pulled four bottles of water from the bag and passed them out.

"I'm not hiding from him. I just don't want to see him because I still have a strong desire to kick him in the balls," I admitted, and they all laughed.

Saylor handed us each a sandwich and a bag of chips, and we settled in our chairs.

"Romeo said River has been in a foul mood for days, and he's been at home sick." Demi unwrapped her turkey sandwich. She'd let me know that the night he'd left with Evie, nothing had happened, as he'd called the guys to come over right away.

But who knew what he was up to since then?

And why should I care?

I didn't. I don't. I won't. I refuse to give him any energy at this point.

"He's kind of always in a foul mood," Peyton said when she finished chewing.

"I've known him my whole life," Saylor said. "He's always been a big grump, but if it's any consolation, he was different with you."

"I agree. It still doesn't excuse what he did, but I think he acted out because he was jealous. And we still don't know what the hell the sticky note thing is about, right?" Demi asked.

"No idea. It's so him to tell me something on a sticky note and forget to give it to me. And then blame me for not knowing how he feels," I ranted. "And . . . and . . . he accused me of fucking Dereck and lying about my relationship. He's an even bigger asshole than I gave him credit for."

"Sometimes people act out when they're hurt. River doesn't let anyone in long enough to be hurt by them, but I think he was different with you." Saylor shrugged. "I'm not excusing what he did; I'm just trying to understand it."

"He doesn't get to have a meltdown and lose his shit on you and be excused. The man needs to grovel if he wants to be forgiven." Peyton raised a brow.

"He doesn't even know I'm here. He hasn't texted or called, so I don't think he cares. And frankly, neither do I," I lied, and they all looked at me sympathetically, like they didn't believe me.

And then Peyton took a swig of her water. "Good. Fuck River and his stupid sticky note and bullshit accusations."

"Wow. Tell us how you really feel," Demi said over her laughter.

"Hey, I did want to talk to you about something." Saylor dabbed her mouth with her napkin when she finished chewing. "I'm looking for a house, because I can't live with my brother much longer. He's hovering and acting like an overbearing parent. I know you want to move out of here and find a place. Would you want to be roommates?"

I'd never had a roommate. I'd lived with my father and had lived on my own ever since.

But something had changed in me since I'd come home. I didn't want to be alone all the time anymore.

My family no longer felt like the small circle it had always been.

"Yes. Let's do it. My lease is up on my apartment back in the city, and I've scheduled movers to bring everything back here, so I've got plenty of furniture to furnish a place."

"Really? Yay. This is great. I found a few cute little houses on the water, not too far from here. Two bedrooms, lots of charm." Saylor waggled her brows.

"This is so fun that you two will be living together. It'll be our new hangout," Peyton said.

"I can go look at a few places with you this weekend," I said.

"Perfect. I'll schedule some tours for us with my realtor. Just don't tell my brother yet. He'll start lecturing me about saving money. But I need my own space."

"If you need to make more money, you can have more hours at Magnolia Beans if you want. Until you get the bookstore open, we can use all the help," Demi said. She'd hired Saylor while she came up with her business plan to open the bookstore next to the coffee shop.

We made small talk for the next hour before they headed back to work. I looked online at the photos of the rentals

Saylor had sent me, so we could choose which ones to see this weekend.

I made my way to my bedroom to pick out my outfit for my first day of work tomorrow, and the unsigned contract was still lying on my desk.

I stared at it, hoping I hadn't made a huge mistake. Dean Langston hadn't taken the news all that well, and I doubted the door would be open for me there in the future.

I picked it up to tuck it into my desk drawer when a small yellow sticky note fell out. It must have been on one of the pages at the back of the contract. I picked it up off the floor and read it.

Or you could just stay here because I love you. Wild River.

My mouth fell open. Had he seriously proclaimed his love on a sticky note? Who does that?

River Pierce.

The man who never lets his guard down.

I knew he'd never told a woman that he loved them before.

So, even though this was the equivalent of breaking up with someone via text, it was a big move for River.

He'd told me that he loved me on a four-inch piece of paper that he stuck to a contract?

I was a weird mix of absolutely giddy and still fuming mad about the way he'd behaved with Dereck. He'd made it clear that he didn't trust me.

But at the same time, I knew River. And in a weird way, I believed that his little outburst was his way of baring his soul and showing me exactly how much he cared. He wasn't used to caring, and it made him feel vulnerable, and I truly believed that his ridiculous response was his knee-jerk reaction to feeling wounded.

But he sure as hell hadn't gone about it the right way. And I was not going to make excuses for him, nor make it easy for him.

I opened the group chat with the girls.

> I just solved the sticky note dilemma.
> He told me he loved me on a sticky note
> stuck to the back of the freaking contract.

SAYLOR

Swoon.

DEMI

It's kind of romantic.

PEYTON

Lame. He should have manned up and
told you to your face.

DEMI

True. But at least you know how he feels.
That's big for River.

> Well, calling me a cheating liar is low,
> even for him.

SAYLOR

You make some good points. But at
least we don't have to solve the mystery
anymore. And he did admit that he loves
you.

> LOVED ME. Past tense.

I knew he loved me. But he'd hurt me, and I'd yet to get an apology. He hadn't even reached out to try to make things right, regardless if he knew I was living here or not.

DEMI

Hey, love by sticky note might be the new thing. Like standing outside someone's window and telling them you love them. This is very modern, in a sweet way.

PEYTON

Pull your head out of your ass, lover girl. He needs to grovel. Apologize. And not on a sticky note. Face-to-face. Man to man.

SAYLOR

She's a woman.

Ummm . . . thank you?

Several memes and emojis followed, and I set my phone down, sat down on my bed, and stared at the sticky note.

I wanted to hate him.

But instead, I held that little piece of paper in my hand and pressed it to my chest. And I wished like hell that we could turn back time and do everything differently.

Because River Pierce loved me, and the truth was, I loved him, too.

33

River

The last few days had been a living hell. I'd come to learn that I actually did have a heart, but unfortunately, I hadn't realized it until it had been decimated.

Ruby Rose has torn me in two.

I'd had Cassie clear my schedule these last few days, and I'd told her I was sick, so the girl was having soup sent over daily from The Golden Goose. But I didn't have an appetite, and that was because I'd decided to get shitfaced every single day since I'd found Ruby with Professor Lame Ass.

Turns out, numbing yourself wasn't all that effective. There wasn't enough booze in the world to not feel this right now. I felt all of it.

Sadness. Hurt. Loneliness.

And for a diehard, content loner, this shit was pissing me off. I hated how quiet my house was now. There was no taunting or endless banter or sarcastic laughter.

No Queenie.

No life. No light. No joy.

I'd lived through some shit in my lifetime, but this was a different kind of darkness.

I'd shut everyone out, and I knew the guys were about done with it, because the last few texts were no longer check-ins. They were concerned.

Today was the first day I hadn't turned to the bottle the minute I'd woken up. I knew I couldn't wallow forever.

I sent a quick text to Cassie.

> Hey. Thanks for the soup, but I'm fine now, so you can stop sending over food. I'll be back at the office tomorrow. You can start rescheduling those clients that we canceled.

CASSIE

> Thanks, boss. I've got soup on the way right now. It's your favorite today, French onion.

I shook my head. Did she ever listen to anything I said? And what sick person on the planet wants a bowl of piping-hot French onion soup? I didn't respond, and I spent the next hour showering for the first time in a few days and getting dressed.

The doorbell rang, and when I opened it, Kingston stood there, holding the container of soup, spoon in hand, as he shoveled it into his mouth.

"This was on your doorstep, and I figured in your sad-sack mood, you wouldn't want French onion."

"Fuck off. You just helped yourself? Why are you here?"

"Because I'm your brother, and it's time to pull your head out of your ass." He followed me into the house and dropped to sit at the kitchen island, as he continued eating.

My meal.

"What if I was sick, and that was sent as the only nourishment I could get in my stomach?" I crossed my arms over my chest.

"I'd still eat it. You're a survivor. You could live off the land. Hell, you'd probably be one of those dudes who could survive on an island and live well. I'm more of a takeout, have-my-meals-made-for-me kind of guy. I like home-cooked meals and being pampered. And I had a few too many beers last night and thought maybe you'd massage my head for me?" He smirked. The annoying bastard was a needy little fucker.

"I'm the one who hasn't been feeling well. How about you massage my head?"

"You hate human touch. I thrive on it. Which brings me to my point." He shrugged before spoon-feeding himself several bites of soup.

"Are you going to fucking make it today?"

"Ah . . . always so impatient." He set the spoon down, letting it rest in the soup. "I came to tell you that I think we fucked up with the sticky note."

"No shit, Sherlock. You made me look like an asshole. I told her I loved her, and she sailed off into the sunset with the professor. Brilliant advice, you dick weasel." I walked to the refrigerator and poured myself a glass of juice.

Kingston chuckled. "I wasn't talking about you telling her you loved her being the bad idea. I'm talking about the fact that you did it on a sticky note. It wasn't the right way to go about it. Ruby isn't really the sticky note type of girl."

No. She's the heart-breaking kind of girl. The kind of girl who worms her way into your heart so deep that you can't breathe without her, and then she just walks away. Completely unscathed.

"Whatever. It was shit advice, and I don't want to talk about it."

"River," he said, his voice serious now. "Look at me."

299

"What?"

"You love her. Telling her was not a mistake."

"I'm over it. I like my life the way that it was. It was a mistake to get that close to her."

"I disagree," he said.

"Of course you do. It's your favorite thing to do," I hissed, going to the cabinet for some pain reliever. My fucking head was killing me. My chest had this dull ache that I couldn't shake. I popped two aspirin into my mouth and chased it down with some juice.

"I know you've been through a lot. I know that losing Mom and Dad the way we did was tough on you. I'm the lucky one, because I don't remember them the way that you do. But you, you remember everything. And you spent months in the hospital after the accident recovering, knowing that our parents were gone. I got off a whole lot easier," he said, catching me off guard with the conversation.

What the fuck is happening?

"Ignorance is bliss. It's not your fault." I cleared my throat.

"You've been really good to me, River. I mean, there is no brother that outshines you," he said, his eyes suddenly welling up with emotion.

"What the fuck are you talking about? Are you sick? Dying?"

He chuckled. "No. I'm worried about you. You're a good man. The best brother in the world. And you deserve to be happy. It's okay that you told Ruby that you love her. That's what life is about."

"Says the biggest playboy on the planet. You've never told a woman that you loved her." I tried to push the lump forming in my throat away and keep my tone light.

"Hey, I don't run from love. I just love a lot of women for a short period of time." He chuckled. "I don't close myself off the way you do, and that's because I haven't been hurt the

300

way that you have. But I've seen a difference in you since Ruby came to town."

I leaned against the kitchen island and crossed my feet at the ankles. "In what way?"

"You were happy. Lighter. Not so broody and angry." He shrugged. "She was good for you."

"And look how the fuck that turned out. It ended the way it started . . . explosive. I'm the one who didn't follow the rules. She was just playing a game."

"Come on, brother. Do you really think that? You know her. That's not who she is. She's as much a straight shooter as you are. She makes no apologies for who she is. She didn't suddenly change overnight."

In hindsight, I knew logically that was true. Hell, I knew who she was. But I didn't know what to fucking think anymore.

"Well, her boyfriend came to move her to the city. She never bothered to say goodbye. I'd say that was a pretty good sign that I was misreading things."

"Do we know that's true?"

"*Do we know that's true?* Were my fucking eyes lying? I saw them together in the kitchen. She's gone, and she never said a word to me after getting the note. So, yeah, we know it's true."

"How do you know she saw the sticky note?"

I groaned. "King, I love you, brother. I really do. But my head is pounding, and my heart—the one I didn't know was a viable organ in my body before Ruby came into my fucking life—is shattered. I can't talk about this anymore or make sense of it. It is what it is. It's over, and I have one more day to wallow in my fucking misery before I go back to work, and I'd like to do it alone."

He nodded, looked back down at his soup, and took a few more bites before pushing to his feet. He walked toward me, reached into his back pocket, pulled out a yellow sticky note, and placed it in my hand.

For fuck's sake.

This nightmare would never end. I glanced down and read it.

I just saw Ruby at Magnolia Beans. Apparently, she lives here now. Who's the best brother now?

"What are you talking about? Didn't she already start her new job at the university? And why the fuck did you write this on a sticky note?"

"I thought sticky notes were your new love language." He shrugged before answering the other questions. "Yes. She started her new job. She works at Fresh Start. She and Saylor are looking for a house to rent. Lots of shit has been going down while you've been wallowing, brother." He shook his head. "Apparently, the girls knew, but Ruby didn't want them to tell anyone. Romeo eventually figured it out and told us this morning, and then I saw her with my own eyes today."

My mind was reeling. I couldn't make sense of it. "How do you know she's working at Fresh Start?"

"Well, for starters, I didn't ask her on a one-sided sticky note. I ran into her. Asked what she was doing there. And she told me she took a job at Fresh Start and that she and Saylor had been looking at homes to rent."

"Her boyfriend was here. I didn't make that up. This makes no sense." I paced around the kitchen, feeling the slightest bit of life coming back to me now.

"Funny you should mention that. I also asked her about Professor Preppy Pants, and she said he'd come to make sure she hadn't turned down the job because of him. They're friends. He was checking on her."

Fuck.

Fuck me.

"Oh."

"Yeah, *oh*, dipshit. You really fucked this one up."

"So, she never signed the contract?"

"Apparently not, but I do believe she's since found said sticky note," he said, moving to the pantry and pulling out a box of cookies.

"How do you know? She told you?"

"Well, I know we shouldn't assume, but she asked me to give you this when I said I was heading over here to see you." He reached into his back pocket again and pulled out another sticky note.

He handed it to me, and I looked down to read it.

You loved me enough to write it on a sticky note, but you didn't trust me enough to talk to me. 🖐

I let out a long breath and ran a hand through my hair. "I guess I read that situation wrong."

"You think? People reading has never been your strength. You're too quick to think the worst. I, on the other hand, am very good at *the reading of the people.*" He popped a chocolate chip cookie into his mouth.

"Oh, yeah? The fucking sticky note was your idea." I stared down at her note, wondering what the hell to make of it. Did she hate me now?

I'd basically accused her of sleeping with the professor.

Of lying to me the whole time we'd been together.

Of jumping from my bed to his.

"Hey, now. We can't win 'em all. But I have a good track record."

"And what the fuck do I do now, genius?"

He finished chewing, and a wide grin spread across his face as he glanced down at his phone, reading a text when his phone vibrated. "The guys are waiting for us to meet them at Romeo's ranch so we can put our heads together and figure this shit out."

"I thought Nash and Romeo were at work. And doesn't Hayes work at the firehouse today?"

"Ride or die, dicklicker. I called them on my way over here.

303

LAURA PAVLOV

I told them that our boy had fucked up royally, and we needed to help him get his queen back. This calls for all men on deck. Go get your shoes on, assmuncher. We need to get going."

I nodded and started walking before turning around, my gaze finding Kingston's. "Thanks for what you said earlier. I'm glad you don't remember much. All I've ever wanted was for you to be happy."

"How about we both give that a try, huh?"

I nodded. "Yep. Not sure I can repair things at this point, but I'll go and hear everyone out."

I hurried down the hall and slipped on my shoes, my mind still reeling.

Ruby lived here now.

She hadn't left me for the professor.

She hadn't left me at all. But she also hadn't told me about her change of plans, which meant she was pissed at me. Possibly hated me.

I owed her a lot more than I'd given her.

I had no idea if it was too late to fix the damage I'd caused, but I needed to try.

Kingston was at the door, holding his keys in his hand. "Let's go."

I followed him out, and a yellow sticky note stuck to the door caught my eye.

Love you, brother.

My chest squeezed.

Maybe sticky notes *were* my new fucking love language.

34

Ruby

"Hello?" I called out when I got to the barn at Demi and Romeo's ranch house. She had texted me and asked me to meet her out here, because she wanted to show me the progress they were making.

"Please don't be mad at me." Demi winced as she came striding toward me, with Romeo and all the guys behind her. My eyes locked immediately with River's, who was watching me the way he always did.

Unbelievable.

"What is this?"

"Romeo clearly can't keep a secret, and honestly, Ruby, you can't avoid him forever." She squeezed my hand when she moved in front of me, apology written all over her face.

"I wasn't avoiding anyone. He's the one who called me a liar and behaved like a petulant child. He could come find me anytime he wanted."

"*He* didn't know you were here," River said, closing the distance between us.

"So, if I didn't live here, the apology would never come?" I crossed my arms over my chest and glared at him. Demi and the guys took a few steps back, and she gave me an awkward wave before they all hurried out of the half-built barn.

I turned my attention back to River, who was looking ridiculously sexy with his disheveled hair and his biceps straining against his black tee. I saw the exhaustion in his eyes, and my instinct was to throw myself into his arms.

I will not forget that this man accused me of horrible things. He doesn't trust me, and that's unacceptable. If we have any chance of moving forward, he's got to understand that, so this shit doesn't ever happen again.

"Well, if you didn't live here, I wouldn't have known you weren't with the professor. That what I saw that night wasn't true. That I misread the situation."

"You misread the situation? That's what you have to say?" I questioned, because this was far from an apology.

"Queenie." His voice broke, and my chest squeezed at how vulnerable he sounded. "I've never felt this way before. I fucked up, and I don't know what to do about it."

"Did you honestly believe that I was back together with him and that I'd played you the whole time? I mean, how can you say that you love me and then think I would do that?" A lump formed in my throat as I looked up at him.

He scrubbed a hand down his face. "I'm an asshole."

"Seriously? I mean, it's been days. You never reached out to apologize. If I had moved, you just would have never talked to me again?"

"Of course not. I would have wallowed for a few days and then pulled my shit together. I was hurt. I was freaked out that I'd told you that I loved you and you hadn't responded."

I knew he was trying, but he couldn't react like this every time he misread a situation.

"River. You told me you loved me on a sticky note. One that you stuck to the back of a contract. What if I hadn't ever found it?"

"I'm not good at this, Ruby." He moved closer, reaching for my hands and taking them in his. "I know I fucked up."

I let out a long breath. "Your friends dragged you here. You didn't come on your own. You need to figure your shit out. I'm scared, too. And you hurt me. A lot."

"Well, I didn't see you coming to my door to explain things."

I tugged my hands away. "That's because you didn't give me a chance. I was planning to come talk to you that night, but instead, you showed up at the bar acting like a lunatic. I'd just accepted the position at Fresh Start, and I was excited to tell you. Nervous that maybe you didn't feel the same way about me, but I was still willing to put myself out there. Do you know how it made me feel that you thought I was lying the whole time we were together? And still, here we are, with your friends dragging you to talk to me. That's not good enough. None of this is good enough. And I'm tired of settling. Figure your shit out, and after you do, then come and find me." I stormed away. This was not the apology I wanted. A future was built on trust, and if we didn't have that, there was no point.

"Me not trusting you had a lot more to do with me than you," he said. I was surprised by the admission, and I came to a stop.

"Agreed."

"I'm not used to putting faith in other people, and the way I feel about you—it scares the shit out of me."

"Well, then, I guess you better figure out what you want to do about that. Because this—" I shrugged, "—isn't good enough. Next time you come talk to me, come because you want to. Come because you know what you want."

And I strode out of the barn, leaving him standing there.

Along with half of my heart.

As much as it hurt, I knew I'd done the right thing. I knew who River was, and I had faith that he would figure it out.

That we would figure it out.

I wasn't taking a risk on a man who wasn't willing to fight for me. To apologize when he was wrong. And look me in the eye and tell me that he loves me.

When I fell into bed a few hours later, I cried myself to sleep, just as I did the next several nights.

Yeah, apparently, that was my new thing.

I cried daily now.

I hadn't heard from River, and I missed him terribly.

A part of me worried that maybe we were both incapable of love.

Two broken people who were better off on their own.

I needed to know that River wanted this.

Wanted *me*.

I parked in the employee spot that Terrence had appointed as mine, and I made my way inside the building.

Jenna was sitting behind the front desk, whispering to Terrence, when I walked up and said hello. They both looked at me with weird smiles on their faces, and I brushed at my cheeks and my mouth. "Do I have food on my face or something? Why are you looking at me like that?"

"What?" Terrence asked. "No. I don't see anything. I don't know what you mean."

"Me either." Jenna chuckled.

I narrowed my gaze at both of them and walked down the hallway leading to my office. When I pushed my door open, my eyes widened. The wall behind my desk was covered from the ceiling to the floor in little yellow sticky notes. It looked like wallpaper the way every single inch of space was covered in yellow paper with handwritten notes on each one. I dropped my purse onto my desk beside a gigantic floral arrangement and walked to the wall, taking my time to read each one.

I'm sorry.

Every fifth or sixth note said those two little words. My

eyes scanned the space, taking in the other messages. There were too many to count.

I love you.

Why is it bad to tell someone that you love them on a sticky note?

I should have told you how much I love you at the barn.

I want to make this up to you.

Sorry for accusing you about the preppy professor.

I'm an asshole.

A wild river.

I miss you.

I miss you so much I can't fucking function.

Queenie, please forgive me.

I know what I want.

I want you. Only you. Always you.

The sentiment went on and on as I bent down to read the messages on the lower half of the wall.

The sound of a throat clearing from behind me had me whipping around. Terrence stood in my doorway with a wicked grin on his face. "Apparently, this is the new way to grovel?"

"Did you know about this?" I asked.

"He asked if he could come in after we closed last night, so I stayed here and let him do his thing."

"That was nice of you."

"I got to meet Beefcake. He was really giving River a hard time for messing things up with you."

I nodded, pushing back the tears. I loved this man, but he'd hurt me. I'd never been good at forgiving people, but I was so happy that he'd come, so maybe I was changing.

"He's the coolest kid around."

"Agreed," Terrence said, taking a step back. "I think anyone that goes to this much trouble to apologize deserves to at least be heard out. He said to tell you to read the card on the flowers when you're done with the sticky note wall."

I heard him laughing as he pulled my door closed and left.

The vase sitting on my desk was filled with what must be three dozen red roses, and I reached for the card.

Queenie. Please meet me at the cove tonight after work. I just want to talk to you. River

I sighed and dropped to sit down as my phone started vibrating.

DEMI

Are you at work yet? I heard you were getting quite the surprise this morning.

SAYLOR

I love surprises. What is it?

PEYTON

I hope it's a naked man with a giant penis.

PEYTON

Or waffles with fresh bananas would be a close second.

I stood back and took a screenshot of the flowers and the wall covered in sticky notes.

SAYLOR

My heart just exploded. Holy swoons! That is so romantic.

PEYTON

It's so sweet, but kind of in a serial killer sort of way. But I'm here for it.

DEMI

I think it's amazing.

So, do we think I should meet him at the cove tonight and hear him out?

DEMI

YES! You asked him to figure his shit out, and I believe that's what he's been doing.

SAYLOR

Agreed. His first apology wasn't impressive. Let's see what he does today.

PEYTON

Hear him out, but make him grovel. And I mean, really grovel.

I can do that. I'm the queen of enforcing the grovel. 😊

I tried to focus the rest of the day, but my mind was on River.

My phone rang just as I was getting ready to leave so I could run home and change clothes before taking the kayak out. He hadn't told me a time, so I just planned to go when I got home.

My mom's face lit up my screen, and I didn't even cringe the way I normally did. It hit me in that moment that I'd come a long way. So had my brothers. Things were so much better with my family now—and my mom was the only one left who hadn't changed at all.

And I doubted she ever would.

But I'd changed the way I responded to her, and I would continue to do that for my own sanity.

"Hello," I said, as I reached for my keys and grabbed my purse.

"Hey." Her voice was sulky and sad. "Where are you?"

"I'm just leaving the office and heading home."

"I'm out of cigarettes and beer, and I just don't have the energy to go pick them up. I need you to stop by the store on your way and just drop them off."

I let Wendy's words sink in and calmly responded. "That doesn't work for me."

"You live here now, so being long distance is not an excuse that works anymore," she said, her tone harsh with resentment and attitude.

"Agreed. So, we'll have to set some new boundaries now that I'm living here full time. Running to get you smokes and booze after I worked a full day is not something I have time to do, nor am I willing to pay for them. I offered to help with your rent, and even though my pay is not as much as it would have been if I'd taken the job at the university, I will stay true to my word and honor our agreement for three months until you pick up more shifts and get on your feet. That is what I have to offer you."

She was quiet on the other end, and I walked toward the elevators, waving at Jenna as I passed her desk.

"Fine. Then I'll ask your brothers. Are you fine with putting this on them?" She sounded smug, and it annoyed the hell out of me.

"Sure. They're grown men. They'll eventually get sick of it and tell you no. You could also get out of bed and go get it yourself and stop dragging everyone down with you."

"Right, as if that ever worked with you. You're so high and mighty with your fancy education and your big job. You think you're better than me—" Wendy went on with other insults just like she normally did. Something about being my mother, respecting my elders, and all the psycho tricks she'd been pulling for years.

A maniacal laugh left my mouth as the elevator doors opened. "You say it like it's a negative thing that I've worked hard at school and secured a great job for myself. I'm not engaging in this conversation. You've got three months to start paying your own rent. My offer still stands if you'd like to have dinner next week and catch up." I was trying to change the dynamic of our relationship, so it wasn't me always going over there and helping her. I wanted to try to have a normal relationship to some extent, but I was going to be okay either way. I didn't have any expectations where my mother was concerned.

"I would like that," she said, surprising me.

"Great. I'm in an elevator, and I'm going to lose the call. I'll text you tomorrow and we can pick a day to meet. Have a good night."

"Yeah, you, too," she said, sounding caught off guard by the conversation.

It hadn't gotten heated. I hadn't reacted to any of it, and it felt damn good.

I ended the call and leaned against the wall of the elevator and smiled.

Things were coming together.

My heart wasn't aching the way it had been the last week, because I knew we were going to figure this out.

I'd make him grovel, but I already knew the outcome.

I missed him terribly.

I loved him.

I wanted to hear him say it. Wanted to hear him apologize, *really* apologize for being a complete jackass about Dereck.

But I knew he was a good man.

I knew he was the only man who'd ever own my heart, so there was no other option than to fix this.

Because nothing worked without him.

I hurried home and changed into a tank top and a pair of jean shorts before climbing into my kayak. It was completely dark out by the time I was out on the water, and I had only the moonlight to lead me to the cove. I could get here in my sleep, though, so it wasn't a problem. It was even more peaceful at night.

The sound of the birds rustling in the trees above and the light breeze bustling around me calmed me.

It didn't stop the butterflies fluttering in my belly, though.

I wasn't fighting it anymore. I'd never been that girl that got all fluttery around a guy. But River Pierce gave me all the flutters.

My Wild River.

Even when I was angry as hell at him, it didn't matter.

I still loved him.

As I came around the corner, I gasped when I saw the area lit up in little white twinkle lights. There were lights on the trees and bushes, and I could see River sitting on the shore, his kayak tied to the old, weathered dock there. I glided through the water, my heart beating so fast it pounded in my ears.

"You came," he said.

"That's what she said." I chuckled because I couldn't help myself.

He walked toward me, not caring that the bottoms of his jeans were getting soaked as he stepped into the water, and he laughed. He reached for the front of my kayak and tugged it over to the dock, tying it off beside his. He offered me a hand and helped me out.

"How long have you been here?" I asked.

"Pretty much all day. I was setting this up, and I didn't want to miss you, so I just stayed and waited. Hoping you'd come." He guided me over to a blanket, and we both sat down. There were a few lanterns with candles.

"You know when I told you to figure your shit out, that didn't mean that you had to cover my office wall in sticky notes and light up all these trees and bushes. You could have just come and talked to me."

He rubbed a hand over his jaw and nodded. "I'm not used to caring this much. I fucked up, and I want to fix it. I *need* to fix it. And I was stunned that you'd decided to stay that day I saw you at the barn. Stunned that I'd been such a fool about the way I'd handled things. I didn't know what to say, so I managed to make things worse."

"You didn't make things worse, you just—didn't make them better." I shrugged. "You said some awful things. Some pretty unforgivable things."

"Yep. I was an asshole. I saw that preppy fucker and lost my shit. Jumped to conclusions." He cleared his throat. "I'm not even sure why I did it, except that I was scared. I thought I'd lost you, and—God, I'm sorry, Queenie. I'm so fucking sorry."

I listened, taking in his words. "I get that. But what does that mean now? We're both scared, River. That's not going to change just because I live here now."

"I'll tell you what's changed." He cleared his throat. "I love you, Ruby. I love you in a way I never knew I was capable of. And I will fight for you, for us, every fucking day. That's what's changed. I realized these last few days that I was never afraid of loving you. It was losing you that scared the shit out of me."

The lump in my throat was so thick it was difficult to speak. "I love you, and I understand being afraid because I'm afraid, too. But we need to have some ground rules if we want to move forward. If we want this to work."

"I want that. Tell me your terms," he said, a wickedly sexy smirk on his handsome face.

"For starters, no more accusations. We're both straight shooters, so how about we just talk things out?"

He nodded. "I can do that."

"No more tantrums or meltdowns. If you're bothered by something, just tell me."

He shrugged. "Done. What's next?"

I tried not to laugh because he was so intense and serious at the moment. It took everything I had not to climb into his lap. I'd missed him. Missed everything about him. "No more sticky note communications. If you feel a certain way, just tell me. And I'll do the same."

"But that whole wall of sticky notes was impressive as shit, wasn't it? Even Beefcake was impressed. He asked Nash if he could have a sticky note wall in his bedroom, and he wants notes from all his favorite girls, including you."

I tipped my head up to look at the moon and chuckled. "He's six. It makes a lot more sense for a six-year-old to communicate via sticky note."

"Okay. No more sticky notes. Although you did a fabulous job telling me I was an asshole on the sticky note you sent over with King."

"It seemed fitting at the time." I turned my head to look at him, his dark gaze locking with mine.

"Well, I sort of did something drastic because I really wanted to win you back after my lame attempt at an apology the other day. But now I realize I might have fucked up again because you just made this new *we-have-to-talk-everything-out* rule."

I cocked my head to the side. "You covered my wall in little yellow papers and lit up this entire area in twinkle lights. What could be more drastic?"

He reached a hand over his shoulder and grabbed a handful of his tee before tugging it over his head. A large bandage covered his chest, and my eyes widened as he peeled it back. The word *Queenie* was inked there.

"You're permanently on my heart, because it belongs to you, Ruby. I don't know how it happened, but I fucking love you. I want you with me always. So, I put you right here, where I can keep you forever."

My teeth sank into my bottom lip as a tear slipped down my cheek. "We can make an addendum to that rule about having to talk everything through. Ink is different."

"Yeah? You like it?"

"I like it," I whispered, pushing up on my knees and gently tracing a finger around the surrounding area. "I love you, River Pierce."

"Is that so?" His voice was smooth and sexy as he covered his tattoo with the bandage and pulled me against his chest.

I tipped my head up and smiled. "It is."

"I love you. I'm sorry I fucked everything up. I was going out of my mind. I didn't want you to leave, and I didn't know how to say it. How to tell you how I felt. And lashing out at the professor came more naturally to me."

I laughed as the light breeze moved around us before I mimicked his words back to him. "Is that so?"

"It is." He pushed the hair away from my face and tucked it behind my ear. "You're so fucking beautiful, Ruby. And I'm probably going to fuck things up a lot, but I'm going to try hard not to."

"I don't expect you not to mess up. I'm sure I'll mess up plenty, too. But we just need to talk about things as they come up."

"Speaking of things coming up," he teased, thrusting against me, and I felt just how much he'd missed me.

How much he wanted me.

And I couldn't remember a time I'd ever been happier or more content.

Right here. Right now.

With this man.

35

River

Ruby and I were insatiable after being apart for a week. We'd had sex down by the water, back at my house two more times, and now she'd convinced me to take a bath with her.

Apparently, relationships were all about compromise. I wouldn't know because I'd never had one.

But there wasn't anything I wouldn't do for this woman, and that included soaking in a bowl of unusually hot water. It meant that her naked body was pressed against mine.

That made it a win.

"So, we've established some new ground rules," I said, as her back was pressed to my chest, careful not to rest it against the bandage, and our fingers were intertwined on one hand. The bathroom was dark, aside from the two candles she'd lit. The candlelight flickered against the walls, and I couldn't remember a time I'd ever felt this content.

"Yep. I think we can both live with those terms." Her voice was all tease. "Do you have anything to add?"

"Is it too soon to ask you to move in with me?"

Her body stiffened, and then she pulled some sort of mermaid move and flipped over onto her stomach so she could look at me. Her eyes scanned the bandage that we'd covered with a waterproof strip on top and then looked up at me.

"It's not too soon. I don't think there's a time limit on when it's appropriate to love someone." She put her finger to my lips when I started to speak like I'd won this one. "However, your little stunt last week left me uncertain about where we stood. I've agreed to move in with Saylor, and I actually think it's good for you and me to find our footing together and have our own places while we do that."

"So, basically, if I annoy you, you have a safe house?" I barked out a laugh.

"I didn't think of it like that, but yes, it gives us time to get used to this. We've both never had a relationship that was this . . ." She paused to think about it.

"Awesome. Amazing," I said.

"Intense." She smirked. "These feelings are new for both of us. So how about we keep doing what we were doing? We can spend our nights together, but sometimes we can be here and other times at my new place."

"All right. I can live with that. And when you're ready, you can move in here." I stroked the hair away from her gorgeous face.

"Deal."

"How do you feel about marriage and kids?" I asked before I could stop the words from leaving my mouth.

Where the fuck did that come from?

"Wow. I can't believe you didn't ask me this on a sticky note." Her lips turned up in the corners, and my fucking chest ached at just the sight of her. "I never thought either were for me, but I also never thought I'd tell a man outside of my father that I loved him. Never thought I'd want to move in

320

with a man or spend every night with him. So, I'm open to negotiations when the time comes. How about you?"

"Same. Never thought about either, and I'm definitely not there yet, but I can see it. I think about it. That last day you woke up in my bed, I just watched you sleep, and all these thoughts were flooding my mind."

"That would normally be super creepy, but I can't lie and say I haven't watched you sleep many times. You look so peaceful when you sleep, and it's the one time you aren't aggravating me." She chuckled.

"I like aggravating you, Queenie. I want to spend the rest of my life aggravating you."

"Well, you did go all in on the tattoo. I think you're kind of stuck with me now."

"I hope so," I said, tugging her mouth down to mine and kissing her hard.

Kissing her like she was mine.

* * *

"You think you two will get married someday?" Cutler asked, as he held Ruby's hand in his, and the three of us walked toward the barn together on Demi's parents' property.

This was where they came to ride every Saturday. It was one of the most beautiful places in Magnolia Falls, and where Romeo wanted to ask Demi to marry him.

"I'd ask her today if I thought she'd say yes," I said, and she shook her head with a big smile on her face.

"I think it'll happen, and I can't imagine there being a day that if he asked, I wouldn't say yes." She raised a brow as if she'd had the better answer.

"Well, today is about Uncle Ro and Beans." I saw the group standing near the barn.

We'd been surprised that Romeo wanted everyone here

when he proposed, because he was a fairly private guy. But he knew his girl would want all the people she loved to be there, and that was what he'd wanted for her.

That was what you did when you loved someone. I used to give him shit, but now I got it. I understood it.

Nash came jogging up beside us, scooping up his son in one swift move. He held up the ring Romeo had left in his glove box. "Got it. And we're cutting it close. He just texted that they are on their way back from their ride. We need to get everyone in the back room at the barn."

Ruby, Peyton, Saylor, and Demi's mom and grandmother had been decorating that back room all morning with Romeo. Ruby said it looked like something out of a movie.

Turns out, me and my boys were romantic as shit.

Never would have guessed it, but I'd been the one putting up a wall of sticky notes a few weeks ago, so you never know what you'll do when you find that one person who makes you feel whole.

Ruby Rose had taken all my broken pieces and put me back together without even trying. Just by breathing. Existing.

We started jogging toward the barn, Cutler all laughs as we hustled everyone into the back room.

"Hey, River," Slade, Demi's brother, said. It was the first time I'd seen him in years, and I'd spent a lot of time hating this dude, but today, I was going to give him a chance. He'd put in the work, and he was coming to live in Magnolia Falls in a couple of months, and I was ready to put the past in my rearview.

Maybe it was because I had something I was looking forward to.

A future with this woman beside me.

With these people surrounding me.

"Hi. I'm glad you made it. Romeo really wanted you here, and I know your sister will be happy to see you." I shook his hand and looked up to see his mom watching us with watery eyes.

Demi's father was there, standing in the back corner, looking like an outsider. I still had my issues with the man after all he'd done to me and Romeo, but I was trying to get over that because of Demi. Even she hadn't made a lot of progress in their relationship, and he and Demi's mom were still separated, but he was here.

He'd shown up.

And sometimes that was all that mattered.

Showing up for the people you love. The rest would work itself out.

I nodded at Demi's father, and he smiled in return.

Well, I was trying.

Everyone was making their rounds and saying hello, and Brinkley and Lincoln had flown in and made it just in time. Lionel hugged us both before attaching himself to Lincoln because he was a big football fan. Nash and Cutler went to say hello to a few people as Kingston strolled over our way.

"Well, look at you two. You're glowing, brother." He smirked, the cocky little fucker.

"And you're so full of shit your eyes are brown." I loved to dish it back to him.

His head fell back in laughter, and a few of the ladies shushed him, but he didn't care.

"I guess I was born full of shit, then?"

"I think what he meant to say was *thank you*," Ruby said, wrapping her arms around my brother. I loved how close they were. Kingston and I didn't have a lot of family, with Grammie being our last living relative that we knew of. But we'd found our extended family here. Most of them being right in this room with us.

"Oh, I have something for you." Kingston reached into his pocket and pulled out two sticky notes, because he was a wiseass and never missed an opportunity to fuck with me.

He handed Ruby hers first, and she looked down before reading it aloud. *"You look beautiful today, Queen Ruby."* She shook her head and smiled. "You wrote this before you saw me."

"What can I say? I can see the future. I knew you'd show up here in your pretty gray sundress, looking like a vision."

"Are you done flirting with my girl, asshole?"

He handed me a sticky note, and I looked down and read it to both of them. *"Grammie needs more flowers for her garden. Stop slacking on the job, you sack of shit."*

I glared at him as he used his hand to cover his laughter. "Demi's mom is calling me over. I'll be right back. Hey, flip that note over, brother. There's more on the back."

He walked away, and Ruby glanced over, and we read it together.

Happiness looks good on you, brother. And yes, I'm telling you that I love you on a sticky note.

"This sticky note thing has taken on a life of its own," Ruby whispered as she leaned against me. "But he's right. Happiness looks good on you."

"Yeah? I can live with that, I guess. I just don't want to tarnish my reputation for being an asshole."

"Your reputation is still solid; don't you worry about it."

Hayes, Nash, Cutler, and Kingston all walked over, with Peyton and Saylor right behind them, just as Lincoln and Brinkley hurried over to us.

"Okay, Romeo said they are two minutes out," Nash said, making sure they all heard him. Everyone stopped talking, and I glanced around the space. They'd covered it in those lights I'd used a few weeks ago when I'd tried to impress Ruby. There were hay bales and buckets of flowers all around. We were having dinner after this out on their property.

Voices came from the other side of the door, and Cutler's eyes widened, and I waggled my brows at him. He used his chubby little hand to cover his mouth, and Nash raised a brow in warning to keep it quiet.

Demi was laughing, and Ruby found my hand, knowing they were close.

"I think dinner's probably ready. Why do you want to go in here?" Demi said as the door started to slide open.

"I have a surprise for you, baby," Romeo said, and Peyton held up her fingers like she'd warned us she would in the three hundred fucking texts she'd sent about how this would go down.

When she held up the third finger, we all shouted, "Surprise!"

Demi startled, Romeo laughed, and everyone cheered. Demi's gaze moved around the group, and her eyes were wide as they stopped on her brother. She ran toward him and threw herself into his arms. "What are you doing here?"

"You're about to find out," Slade said as he set her back down on her feet.

Romeo was right there when she turned around. The romantic fucker had dropped down on one knee.

Damn, the dude was smooth.

"Oh my god," she whispered. "What are you doing?"

Nash must have slipped him the ring already because he pulled it from his pocket and held it in his hand. "You know I'm a man of few words, so I'll keep it short."

Everyone chuckled, and I glanced over to see Lincoln, Brinkley, and Tia standing beside Romeo's mom and grandmother, and they were all smiling.

"I love you, Demi. I love you so much it hurts sometimes. But you know I can take pain like a champ." His voice was all tease, and everyone laughed, including Demi, who decided to take that moment to drop down on her knees in front of him.

"Baby, I'm kind of doing my thing. What are you doing down here?" he asked, and everyone was smiling at them.

"I want to be close to you." She swiped at the tears running down her face, and I turned to look at Ruby, who was crying just as hard.

This strong woman, who could handle just about anything, had a tender heart beneath it all. Something I'd come to recognize and cherish.

My woman was strong and brave and caring and sensitive all at the same time.

And I fucking loved it.

I wrapped an arm around her shoulders, and she leaned into me, like she couldn't get close enough.

"I want to wake up with you every day and fall asleep with you every night and build our home together that we'll fill with lots of kids when you're ready. Will you marry me, baby?"

Demi threw her arms around Romeo's neck and hugged him as she shouted out a very clear *yes,* and everyone whistled and hollered. He slipped the ring onto her finger and pulled her to her feet before tipping her head back and kissing her.

I found Ruby's hand as we all made our way out of the barn and took our time congratulating them, before going to the back of the house to eat. Ruby took that moment to tug me away from the group, leading me down a little trail.

"This is where we ride when I come out here on the weekends. Look at that view." She stood beside me as we looked out at the turquoise water in the distance.

I looked down at her wearing her pretty gray sundress with her long, dark hair tumbling down her shoulders and back. My gaze locked with hers. "I like this view, looking at you, best of all."

"You don't think you'll tire of it?" she teased.

"I promised you forever, and I'm a man of my word."

"I'm going to hold you to it." She pushed up on her tiptoes and kissed me.

And I knew in that moment that forever would never be long enough with Ruby.

But I'd take what I could get.

Epilogue

Ruby

Fall was here, and I was enjoying every second of it. It was my favorite time of year, seeing the leaves change and enjoying the cooler weather. The town was festive, with pumpkins and hay bales everywhere you turned.

We were all going trick-or-treating with Cutler. He was the coolest kid I'd ever met, and if I were guaranteed to have a kid like Cutler Heart, I'd probably sign on to have a dozen.

River and I talked about the future often now. It was something I'd never done in the past. But now, I enjoyed looking forward. Dreaming about things I never thought I'd want.

I guess love had a way of changing things. It had for me.

Being loved by River Pierce had exposed a new side of me.

I cried when I was sad, and I cried when I was happy.

I didn't shame myself for feeling things. I didn't try to be stoic when something hurt me. I talked about it, and my boyfriend . . . well, he threatened to beat up anyone who hurt me. And then we talked some more until we both felt better.

At the end of the day, for the first time in my life, I didn't feel like I was going through the motions.

I was living.

It didn't hurt that my roommate was an avid romance reader, and I'd found this whole new world that I loved escaping to. Turns out that I'm a big, sappy romantic deep down.

Saylor couldn't wait to get her bookstore open, and me, Demi, and Peyton were her biggest cheerleaders.

That was another thing that I'd found being back in Magnolia Falls.

Girlfriends.

Something I'd never had before, and now, I couldn't imagine my life without them. Women lifting other women up—it was powerful.

My father was making so much progress, eating healthy and taking much better care of himself. I loved that I got to see him almost every day, now that I was living back in Magnolia Falls, and he came and had dinner with River and me every Sunday.

It didn't hurt that my brothers were thriving. They were both holding down jobs and finally living on their own, and they'd yet to miss a rent payment. I saw them often and they didn't only come to me when they needed me. Although, they came to me for advice every now and then, and I would be lying if I didn't admit that I liked it.

My mom and I were a work in progress, and I was okay with that. We'd had lunch twice now, and though we still had a ways to go, it was better than it had been in a very long time.

I never thought I'd say this, but life was good.

Really good.

We walked house to house, as Cutler ran up and rang the bell and then did the most adorable happy dance each time he got more candy.

We all had our Magnolia Beans cups filled with warm pumpkin goodness as we walked street after street, because this kid was not going to miss one house if he had anything to say about it.

"Thank God this is the last house," River whispered in my ear.

"Stop being ridiculous. He's loving it."

"You know what I love? This costume you're wearing." He nipped at my ear, and I chuckled.

"I'm wearing black jeans, a black sweater, and a crown. It's not much of a costume," I said.

"What can I say? My evil queen turns me on," he said.

"And what are you supposed to be?" I raised a brow because he was wearing jeans and a sweater.

"I'm a lawyer."

I smiled. "It's not a very lawyerly outfit."

"Damn straight. If I ever start looking lawyerly, you better smack me upside the head."

"You can count on it." We walked up the walkway to Nash's house, and Cutler sprinted into the kitchen to start going through his candy.

"I ordered pizzas. They'll be here in thirty minutes," Nash said, as we settled on the big L-shaped couch in his family room.

"Thanks, I'm starving," Kingston said, as he dropped to sit beside me.

"It's a big week." Demi sat between Romeo and Saylor. "Construction starts on the bookstore on Monday."

"I'm so excited about it. And with me working at the coffee shop, and the bookstore being right next door, I can be watching the progress in real time," Saylor said.

"You sure you can make a living doing this?" Hayes took a pull from his beer and settled his gaze on his little sister.

He'd worried when she'd moved into her own place and was grateful that I was rooming with her so she wouldn't be alone. But the guy worried about her a lot. I got it, because I had always been that way with my brothers. But I knew this was different. He'd always been like a father to Saylor. They hadn't had an easy upbringing, and I knew some stuff had gone down with their mother's husband, but she didn't talk about it. She wanted to be independent, and it frustrated her that Hayes was so protective.

"Well, I've done all the research. I have a business degree. I love books, and I'm turning my passion into my career. So, yeah, I think I can make a living doing this. And if I can't, then I'll figure something else out." She stared at Hayes, and everyone was quiet, because there was definitely tension there, but we all understood both sides.

His need to protect her and her need to prove that she could take care of herself.

"She's going to kill it," Kingston said, breaking the silence. "And Ruby passed on this romance book to me, and let me tell you, I'm all about it now. Damn." He whistled. "I need to step up my game with the ladies. This dude in the book is one hell of a lover."

The room erupted in laughter, aside from Hayes, who didn't seem humored by the comment at all.

"Are there that many people reading romance books?" Hayes asked.

"No. It's a very unpopular genre. That's why I'm opening a store selling romance books, because I want my business to fail," Saylor said, not hiding her irritation, which was rare for her. She was a ray of sunshine most of the time. But the pressure of getting this business off the ground, taking out a loan, and making all sorts of decisions was weighing on her.

"I know you're smart, Say. I'm not questioning that. I just want to make sure you don't get in too deep." Hayes softened his gaze and set his beer down.

"It's always a gamble when you go into business for yourself. And the bookstore won't only have romance books although that will be the primary genre, there will be others as well. But I'm nervous enough, Hayes, and I don't need you planting all these seeds of doubt. I'm excited about it, and I need you to get on board."

"Yeah, you got it. I'll stop with the comments," he said, pushing to his feet. "Anyone need another beer?"

"I'll take one," Kingston and Romeo both said at the same time.

The doorbell rang, and Nash went to answer the door for what I assumed was the pizza.

"It's going to be great," Demi said, bumping her shoulder into Saylor's. "I was really nervous, too, and my parents were not sure a coffee shop was a good idea. But Magnolia Beans is thriving, and the bookstore will be no different."

"He's just worried about you." River wrapped an arm around me as he spoke to Saylor.

"Yeah, worrying is his love language. Right, baby?" Romeo chuckled.

"Yep. Especially when it comes to Saylor," Demi said.

"I'm a grown woman." Saylor shook her head with irritation. "I had a date last night, and Hayes insisted I call him when I got home because he thinks Lucas Kraft is a tool. But he hated the last guy I dated, too."

"Well, I hate to break it to you, but Lucas Kraft is a douchebag," River said over his laughter.

"And why do you say that?" I raised a brow. I agreed with him, but I wasn't going to burst her bubble. She'd been excited to go on a date, as she hadn't been out since she and her college boyfriend broke up months ago. She hadn't yet told me how things went last night, and I had no real reason for not liking Lucas other than his teeth were a little too white, and he was pretty full of himself.

"For starters, he refers to himself in the third person. He came to see me over a year ago about suing his parents because they got rid of his superhero collectibles when he was in college. He wanted to be reimbursed for the toys that they actually bought him."

Saylor covered her mouth with her hand. "I'm not totally surprised. The date was a total disaster, but that's not the point. I can take care of myself."

"Well, he came into the coffee shop this morning and told me you guys had a great time last night. So, I don't think Lucas has any idea that it didn't go well." Demi chuckled.

"Yeah, that's because I never spoke. He talked the entire time about himself. And he had me split the bill with him, and he had a full entrée and three cocktails, while I had one drink and an appetizer."

Laughter filled the space around us.

"What an asshole," Kingston said. "I've got your back if he gives you a hard time."

"I thought you were a lover, not a fighter." River raised a brow at his brother.

"I'd throw a punch for Saylor, no doubt about it." He winked at her, and I didn't miss the way her cheeks flushed.

I'd noticed the way they always seemed to gravitate toward one another when we were all out together. Maybe it was just all the romance books I was reading lately that had me noticing things more.

River had mentioned that Saylor lived with them for a few months during the time he was away at Fresh Start, but he didn't say much about it. He said it wasn't his story to tell, and I hadn't pushed.

"Thanks, King." She smiled.

"And we'll make that bookstore everything you want it to be," Kingston added.

"I know you will," she said, just as Nash called out to come and eat.

Everyone moved to the kitchen, and River tugged at his brother's hoodie, holding him back.

LAURA PAVLOV

"You watch yourself there, little brother. Sisters are off limits, and you fucking know that." River kept his voice low, so only the three of us could hear him.

"Dude, don't be an asshole. I'd never go there. Saylor's like a little sister to me."

River nodded. "All right, good. She's far too sweet for you anyway."

"Hey, I'm the sweetest guy I know. Right, Ruby?" Kingston chuckled.

"You're pretty sweet—for the town playboy," I said.

"I can't help it if the ladies love me."

"Yeah, it's a real curse," River groaned as we walked toward the kitchen.

He intertwined his fingers with mine and tugged me back as his brother made his way over to the pizza.

"You ready to marry me yet?" River whispered in my ear. He did this often. Told me pretty much every day that he'd tie the knot with me the minute I was ready.

"What are you going to do the day that I say yes?" I teased, as I turned with my chest against his.

I was so in love with this man, it was hard to wrap my head around it.

"I'm going to haul your sweet ass over my shoulder and race down to the courthouse and officially make you mine."

"I'm already yours," I said, tipping my chin up to meet his heated gaze.

"Yeah, you are."

I pushed up and planted a kiss on his mouth. "I love you."

"I love you," he said.

"Get a room!" Hayes shouted, and everyone laughed.

"Trust me, I'm trying to get her to move in with me. Sorry, Saylor, I know you like rooming with her, but I kind of want her all to myself."

Saylor shook her head and laughed. "She's either at your house every night or you're at ours."

"He's such a greedy bastard," Kingston said. "Sorry. Earmuffs, Beefcake."

Nash rolled his eyes. "You're supposed to say earmuffs before you say the bad word, you douchedick."

"Hey, douchedick is as bad as bastard."

"Yeah. I'm aware. Do you see his hands over his ears?"

"You're welcome. I'm the reason he's covering them up." Kingston smirked and looked over at his brother.

"I'm only greedy about one thing, and that's my girl," River said.

"Cheers to that." Romeo held up his beer and clinked it with River's.

I leaned against his shoulder, grateful for this found family I'd come to love.

And this man who'd given me the fairy tale I didn't even know I wanted.

River had shown me what love was.

We'd been two broken souls that had healed together.

And I'd never been happier.

Forever had started for me the first time he'd kissed me.

And every day since.

Acknowledgments

Greg, thank you for giving me the fairy tale. I love you endlessly.

Chase & Hannah, thank you for always cheering me on and being in my corner. I am so incredibly proud of both of you and love you to the moon and back!

Willow, thank you for always making me laugh when I need it most! You are such a bright light every single day, and I am forever grateful for your friendship! Love you!

Catherine, you are the Ben to my L-Lo! So thankful for your friendship! T&T forever. Love you!

Kandi, I'm not sure how I ever existed without you. I love our chats, the laughs, the donuts, the encouragement, and all the magic of YOU! Forever thankful to have you in my life! Love you!

Elizabeth O'Roark, thank you for ALWAYS making me laugh, and for letting me pressure you into giving me all of your books early! I am so thankful for your friendship! Love you!

Pathi, I would not be doing what I love every single day if it wasn't for YOU! I am so thankful for your friendship, and for all the support and encouragement! I'd be lost without you! Thank you for believing in me! I love you so much!

Nat, I cannot begin to put into words how much I appreciate you! Thank you for letting me pass every single thing I can to you! LOL! You have created a monster! I'd truly be lost without you. So yes . . . you've got a stage five clinger on your hands. I'm SO GRATEFUL for you and I love you SO MUCH!

Nina, I'm just going to call you the DREAM MAKER from here on out. Thank you for pushing so hard for me, for believing in me and for making my wildest dreams come true. I love you forever!

Kim Cermak, thank you for being YOU! There is just no other way to say it. You are one in a million. I am endlessly grateful to have you in my corner, but most importantly, to call you my friend. Love you!

Christine Miller, Kelley Beckham, Sarah Norris, Valentine Grinstead, Amy Dindia, Kate Kelly and Ratula Roy, I am endlessly thankful for YOU!

Meagan Reynoso, thank you or reading all my words early, giving fabulous feedback, and working so hard creating the PR packages with me. I love you!

Logan Chisolm, I absolutely adore you and am so grateful for your support and encouragement! Love you!

Kayla Compton, I am so happy to be working with you and so thankful for YOU! Go Niners! Love you! Xo

Doo, Abi, Meagan, Annette, Jennifer, Pathi, Natalie, Caroline and Diana, thank you for being the BEST beta readers EVER! Your feedback means the world to me. I am so thankful for you!!

To all the talented, amazing people who turn my words into a polished final book, I am endlessly grateful for you! Sue Grimshaw (Edits by Sue), Hang Le Design, Sarah Sentz (Enchanted Romance Design), Emily Wittig Designs, Christine Estevez, Ellie McLove (My Brothers Editor), Jaime Ryter (The Ryters Proof), Julie Deaton (Deaton Author Services) and the amazingly talented Madison Maltby, thank you for being so encouraging and supportive!

Crystal Eacker, thank you for your audio beta listening/ reading skills! I absolutely adore you!

Ashley Townsend and Erika Plum, I love the incredible swag that you create and I am so thankful for you both!!

Jennifer, thank you for being an endless support system. For running the Facebook group, posting, reviewing and doing whatever is needed for each release. Your friendship means the world to me! Love you!

Paige, ahhh . . . mother loves you so much! I love our chats, our laughs and all the magic that is YOU! So thankful of your friendship and to have you in my lie!

Rachel Parker, so incredibly thankful for you and so happy to be on this journey with you! Love you so much!

Megan Galt, thank you for always coming through with the most beautiful designs! I'm so grateful for YOU!

Amy, Rebecca, Lauren & Willow, I wouldn't have been able to finish this book without you! I am so thankful for your support and your friendship!! Thanks for sprinting, for pushing me and supporting me on this journey. Love you!

Sammi, Marni, Monica, Corinne, Melanie and Jessica, so thankful for your friendship and to be on this journey with you! Love you so much!

Gianna Rose, Stephanie Hubenak, Rachel Baldwin, Kelly Yates, Sarah Sentz, Ashley Anastasio, Kayla Compton, Tiara Cobillas, Tori Ann Harris and Erin O'Donnell, thank you for your friendship and your support. It means the world to me!

Mom, thank you for being my biggest cheerleader and reading everything that I write! Love you!

Dad, you really are the reason that I keep chasing my dreams!! Thank you for teaching me to never give up. Love you!

Sandy, thank you for reading and supporting me throughout this journey! Love you!

To the JKL WILLOWS . . . I am forever grateful to you

for your support and encouragement, my sweet friends!! Love you!

To all the bloggers, bookstagrammers and ARC readers who have posted, shared, and supported me—I can't begin to tell you how much it means to me. I love seeing the graphics that you make and the gorgeous posts that you share. I am forever grateful for your support!

To all the readers who take the time to pick up my books and take a chance on my words . . . THANK YOU for helping to make my dreams come true!!

ONE PLACE. MANY STORIES

Bold, innovative and
empowering publishing.

FOLLOW US ON:

@HQStories

Ruby Rose declared me the enemy before I had a chance to defend myself. I may be an attorney, but this girl had appointed herself judge and jury. And I'd never minded a good verbal sparring.

But the more we fought – the more I craved her. Until our arguing turned into a bit of a wager, one I was determined to win.

One time. Sixty seconds.
A secret only we would share.

But from the minute we crossed the line, there was no turning back. Ruby Rose may have given me more than sixty seconds, but she wasn't offering forever. And now my world doesn't work without her in it.

But how do I convince her to stay, when she already has one foot out the door?

www.HQstories.co.uk

ISBN 978-0-00-871957-9

9 780008 719579

UK £9.99